GUARDING HIS MIDNIGHT WITNESS

Anna J. Stewart

HARLEQUIN

ROMANTIC SUSPENSE

ROMANTIC SUSPENSE™

Recycling programs
for this product may
not exist in your area.

ISBN-13: 978-1-335-62675-2

Guarding His Midnight Witness

Copyright © 2020 by Anna J. Stewart

All rights reserved. No part of this book may be used or reproduced in any manner whatsoever without written permission except in the case of brief quotations embodied in critical articles and reviews.

This is a work of fiction. Names, characters, places and incidents are either the product of the author's imagination or are used fictitiously. Any resemblance to actual persons, living or dead, businesses, companies, events or locales is entirely coincidental.

This edition published by arrangement with Harlequin Books S.A.

For questions and comments about the quality of this book, please contact us at CustomerService@Harlequin.com.

Harlequin Enterprises ULC
22 Adelaide St. West, 40th Floor
Toronto, Ontario M5H 4E3, Canada
www.Harlequin.com

Printed in U.S.A.

Bestselling author **Anna J. Stewart** is living her dream writing romances for Harlequin's Romantic Suspense and Heartwarming lines. In between bouts of binge-watching her favorite TV shows and movies, she puts fingers to keyboard and loses herself in endless stories of happily-ever-after. Anna lives in Northern California, where she tries to wrangle two rapscallion cats named Rosie and Sherlock, possibly the most fiendish felines known to humankind.

Visit the Author Profile page at Harlequin.com for more titles.

For Lindell Costa.

A woman who made it all look effortless.

Chapter 1

"Welcome back, Detective."

Jack McTavish dropped out of his SUV and tried not to cringe at Deputy Scott Bowman's guarded tone. He'd heard the same inflection from countless others during his long weeks of convalescence. So he'd been shot eight months ago. So one of the bullets had missed his heart by mere millimeters. And okay, yeah, he'd flatlined twice during surgery and once more in recovery. In the days that followed, he'd come roaring back by challenging his surgeon more than any other patient of his, ever, no doubt leaving him questioning his career choice. But none of that, at least in Jack's opinion, gave his fellow officers and detectives permission to eye him as if he had just returned from the dead.

He wasn't dead. Not by a long shot. But apparently he still had to prove it.

"Thanks, Bowie. It's good to be back." Jack reached into his car for his double-shot espresso and checked to make sure he'd clipped his badge to his waistband before verifying his sidearm was secure. He resisted the now familiar urge to scrub uneasy fingers over the still throbbing scars across his chest and side. *Psychosomatic*, according to his physician sister, Ashley. *Ghost pain*. Easy for her to say. He was completely healed, but knowing that in his head didn't prevent the occasional panic attack and nightmares that continued to plague him. When he actually slept.

"So, what are we dealing with?" Jack fell into step beside the deputy as they headed down the dimly lit street. His LT hadn't been very forthcoming with information about the call, only that the person had specifically requested a detective when she'd called 9-1-1. "Crackpot or attention seeker?"

"Jury's out."

Jack didn't have to look at Bowie to know the legacy cop was grinning. A grin served as the kid's default expression. The twentysomething deputy with a little more than three years under his belt was also one of the most organized and reliable officers Jack had worked with in his nearly twelve years on the job. Which was why Jack had specifically requested him as his partner while his usual cohort Cole Delaney finished his vacation. Besides, Bowie was looking to earn his detective's badge, and Jack was happy to play mentor for the time being. "Tell me what you do know, Bowie. Who's the caller?"

"Greta Renault. Resident across the street. Claims to have witnessed a crime from her window but wouldn't give any details over the phone. The dispatcher couldn't shake the feeling something was off, so rather than list-ing it as a nuisance call, the supervisor called the lieu-tenant who—"

"Who decided my first day back on the job should start with a bang. Awesome." Jack's first question was what this Greta Renault had been doing spying out her window at this time of night. In his experience, calls like this were a cry for help, in more ways than one.

"A patrol unit did a quick sweep, didn't find anything amiss. I did a walk-around while I was waiting for you," Bowie continued. "I didn't see anything either around the caller's building or the one in question. I did knock on the door of the office complex and spoke with the night security officer. He said as far as he knew, he was the only one in the building. Which makes sense as it's still under construction in some parts."

"Sounds like someone's been watching too much Hitchcock." Jack took in his surroundings as they headed toward the caller's front door. Nothing like dead of night silence to ease a cop's mind. This time of year in the Sacramento Valley, when April was sliding into May, the weather had yet to decide which direction to go. Cool nights and warmish days interspersed with surprise thunderstorms and retina-blasting sunshine. Personally, Jack preferred crisp nights like this. Noth-ing could hide in the silence. Even the quietest cough couldn't go unnoticed while shadows caught in the beams of determined streetlamps.

A twinge of envy nudged at him as he looked up at the impressive structure that reminded him somewhat of a New York City brownstone. He'd always liked this part of town, the way historic Sacramento, California, meshed with newer, flashier and less interesting architecture. Such a stark contrast to his two-bedroom condo in the family-heavy suburb of Elk Grove. This recently restored landmark brick building where the witness lived was situated within walking distance to the new downtown arena, a nice neighborhood grocery, the capitol building, and the ever popular Old Sac, the tourist trap that had caught Jack up in its temptations on more than one occasion since he'd moved here almost three years before. This part of town, with its combination of corporate offices, hole-in-the-wall restaurants and reputation-building art galleries tended to be a bustling part of town during the day. At four in the morning? Not so much.

"What do we know about Miss Renault?" Jack sipped his cooling jolt of caffeine and tried to ignore the haunting sound of his sister's disapproving tsks. He'd done everything she'd instructed during what seemed like his endless recovery, including cutting down on red meat and upping his intake of kale. He was not, however, willing to give up coffee. No matter how much Ashley grumbled at him.

"We don't know much," Bowie said. "She only moved to Sacramento last summer, but two years before she bought this building and had it renovated into loft apartments. She's currently the only occupant, though. Must be weird, living in this big a building all alone." Bowie craned his neck to look up. "Bet it would play with your head."

Jack agreed. He knew how the solitude could push in on a person and keep them on edge. "You liking these early hours?"

"Not particularly, sir. But it's part of the job."

That it was. Knowing Bowie, however, the deputy had already rearranged the times and days he spent volunteering at local teen centers and the Y teaching self-defense classes to kids of all ages. "So what do you think?" Jack glanced up at the four-story facade. "Want to lay odds on what this turns out to be?"

"Ah." Bowie glanced at Jack with a familiar twinkle in his always appraising eye. "I'll put twenty on our witness having partaken in some recreational smoking products."

Jack chuckled and pressed the one intercom button outside the custom wood and glass-etched door. "There's that sense of humor that keeps us all sane. I'll take that bet. But I'll go with lonely. Someone needs some attention."

"Safe bet," Bowie mumbled.

Jack bit the inside of his cheek. He didn't like the idea of anyone thinking he preferred to play anything safe, but the truth was…that's exactly what he planned to do. He had to if he was going to convince his superiors that he was ready to be on the job again. Because he'd realized one thing while he'd been lying in bed, going out of his mind with boredom: without this job, he had nothing. He pressed two fingers against his heart as doubt surged. Doubt that had him considering putting in for a promotion if he didn't think he'd die a lot sooner stuck behind a desk.

He hit the buzzer again.

"Yes?" A calm, slightly breathy, coherent voice drifted out of the state-of-the-art intercom speaker.

"Detective Jack McTavish and Officer Bowman from

Major Crimes, ma'am." Jack leaned in and pressed the button as he spoke. "We understand you'd like to report a crime?"

Silence echoed on the other end. Jack frowned at Bowie, who shrugged.

"Ma'am?" Jack said again.

"I didn't think you were coming."

Translation: they'd taken their time getting there. "I apologize for the delay, Ms. Renault. If you could buzz us up, we'd like to speak with you."

Another hesitation. "All right. Fourth floor."

"Thank—" his response was cut off by the shrill buzzer and the lock unlatching. "This should be interesting." He pulled open the door and stepped inside.

"Elevator, nice." Bowie gave an appreciative nod toward the restored, old-fashioned iron car.

Silence filled the space as the front door closed behind them. Impressive locks and security, Jack noticed. High-end marble extended across the expansive foyer. A large circular table sat in the center of the area, filled with a spray of flowers Versailles might appreciate. High ceilings, carved crown molding. Elegant and tasteful despite the odd trace of turpentine lingering in the air.

He headed for the stairs and ignored Bowie's disappointed sigh. Jack hadn't been burning up his treadmill every morning to take elevators. He wasn't about to give anyone an excuse to doubt his fitness for the job. Not that Bowie, or any other officer he worked with in the Sac PD, would rat him out if Jack took the less stressful option.

"You hear from Cole and Eden?" Bowie asked as they rounded the second floor landing.

"Talked to Cole yesterday. They'll be back next week." Jack flinched as his chest twinged in protest, this time maybe not so imaginary. "Eden came across more evidence in that cold case she's been chomping on and talked Cole into staying in Flagstaff a while longer."

As much as Jack missed his partner, he was glad to be working this case without him. Even Cole had joined in the chorus of naysayers, suggesting Jack consider taking more time off.

When he pulled open the door to the fourth floor, his heart pounded heavy in his chest. He stepped aside to let Bowie pass and bent over for a moment to take a long, deep breath.

"Pull it together, man." Jack gave himself a good shake and stepped into the hallway just as Bowie knocked on the only door in sight. It opened at Bowie's touch and for an instant Jack wondered if Ms. Renault employed a ghost as a butler.

"Hello?" Bowie called, his hand heading for the snap on his holster.

Sweat broke out on Jack's forehead. Instinct had him mirroring Bowie's action even as his hand shook. He'd been caught off guard once—he wouldn't let it happen again. "Miss Renault?"

"Come on in!" a voice from inside called.

The tension strangling Jack's spine evaporated, and he patted Bowie on the shoulder as if he hadn't been worried. "You spook too easy." Jack sniffed the air. "No recreational smoking in here. Get ready to pay up."

"You haven't won yet," Bowie mumbled and followed Jack inside.

"Miss Renault? Detective Jack…" Jack trailed off as he caught sight of the apparition moving toward them. *Apparition* seemed the only appropriate way to describe her, given the way Miss Renault glided across the room, light on her feet, dark silk pajamas flowing around bare feet. The deep V at the neck gave a hint as to lush, full breasts and creamy skin. Stark, silver-blond hair sat piled on top of her head, and she wore thick, black-rimmed glasses perched on her narrow nose. But her eyes, Jack thought. The eyes behind those glasses stole the breath from his lungs. Indigo. With sharp shards of gold that made him think of Van Gogh's *The Starry Night*. She looked at him with those eyes now in a combination of irritation, suspicion and…interest?

"McTavish," Bowie finished for him and elbowed him in the side. "Detective Jack McTavish."

Jack pinched his lips tight and stepped forward right onto Bowie's foot. The officer let out a whimper he attempted to cover with a cough.

"A pleasure. And it's Greta, please." She held out her free hand as her other held a stark white teapot, steam billowing from the spout. "I assumed when no one arrived shortly after I called…" She trailed off in much the way she had over the intercom. Her eyes glazed over just a bit, and she swayed.

"Ma'am?" Jack bolted closer, wondering if this wasn't some sort of seizure disorder. Was it? She was still there, wasn't she? "Greta?"

"Hmm?" She blinked, lifted her chin, and even in the dim light of her spacious loft, her cheeks exploded with color. "Oh, heavens! I'm sorry. I've been working, stuck, actually. You know, when you can't figure out where…" She went quiet, turned around and disappeared around the corner, leaving the faint hint of jasmine and paint thinner in her wake.

"I'd like to amend the conditions of our bet." Bowie moved in behind him. "I'm going with kooky."

"Maybe." Greta Renault certainly seemed unique, and unique had always fascinated him. Unique had also gotten him burned more times than he could count. He followed her as if in some kind of trance and found her, to his surprise, sitting cross-legged on her wide and deep kitchen island, doodling on a pad of paper. "Greta?"

"Uh-huh." She held up a finger for a flash of a moment. A thin, embossed leather bracelet adorned her wrist. "Just a second. I had an idea, and I just…need… to…" Her fingers flew across the paper as if they had wings. The sharp lead scraped in the silence, an oddly comforting sound that drew him closer. "Okay, yeah. Yes. This will work. Oh, this is perfect." She tilted her head up and smiled at him, a smile so wide and joyous, his knees went week. "You, Detective Jack McTavish, are a lifesaver. Definitely an inspiration. One look at you and bam!" She smacked her palm against the side of her head. "The ideas are flowing again. Thank you."

"My pleasure." Jack looked at Bowie as the deputy circled the kitchen and scanned the countertops, no doubt looking for medications or drug paraphernalia. Jack didn't see a trace of anything in the room other than utter and complete organization. Not even a stray toast crumb to be found.

Greta hopped off the island and poured herself a cup of dark, aromatic tea. Nope, Jack told himself as he finished his coffee, kooky definitely wasn't a bad thing. But he was here for a reason; a reason he was going to have to report back on soon. Which meant he didn't have time to be entertained. "Greta, I don't mean to be rude, but why did you call the police?"

"The police?" Her face clouded, her smile dipped.

"You called 9-1-1 at just after eleven." Bowie clarified as he glanced at his notebook.

"Oh, right." Her eyes flashed and cleared. "The murder."

"The murder." Whatever he'd been expecting to hear, that wasn't it. Jack leaned an arm on the counter and kept his tone even as he saw Bowie roll his eyes so hard they should have fallen back into his skull. "You witnessed a murder?"

"Mmm-hmm." When she nodded, a strand of long, silver-blond hair fell over one eye. "I was afraid when you didn't arrive, I might have…" She trailed off again, pushed the unspoken thought along with her hair away. "Never mind."

"Where was this murder exactly?"

Jack straightened at the strained patience in his deputy's voice.

"Across the street. In that new building." She sipped her tea. "I can show you." She set her cup down and floated out of the kitchen before either of them could respond.

She reminded him of a sprite, Jack thought. Or perhaps a siren. He had the sneaking suspicion she could lure him into the afterlife and he'd gladly follow. And that, he told himself, would be a very bad idea.

"Don't mind Cerberus." Greta flicked dismissive fingers toward the sleek gray cat perched sphinx-like on the top of one of the bookcases. "He's harmless. Mostly," she added when Cerberus batted a paw at Bowie's head and hissed as they passed.

Jack tried to focus on his surroundings as he followed her down the wide hall. The loft in its entirety was enormous, with a maze of copper pipes twisting against the ceiling. Expansive skylights allowed for a starry night view as the sun had begun its rise. Her furnishings for the living room, besides the array of neatly arranged bookshelves, seemed both comfortable and practical. The medium-sized flat-screen was off. An orderly stack of DVDs sat on a short sleek table below. To his right, floor-to-ceiling windows encompassed the entire north wall and were draped with a shimmery gray fabric with gauzy white overlay that pooled on the floor. The hardwood floors had been refurbished with just enough give he could hear her bare feet slap as she led him deeper into the unknown, to the narrow door at the end of the hall.

The smell of paint and turpentine grabbed him around the throat as he stepped inside an artist's studio that would have brought the old masters to tears.

Thick, paint-spattered beige tarps had been spread across the floor. Built-in cabinetry with glass doors allowed a person to see the arranged brushes and paints and other supplies inside. A small speaker system was situated on the counter by the door along with a pod coffee machine and a collection of pristine white mugs.

Jack couldn't recall ever seeing anyone's house look so tidy and efficient. Sparse even.

Greta stood in front of a half-finished canvas that was almost twice her height. The explosions of colors—blacks, purples, blues, with splashes and dots of pinks and red made him feel as if he'd stepped out of the earth's gravitational force and into the spinning universe. She'd only covered half the canvas in paint, however, as if it had been cut off, waiting for whatever its creator deemed necessary.

Jack was about to clear his throat when he caught sight of a painting across the room. A seascape seen from atop cliffs. Pastels and primary colors intermingling in unnatural yet symbiotic waves. And there, standing at the very edge of the most delicate rock, a solitary female figure stood, arms outstretched as if embracing the coming storm.

A woman with shimmering silver hair.

"Crashing Waves."

"Excuse me?" Bowie's question broke through Jack's trance.

"You know it?" Greta's voice just over his shoulder should have surprised him, but it didn't. He'd known she was there before she spoke.

"I—yes." He nodded. Now wasn't the time to admit he had a signed print of the painting over his sofa. It had been one of the few items he'd brought with him from Chicago. He could still remember the moment he'd first seen it in the gallery a little more than four years ago; the first showing for the artist responsible. His date for the evening hadn't appreciated his shift of obsessive attention. His bank account hadn't appreciated the purchase price. But something about the piece, about the woman facing the forces of the darkness closing in on her, had spoken to him.

Now, standing in Greta Renault's studio, Jack glanced at the signature. "*G. Renault.* I should have realized." Bowie had told him their supposed witness was an artist. "Your work is spellbinding."

"Thank you." The smile she gave him illuminated the dark spaces inside of him. "There's little an artist enjoys more than the expression you're wearing on your face at this moment, Detective McTavish."

"Jack," he corrected automatically.

"Miss Renault." Bowie cleared his throat. "About this murder?"

Jack turned in time to see the light fade in Greta's eyes.

"Yes, about that." She managed a strained smile, crossed her arms over her chest and walked over to where she perched on a high stool by the long, narrow window. "I was just finishing for the night, so it must have been around eleven. I like to work late. Fewer distractions. Not as much noise out there." She tapped the side of her head. "Or in here. You know?"

Jack nodded. He did know.

"I had just turned out the light to go fix some tea when one came on across the street. There." She pointed to the steel-and-glass building. "Third floor, corner office. It stopped me cold."

"Is that unusual?" Jack pulled his attention away from her paintings and refocused on his purpose for being here. Aside from the dim glowing lights in the building she indicated, no doubt for the janitorial staff, the entire space looked bare-bones empty. The stark steel and chrome seemed jagged and cold next to the warmth of the building he was currently in. "To see lights at night over there?"

"Other than the security ones, yes. That's why I kept watching. I do that. Watch people. They're fascinating." Her voice sounded almost wistful. "From a distance, obviously. I've been keeping tabs on the construction, of course, but this was different."

"Could you see who came into the office?" Bowie asked.

"Not at first." Greta shook her head, squinted as if trying to remember. "There were two men. Both wore suits. One was a bit more tailored than the other. Polished, even. The other was older, heavier, especially around the middle. Rumpled. He wore glasses, round, with thin frames."

"That's pretty good eyesight," Bowie said in a way that had Jack gnashing his teeth.

"The heavier man had a mark, here." Greta touched her hand to the side of her neck, trailed it up her left cheek. "I wondered if it might be a wine mark? One of those birthmarks people are born with." She shivered. "He was so angry."

"The man with the birthmark?" Jack asked.

"No. The other one."

"Angry." Bowie continued to scribble. "And you know this because—"

Jack shot a look at Bowie who, near as Jack could tell, wasn't even trying to hide his disbelief. If Greta noticed, she didn't let on.

"People change demeanor when they're angry." Greta's eyes remained pinned to the now dark office. "The body, it tenses, tightens, like a spring. It's like it's ready to strike. But he didn't. The older man, I mean. But the younger one did. Fast. Next thing I saw, the first man was lying on the floor, not moving. Then the younger one was standing over him." She turned glassy, shocked eyes to Jack. "That's when he turned and looked out the window. I think." She visibly swallowed. "It felt as if he looked right at me."

"Looked at you?" Jack moved in to block her view, as if he could pull her out of the memory. "This man saw you?"

"I know how that sounds." Her fingers brushed against the hollow of her throat. "My lights were off so I can't be sure. I couldn't, didn't move. All I could do was stare back."

"What did he do then?" Jack asked before Bowie could.

"He walked over to the window, put his hands in his pockets and smiled."

"He smiled," Bowie said.

"Yes." Greta nodded.

"So you got a good look at his face," Bowie pushed and moved in. "You could give a description to a sketch artist?"

"She's an artist, Bowie," Jack reminded the deputy with a bit of bite in his voice. "She could draw him herself."

"I could," Greta said without hesitation. "But I don't have to. I know who it was."

"You do?" Jack wondered if he'd ever stop being surprised.

"It was Doyle Fremont."

The energy coursing through him drained in an instant. Jack sat on the edge of the table behind him. "Doyle Fremont as in the tech tycoon and real estate developer?"

"Yes." Greta's eyes went wide. "I know it sounds strange, and believe me, I debated calling, but with that man just lying there, how could I not?"

"You said the heavier man was just on the ground. Did he fall over or was he struck?"

It was a moment before she shook her head. "Not that I remember."

"Is it possible he had a heart attack and collapsed?"

"I...maybe?" But she didn't seem convinced. "If he did, why didn't Doyle Fremont call someone? Why focus on me?"

Why indeed? Jack was both shocked and grateful Bowie refrained from responding, but he knew what the deputy was bound to ask. The same question Jack was obligated to. "Is there anyone staying here with you, Greta? Anyone who might be able to corroborate—"

"No. I live alone." The way she folded in on herself, curled her arms tight around her waist, flinched into the darkness, Jack could all but feel the regret and uncertainty in her. She wasn't happy about any of this.

"Just to clarify." Bowie cut in before Jack could push further. "You're saying you saw Doyle Fremont arguing with an older, heavier man with a birthmark and that when that argument got heated, Fremont killed him. How?"

"How?" Greta's brow furrowed as she slumped a bit on the stool.

"Yes, how. Did he shoot him?"

"Ease up, Bowie," Jack murmured. It was clear Greta believed something had happened. Jack looked back at the empty office building. But if he believed his eyes…

"No, he didn't shoot him." Greta shook her head as her cheeks began to flush. "No, I didn't hear a shot. I didn't see a gun."

"Then did he stab him?" Bowie's voice rose ever so slightly. "Was there a knife?"

"I…maybe?" She frowned. "I don't know." She seemed to be talking to herself now. Questioning herself.

Bowie sighed. "Ms. Renault—"

"You said you thought Mr. Fremont saw you. Looked at you and smiled." Jack stood back up, stepped slightly in front of Bowie to take charge once more. "What did Mr. Fremont do then?"

"He turned and walked away. The next thing I knew, he turned off the lights. I couldn't see anything after that. That's when I called 9-1-1."

"So the body should be there." Bowie turned irritated eyes on Jack and mouthed the word *kooky*. "If there is a body."

Jack's normally expansive temper strained.

"You don't believe me." Greta's voice went cold, as if Bowie's accusation had doused a fire inside of her. "You think I'm seeing things. Making things up." Her eyes sharpened with a glint of steel.

"We didn't say that," Jack answered before Bowie could. He would have thought the deputy would use a bit more diplomacy than was currently on display. Even if she was disturbed, even if what she'd seen wasn't real, she didn't deserve to be treated with anything other than respect. "Greta—"

"This was a mistake." Greta jumped off her stool and, head held high, walked out of the studio. "I want you to leave."

"What on earth is wrong with you?" Bowie whispered as he shoved his notepad into his pocket. "I expected you to be a little off after all these months, Jack, but don't tell me you believe this ridiculous story. Doyle Fremont, one of the biggest money men in the country, murdered someone? Please."

"I don't know what I believe." Other than Greta Renault was convinced of what she'd seen.

"So, you're what? Going to humor her? Why? Because she's a knockout?"

Jack didn't appreciate the sarcasm or the accusation. "Because whether what she saw actually happened or not, she believes it did. Either way, she needs help, Bowie."

"And you think you're the one to give it to her?"

"Clearly, you aren't," Jack snapped before he followed Greta into the other room. He found her holding the front door open, eyes and jaw set as she intently stared at anything other than him. "Greta, I apologize—"

"Don't." She flinched, and try as he might, he couldn't find a trace of the welcoming, bewitching woman who had let them into her home. "Just don't. I made a mistake. I knew I shouldn't have called. I shouldn't…" She stopped, took a shuddering breath. "I shouldn't have expected you to listen to me."

"I did listen," Jack tried again, but she inched the door closed. "Greta—"

"I did not imagine this." She looked Jack square in the eyes, and he saw the hurt swirling in the blue depths. Hurt and disbelief and, surprisingly, anger. "I know what I saw, Detective. And if you aren't going to do anything about it, I will."

She closed the door in his face.

Chapter 2

"I know what I saw." She should have those five words included on her next tattoo. Greta snapped the lock on the door and returned to the kitchen to top up her tea. Moments later, she curled up into the corner of one of the two sofas bookending the massive yet dormant gas fireplace, fingers tapping restlessly on her knee.

People. The main reason she preferred keeping to herself, staying in her home for long stretches of time, was people. It wasn't healthy, as her friend Yvette kept telling her. And she knew the more time she spent alone, the harder it was to interact with anyone out there. But what was she supposed to do when something out of the ordinary happened, besides having to invite the outside in?

Cerberus leaped from his perch atop the bookcase

and joined her, twining and weaving his way into her lap and under her arm. Greta hugged the cat close, closed her eyes and focused on the way her heart hammered in her chest. It was better than having the memory of that man lying motionless on the floor.

She'd given in to her first impulse and called 9-1-1. It hadn't crossed her mind not to until she heard the voice on the other end of the phone. Another night. Another 9-1-1 call. Another murder. One that had hit much closer to home.

"Don't do that. Don't go there. That's not where you exist anymore." In her haste, she'd shattered her protected, carefully built world and invited a pair of detectives into her home. Detectives who seemed more interested in finding the right punch line than investigating a crime. Or at least one of them had. The other one...

Detective Jack McTavish. She inclined her head, frowned into the fading darkness even as the cinnamon tea sat spicy on her tongue. He'd been nice. Understanding. To a point. He knew her, knew her work. Maybe that had earned her the benefit of the doubt.

Did they think she didn't know how far-fetched her story sounded? Even in her self-created bubble, she knew who Doyle Fremont was. And that, more than anything, could be why she'd been so shocked at what she'd seen. Regret pulsed through her. If only she had gone to sleep earlier, instead of extending her session to ten-plus hours. If she'd been asleep, she could have been dreaming about better times. The ones in the past and, hopefully, the better ones to come in the future.

But she hadn't been sleeping. She hadn't slept in days

as the pressure about her upcoming show had continued to build. Insomnia was nothing new; it was one of the unhealthy ways her body dealt with stress. When she seemed to hover between worlds, where the veil between reality and dreams sometimes tangled. Greta chewed on her thumbnail. She remembered the pulse-pounding electronic club music coursing through the soundproof loft. The smell of fresh paint. She was never more awake—or alive—than when her brush touched the canvas.

She brushed tentatively over the leather bracelet she wore every day as a reminder that nothing was permanent, not even pain. She searched for the solace the Celtic symbols for courage, strength and compassion provided and, finally, edged away from the darkness.

Cerberus began to purr, pulling out of her hold and curling into a tight ball of protection in her lap. Greta continued to stroke his fur, grateful for the accepting company even as the image of a kind, masculine and handsome face drifted through her mind.

Detective Jack McTavish.

The sight of him had erased everything else in her head, just long enough to capture him on paper. It wasn't often inspiration struck with the force of lightning, and that it still could release a torrent of adrenaline that had sent her buzzing. It hadn't just been his looks, which were impressive. Something about him felt familiar in the gentle way he'd spoken with—and not to—her. Empathy wasn't usually so openly transmitted, but beneath his attempt to connect with her, she picked up on the ache, on the sadness. The loneliness.

It had been clear in his eyes, eyes that from the moment she looked into the rich blue depths had transported her out of her controlled, solitary world into one of exploding colors and echoes of laughter on the wind.

"Okay, you have got to get some sleep." Greta groaned. She didn't need her erratic imagination taking her to places she dare not go.

Not for the first time tonight, her fingers itched to reach for her cell and call Yvette. Yvette, who knew more about Greta that just about anyone else. Yvette, who had been her only friend for what they'd laughingly called *banishment education*, shipped off to boarding school overseas. In Yvette's case because of obscenely rich parents who were completely uninterested in overseeing even the tiniest detail of their child's life. And in Greta's case because her parents were dead.

Surrendering to Yvette's push for Greta to step into the real world had brought her to Sacramento, where her recently married friend worked as the mayor's deputy PR person. Which made what happened tonight Yvette's fault, Greta thought with a smile. Oh, how she'd love to throw that at her friend the next time she saw her. But she wouldn't. The last thing she needed was for Yvette to worry about her. A worry she'd set aside ever since Greta had taken up residence in her new home.

The swirling in her head returned, tempting her to surrender to the welcome, infrequent undertow. The promise of elusive sleep both energized and exhausted her.

"I know what I saw," she murmured again. The privacy and solitude she'd eked out over the past few years fractured, cracking beneath the weight of her determination to cling to the truth as she saw it. The promise she'd made to Detective Jack McTavish floated back.

The police didn't believe her, but she couldn't, she *wouldn't* let that stand.

Doyle Fremont was a killer.

She just had to prove it.

"Bowie says your midnight witness was hot."

The cacophonous birthday-induced celebratory atmosphere of the Major Crimes squad at the Sacramento Police Department roared in Jack's ears as he leaned back in his office chair. He'd survived his and Bowie's visit to Greta Renault's home three days ago, but he wasn't so sure about his welcome back party. He did appreciate the mock chalk outline on the floor in front of his desk—cop mentality and humor at its finest. It was just about the only thing to have brought a smile to his face since he'd interviewed their enigmatic witness.

Something about Greta Renault continued to cling to him, call to him. So much so he'd made a few cursory passes at a background check. Maybe it was the haunted look in those starry blue eyes of hers. Maybe it was the way she'd looked at him at the end, as if she'd been expecting exactly the reaction she'd gotten. Normally Jack liked living up to people's expectations.

But not in this case.

"My what?" The scent of burned coffee and sickly sweet cake permeated the air and coated the cops with a thick layer of powdered sugar. He looked up at Tammy, the evidence tech who had come up from the depths of the basement to help the squad rejoice in Jack's triumphant return to the department. "Sorry, Tammy. What did you say?"

Tammy sighed in that overacting, community-theater way she had and hopped onto the corner of his desk. She kicked her feet against the drawers as she dug a fork into a fist-sized slice of chocolate marble cake. "I said Bowie said your witness from the other night was hot." She took a bite and waggled her eyebrows at him. "He also said she's—"

"Let me guess. *Kooky*." The more Jack heard the word, the less he liked it. Especially in relation to Greta Renault. Eccentric, yes. Distracted? Sure. But she was also beautiful, intriguing and talented. Not to mention scared. He'd seen it. He'd felt it. "She's different."

"Uh-huh." Tammy licked the frosting off her fork and snorted. "I'm sure that's what he meant."

Jack frowned. "What else did Bowie say?"

Something in his voice must have snagged Tammy's sensor because she sat up straighter and ducked her head. "Not much."

"Did he happen to mention she's a world-renowned artist whose paintings have been commissioned for some of the most important buildings in the world, including the United Nations?"

"He did not." Tammy arched a brow and took another bite. "He did say her cat might have come directly from the underworld. And you know what they say about cats and their owners."

"What do they say?"

"Um…" Tammy pressed her lips against the fork and winced. "That they're—"

Jack's cell phone rang.

"Saved by the out-of-date ringtone." Tammy jumped off his desk. "Gotta go."

"Uh-huh." Irritation he hadn't been able to shake since leaving Greta's loft surged afresh. He knew cops in general had their own way of dealing with the odd people involved in cases, but he did not like the way Bowie—and now others in the squad—were focusing on Greta's unconventional behavior. Unfortunately, his caseload at the moment was practically nonexistent, which gave him far too much time to think.

He was beginning to wish Cole was here to help him out with this one after all. He needed a bit of camaraderie right now. But his sister would do in a pinch. So, rather than letting the call go to voice mail, he answered his cell. "Hey, Ashley. What's up?"

"Just checking to see if you've popped any stitches yet." His sister's teasing voice did what it always did and soothed the rough edges.

"Ha, ha. They dissolved months ago, and you know it. Or didn't they teach you anything in medical school." Grateful for the diversion, he got up and headed to the stairs. Nothing better to clear his head than some fresh air and open space. "How was your trip? All nice and relaxed from the spa?"

"Funny enough, the trauma surgery convention didn't leave much time for a massage or a mani-pedi."

Neither had taking care of Jack for the past few months, but if there was one thing he knew about his sister, it was that she rarely took time for herself. "When did you get back?"

"About an hour ago." He could hear her opening and closing the bare cabinets in his kitchen. "Thought I'd check in, see how it's going. They have you shackled to the desk?"

How was it going? He hadn't slept more than a few hours the last couple of nights. Every time he closed his eyes, all he could see was that determined expression on Greta Renault's face. How was it going? What a loaded question. "For the most part. Had a case the other night, though. Weird. Strange witness." Great. Now Bowie had him doing it.

"Strange how?"

Grateful she didn't make a joke about it, he let out a pent-up breath. "Strange as in I think I believe her even though her story sounds, well, unbelievable." He winced at his own words. Why was he even still thinking about this? He'd been keeping an eye on the morgue roster. Checked in unofficially with contacts at local hospitals and clinics. No one had reported anyone fitting the victim's general description. When his sister didn't respond, he checked his cell, worried he'd dropped the call. "Ash?"

"I'm here. It's only natural, after a traumatic injury like you had, to question your actions and thought processes, Jack. To wonder whether you're thinking clearly. It also makes sense you'd question every decision you make."

"You told me all this during my recovery." A recovery she'd overseen personally after leaving her job in Chicago. The silver lining to his being shot: he'd given his sister the excuse she'd been looking for to start over somewhere else after her divorce.

"Nice to know you listened," Ash joked. "You say you think you believe her."

"I believe she believes it." Was that the same thing? Or was he so bored he was looking for anything to latch on to? Or…was it something else?

"Sounds like you don't want to believe her."

"I don't." That niggling feeling, that gut-deep instinct he'd honed in the last dozen or so years, was speaking to him again, the same way it had back in Chicago. The fallout from that case had kicked a big hole in his career and driven him all the way to the West Coast. Maybe it was boredom. Maybe he just wanted to prove to Bowie and everyone else that he was still a good cop. Or maybe he just wanted an excuse to see Greta Renault again. "It would make life a lot easier for everyone if she's wrong." Poking at Doyle Fremont with a stick was like tempting a political grenade to go off. The smart play was to just move on and forget about everything.

Including Greta Renault. *Especially* Greta Renault.

"Not like you to take the easy way," Ashley said as more cabinet doors were slammed shut. "Seriously, Jack. Do I have to do all the grocery shopping? How hard is it to click a few buttons?"

"I keep forgetting." When had online grocery shopping become an afterthought? Since Ashley had arrived the week after his shooting, she'd been taking care of all that stuff. Guess it was time to get back to his usual routine. He glanced at his watch. "I'm off in an hour. I'll take care of it when I get home."

"Yeah, well, I'm moving out soon, so you need to get used to living alone again."

"You got a job?" Relief came first, followed by the knowledge that the friendship he'd strengthened with his little sister might be short-lived. They might have driven each other to distraction growing up, but she'd been his lifeline these last few months. That she'd dropped her entire life to help him get better had meant more than he could ever convey. Or repay. "Where?"

"Well, that's the bad news." Ashley sighed. "And so is this granola bar." She coughed and choked. "I think it might actually be sawdust now."

"I think the last owner left that there." Jack lifted his face to the afternoon sun. A perfect day in Northern California really couldn't be beat, not with the gentle breeze whistling through the trees and fallen leaves rustling along the sidewalk.

"Not funny," Ashley grumbled. "Just for that, I'm not going very far. Folsom General was looking for an ER doctor, and they've offered me the position. I start in a month. So lucky you, you get to help me start house hunting."

"Folsom, huh?" Jack couldn't stop the smile from forming. With their parents and other brother still back East, it would be nice to have some family around, and the Sacramento suburb was a great area. "I guess that's far enough away for me to miss you."

"Just for that, I'm not cooking dinner."

"And the good news keeps coming."

"Ha, ha. Glad to hear you sounding back to normal. Hey, Jack."

"Yeah."

"If you even believe this woman for a second, see it through. You've never been one to let the politics of a case get in the way. Don't start now."

"Thanks, Ash." Jack didn't know why the advice helped, but it did. Like his own personal Jiminy Cricket perched on his shoulder, his sister's words pushed him in the direction he was already headed. "I'll pick up takeout for dinner on the way home."

"Sushi, if you're taking suggestions. From Mana."

Of course she'd pick the restaurant completely in the opposite direction. But she was right. Best sushi in town as far as he was concerned. "You've got it. Thanks for calling, Ash."

"Anytime. Don't forget the sake."

Greta had known for years she should expand her interaction with others, but stalking her millionaire businessman neighbor probably wouldn't get her the results she wanted.

No, not stalking. *Surveilling.* Greta kicked free of the blankets and stared up into the predawn sky. It would have been easier to keep an eye on said neighbor if Doyle Fremont was actually in town. After spending a good portion of a day watching through a pair of her grandmother's antique opera glasses for Fremont to return to his office, she'd built up the courage to call Fremont Enterprises to inquire about an appointment. She'd been told Mr. Fremont was out of town and not expected back in Sacramento until...

Greta blew out a long breath. Until today.

Of course that crumb of knowledge hadn't stopped her from checking his window from her stakeout stool in the studio. Every time she went to get a cup of tea or go to the bathroom, she scanned the third-floor office for anything amiss. It was getting, Greta had to admit grudgingly, a bit obsessive.

It added to her list of things to worry about. She had

a major showing in two weeks, a show that could catapult her into the big time. So far she'd been a word-of-mouth artist, perched on the edge of stardom, but this show was going to change everything. There were critics and reporters coming from as far away as New York. Now was not the time to fixate on what was not conducive to her productivity.

Her work was suffering, her creativity stifled even more than it had been before Detective Jack McTavish and his partner had come calling. The block she thought she'd busted through had shown up again thanks to the numerous impressions and images of the handsome detective.

"The handsome detective." Greta actually snorted. "Sounds like an eighties cop show."

She knew what she should do. She should put this whole thing out of her mind and get back to work. She'd reported what she'd seen. It was up to the police whether they followed through or not. But how could she walk away, never knowing for certain if what she'd seen was real?

No. She needed answers. She needed proof that what had happened had actually happened. Her peace of mind, her *future* depended on it.

She'd scoured the internet for news of any mention of a murder or even a body being recovered or found. There had been nothing—at least, nothing matching her memory—and the more time that passed, the more anxious she became.

Even now, days later, lying in bed, she couldn't stop thinking.

She traced along the pattern of the thin, embossed

leather cuff she wore as a reminder that there was always light after the dark. There was always a solution. Even when it seemed there wasn't.

Any hope of peace vanished when Cerberus landed solidly on her chest. He poked his cold, demanding Feed Me nose against hers and had her rolling out of bed. While her tea brewed, she tried to shake off the unease yet another sleepless night had brought, the unwavering sensation that she'd opened the door to something that could never be shut again.

And no, she told herself, she didn't mean Jack McTavish.

Restless, she strode out of the kitchen, drawn down the hall to the painting that had been taunting her for weeks. The canvas that she'd dubbed *Fortress of Tranquility* sat there, in the middle of the room, surrounded by mussed fabric tarps, paint spatter and a slightly askew worktable topped with paints, brushes and jars of mineral spirits and water. She'd given up last night. Walked away when she'd been unable to move beyond the mental block that even now pushed against her mind, but instead of finding peace, she'd turned right into an entirely different kind of nightmare.

So many emotions circled within her, she could barely identify them: fear, regret, anticipation, relief. They tumbled in and around each other like she'd tipped over one of her brush jars, scattering the stained handles into a mess. Now she knew to avoid looking out the windows; she didn't want to be reminded of what she'd seen. She shifted her fractured attention to the painting she'd been struggling with for longer than she cared to admit.

It was humbling to be conquered by a canvas of mostly white. What did it say about her that she couldn't seem to see beyond the vastness that sat like a beacon in the center of a room that had provided so much inspiration in the past? Had she offended her muse in some way? Done something to close the door to imagination and wonder that had, until recently, rarely failed her?

Greta sighed. Painting had been her refuge for as long as she could remember; it had never let her down before.

And that terrified her more than anything she might have witnessed the other night. Without her work, without her painting, what did she have? Why was she alive?

She snapped the thought out of her mind before it could fully form. "There's no going down that path." Her voice echoed in the studio, a crack of sound that shot her back into the reality of the moment. Whining about the situation wasn't going to do a darned thing except exacerbate the hopelessness. She'd spent a lifetime learning to balance on the edge of that cliff. She wasn't going to step off now.

Time to stop wallowing and get to work. But not, she decided, on the piece that continued to evade her. Nope. She needed something new, something completely different that would open her mind back up to possibilities.

Not for the first time, she pulled the canvas down, set it against the wall across the room and unearthed a new one, smaller, but not by much. The prep, the sound of the brush bristles scraping against the taut fabric soothed her nerves.

She never understood why she painted what she did, only that the compulsion needed assuaging. The colors, the form they took, sometimes swirling, sometimes dormant like the ocean after a storm, presented themselves at the end of her brush as if she was possessed. But always, always, amid the forces of nature and darkness, the woman appeared. Tall. Lithe. Silver-haired and faceless, embracing what approached or holding back what attacked. What loomed. What threatened.

Greta bit her lower lip, refusing to stop as the image formed out of the fog as if an answer to a desperate plea. She dipped her brush into the slick oil paint, a flesh tone she rarely used but for some reason had prepared and surrendered. And there, seconds, minutes, hours later, her mind loosened, and a thin ray of idea-laden light burst through.

It was his eyes, Greta realized as she dipped the needle-thin tip of her outlining brush into the glossy blue, that called to her. His face was as perfect on the canvas as it had been inches from her own. She moved in, added a droplet of golden yellow into the blue that had her inner critic singing. Her hand continued to sweep and capture every microcosm of detail she'd made note of when she'd sketched him in the kitchen. Only when she stepped back to examine the nearly finished piece did she pick up on the depths of who he was.

She'd spent most of her life watching, observing. Studying the few who stepped in and out of her path. She'd always purposely kept everyone at a distance, but from the moment she'd first set eyes on Detective Jack McTavish, something inside of her had stirred. Unfamiliar. Tempting. Exciting. And, when she stopped to really think about it, utterly terrifying. It was that fear that kept the brush moving, kept her bare, paint-splattered feet on the wrinkled tarp.

Her apprehension hadn't stopped her from committing his details to memory, such as his sturdy shoulders that told her he could take on a lot. The way his dark blond hair brushed evenly across the collar of his blazer, showing he took pride in his appearance, a supposition seconded by his clean-shaven face at such an early hour.

A nightmare, not a dream, had brought him into her life. Fleeting perhaps, but for long enough to impact her.

Her hand stilled as the fear scuttled to life once more. These emotions, these thoughts, all these rioting sensations had arrived on the wings of a darkness she could only pray she hadn't imagined.

She didn't trust many people; she never had, and chances were she never would, but there was something about Jack McTavish that made her wish her abilities in that direction were stronger. Maybe all she needed was a bit of practice. Maybe it was time to step further out of that self-imposed solitude and...

Greta jumped when Cerberus wound his sleek gray body between her feet and rubbed his head against her calf, his purr at jet-engine setting. She blinked, glancing over at the paint-spattered clock sitting perfectly straight on one of the organized shelves.

Her stomach growled, not an uncommon occurrence when she got lost in her work. She didn't bother to examine what she'd created as she set the paint and brush down and returned to the kitchen to rebrew the tea that had gone cold. Because her stomach demanded it, she toasted up half a bagel.

Still embracing the residual haze that followed her

out of a bout of work, she found herself wandering to the hall window just outside her studio. Before the last of the fog cleared her mind, she sipped her tea and, wedged behind the thin layers of fabric, watched the constant stream of moving vans and construction workers putting the finishing touches on the new Fremont Complex.

Bile rose in her throat. She tried to resist looking at the window. How did they do it? she wondered. How did everyone scuttle about their lives as if nothing had happened? As if everything was normal. As if nothing had changed.

Everything about the other night, right down to the police officers' reaction, told her it had all been some kind of dream.

Except she knew it wasn't.

Didn't she?

Jack pulled his SUV behind an open moving truck parked less than a block from the soon-to-open Fremont business complex.

Ashley had been right yesterday. Stewing about this case wasn't going to do anything than raise his blood pressure. Chances were Greta Renault had been sleepwalking or dreaming or…something. But simply walking away without asking any questions? That wasn't who he was.

He'd just needed a not-so-gentle reminder of that fact.

He leaned over, craned his neck to look up and out of the windshield. "The guy definitely knows how to refurbish a building."

Not to be outdone by the likes of those companies

that maintained a massive presence in the Bay Area, Doyle Fremont was centralizing all of his businesses— real estate, technology research and about a half-dozen other sub-interests Jack hadn't committed to memory— into the block-long, seven-story, all-inclusive structure. Not only did the complex include a dozen apartments, but there would be a five-star lobby restaurant open to the public, a state-of-the-art tech store, a meditation garden on the roof for employees, valet service and its very own custom coffee shop.

Personally, Jack preferred the blood-curdling coffee and stale donuts of the squad room. Which was where he had spent his morning running down basic information on Doyle Fremont and his various enterprises and connections. Near as Jack could tell?

The guy was so clean he squeaked. No one, at least no one in Jack's extensive investigative experience, was *that* clean. No one.

"Dropping off or picking up?" One of the moving men called out to him as he locked up his car. About as tall as he was wide, the mover barely gave a glance to another man in the truck who handed him an over-size box.

"Neither. Job interview," Jack lied. "I'm not parked in a loading zone, right?"

"You're fine. Just go around front. We've got the freight elevators locked down."

"No problem." Jack gave a polite wave and hustled down the street as if he was late for his appointment. Before he rounded the corner, he stopped, pretended to check his phone as he glanced up and across the street at Greta Renault's building. Having been inside the charming space, he recognized the shorter windows as those in her studio while the taller ones were in the hall; the curtains had been reserved for the living room.

One of the curtains shifted slightly, but when he didn't see any sign of Greta, he assumed it was her cat getting his exercise. Jack angled his phone up, snapped a few pictures to remind himself later as to what could be seen from where. He rounded the corner and pushed through one of the heavy glass lobby doors rather than walking through the lazy, roundabout entrance.

If he didn't know better, he'd think the Fremont Complex was already open for business. There was a security counter off to the left, manned by two uniformed guards currently clicking through the multiple screen displays flashing across monitors built into the wall behind them as they adjusted hookups and plugs. Instead of stale, air-conditioned office air, Jack found himself inhaling something close to pure oxygen, no doubt the result of the lush greenery planted around the spacious area. As he looked up, he saw the lobby stretched all the way to the skylighted roof, with an open floor plan outlining the expanse of the building. He remembered reading that Fremont had originally planned to build on the empty rail-yard property, but at the last minute, about eight months ago, he'd changed course and bought this former hotel and invested double the cost in the extensive remodel. Given all that had been done in the time, Jack guesstimated Fremont had sunk a good portion of his fortune into the project. Why the rush? It was only one of a hundred or so questions Jack had.

"Pretty impressive, don't you think?"

"Very." Jack's response was automatic as he faced the man behind him. "Fritz?"

"How ya doin', Jack?" Doug Fritzhugh, a former cop who could have made a living as a pro wrestler, slapped a surprisingly gentle hand on Jack's shoulder. "You don't look too worse for wear."

"Doing okay, thanks." Aside from longing for the day people didn't look at him as if he were a walking miracle, he thought. "Haven't seen you since your retirement party." Jack took in the gray security uniform and shiny gold nameplate. He'd heard through the grapevine Fritz had made a jump up in the world into private high-end security for a well-recognized company. It hadn't taken much to find out where. The answer had been a lucky break for Jack. "I see it didn't take."

"Retirement? Oh, it took just fine for me." Fritz guided Jack out of the way of an oversize leather sofa being carted in from outside. "The wife lasted about a month before she was begging me to get a job. I had a few connections, made a couple calls, and voilà. Head of security for this place."

Jack smirked at the phrase. "You're going to have your hands full. Lots to take care of, I'd imagine."

"Compared to thirty years on the force, this is gonna be a slice of heaven. Well-paid heaven." Fritz lowered his voice and laughed. "You looking to make a change? Wouldn't blame you if you were."

"You know me, Fritz," Jack said. "I never rule anything out. I was driving by a few days ago, thought maybe I'd check the place out. Don't suppose I could talk you into a tour?" He glanced up.

"Well, sure." Fritz shrugged. "Let me get my boys

settled, and I'll show you around. Can't take long, though. The boss is due back today, and we're trying to get as much done as we can."

"Due back? He's been away?" Jack followed Fritz over to the security desk and signaled for a guest badge.

"Los Angeles. Some big fundraising shindig. Quite the deal, from what I hear. My wife pays more attention to that stuff than I do. Here you go. Clip that to your jacket." Fritz handed over the badge that clearly designated him as an outsider. "The coffee bar's already in full swing if you want something. Where do you want to start?"

"How about upstairs?" Jack kept his tone neutral. "Like, maybe the third floor?"

In some ways, Greta thought, surveillance was like watching a movie. All that was missing was a monster bowl of popcorn and butter-covered fingers.

As she had over the past few days, Greta sat on one of her kitchen stools, a bottle of water perched on the sill of the window and her grandmother's antique opera glasses, one of her few prized possessions, held up to her face. They didn't help much, but enough she could scan faces and spot movement. As if she couldn't spot Doyle Fremont in a crowd. Who was she expecting to see? Her murder victim?

Her hands went icy at the thought, and she swallowed hard. Well, that would answer that question, wouldn't it? "Great. Now I'm sounding strange even to myself." Cerberus let out a tiny meow from where he was sitting at her feet. "Sorry, Cerb. I know I'm supposed to be painting, but I can't get this out of my mind."

It was as if the rest of the world had fallen away, her painting, her routine, even her cell phone forgotten, although as far as the latter was concerned, she rarely paid it any mind. She'd already ignored three calls from her friend Yvette because she always knew when Greta was keeping a secret. Only problem with avoiding the phone was that Yvette would get irritated enough to pop by to check on her. Whatever. Greta would deal with that when she had to.

As if reading her mind, her cell rang again. With a growl of frustration, Greta got up, left the glasses on the stool and hurried into the living room to answer the phone. "Yvette, everything's just fine."

"Why wouldn't it be?"

"Uncle Lyndon." Greta sighed and sank onto the arm of the sofa. She really needed to pay attention to her caller ID. "No reason." She cringed at the idea of lying, but it was better than the truth, at least in this case. Lyndon Thornwald, her late father's best friend, had long been the only constant in her life, acting as both her lawyer and legal guardian while she'd been a minor, then as her agent when her career began to take off. "When does your flight get in?"

"I was scheduled to arrive this afternoon."

Greta's stomach dropped. Today? Oh, that wouldn't work at all. She peeked over the back of the sofa and out the window. Doyle Fremont was due back today. Now was definitely not the time to host a houseguest. Except... "Did you say you *were* scheduled?"

"That's why I'm calling. One of my clients passed away this morning, so I'm tied up in New York and can't get out there until next week at the earliest. So unless you want to reschedule your show, you'll need to meet with Ms. Sorenson at the gallery this week on your own."

"Oh." Greta nibbled on a paint-stained thumbnail. "Okay." She'd never handled one of these meetings on her own before. With the attention span of a dying gnat, important details didn't always stay in her mind the way they should. That said, Collette Sorenson, the curator of the renowned Camellia Art Museum, held great sway over the West Coast art world. The last thing Greta wanted to do was alienate a woman who could have a substantial influence on her career.

"I guess I can do that." Even as she said the words, the anxiety built in her chest. This was why she should leave the house more often, so what needed doing outside these walls wasn't so terrifying. "I'm probably in need of a change of scenery anyway." Was she trying to convince him or herself? "Before it's time to move on." She was already closing in on a year, and she rarely stayed anywhere longer than that.

The hesitation was slight on Lyndon's part, but it was there. "So soon?"

"It's been ten months." If there was one constant in her life, it was her determination to avoid anything remotely permanent. Permanent meant commitment, meant promises, and with her uncertain future, she had no business making either. "I was considering Portland."

"If that's what's best."

"You don't think I should move?" Definitely not the reaction she'd expected. "You're the one who's always said the longer I stay anywhere the more likely it is someone will dig up my past. Besides, I like building up my real estate portfolio." Not that she needed to. The family money she'd inherited when she was six years old was more than enough on its own. But she liked the idea of owning bits and pieces around the country and abroad, although she had never gone back to any of them. Some people put pins in maps. She collected real estate. "Unless you think—"

"I think you should do what you want to do, Greta." There was an exhaustion in his voice she hadn't heard before. "I just assumed since Yvette was so close now, you might want to stay a bit longer."

That might have been true before her ill-advised guilt-call to 9-1-1. Greta rubbed her fingers across her forehead. All the more reason she should be relieved Detective Jack McTavish and his sidekick hadn't taken her seriously. She'd spent most of her life trying to bury the past. She certainly didn't need the police digging into it. "Maybe someday I'll stop, but not now. I don't want to take a chance."

"We can talk about it when I arrive. You're certain about meeting with Ms. Sorenson yourself?"

The doubt was there, just like the doubt she'd heard from Deputy Bowman, the doubt she felt in herself. She was rubbish around people; at times she could barely hold a conversation without getting distracted or going off in another direction. An unexpected flash of Jack McTavish exploded in her mind and for a moment, thanks to the image of his dimpled smile, she almost forgot what she and Lyndon were discussing. "I'm sure."

"I'm going to send you a list of things we need to

confirm. Please be sure you go over it. Whatever else you need to discuss with her is up to you."

"All right." She had the entire weekend before she had to go to the museum on Monday, but she was already getting nervous. In a good way. "Was there anything else?"

"Just remember, it's difficult to put the genie back in the bottle. Life is going to change for you after this show, Greta. We all need to be ready for it."

"At least with genies you get three wishes," Greta teased because she felt he needed it. "If I have any questions about the meeting, I'll text you." This must have been what Dorothy felt when she'd emerged from her black-and-white world into glorious Technicolor. All that promise, the hope she'd find down the yellow brick road, it was all just waiting for her. This could be the start to an adventure, something she'd avoided all her life. All she needed to do was take the first step. "This is the right move. It's my work, my future. I need to take better care of both."

His silence didn't last quite so long this time. "I worry about you, Greta," he said finally. "I don't want—"

"I know." Greta swallowed around a suddenly tight throat. "I know what you're afraid of. But I'm not my mother." She squeezed her eyes shut against the past and the pain. Against the terror that the darkness would swallow her as it had her mother. That she would become a danger not only to herself but to those around her. All the more reason to keep her life as solitary as possible. No matter how lonely it might be. "And you will be here for the show, won't you?"

"I wouldn't miss it." She could hear the scratching

of the eagle topped fountain pen she'd given him when she was ten years old. No doubt he was scribbling on a piece of monogrammed stationary. The idea made her lips twitch. Lyndon Thornwald was so old-school that history textbooks could use him as a footnote. "Just let me know how the meeting goes."

"I will give you an update as soon as I have one," Greta promised and after a few more minutes, they hung up.

She wasn't entirely sure what excited her more: taking a professional meeting all on her own or having the perfect excuse to take her time exploring the wonder of the Camellia Art Museum, which currently hosted a small, privately owned Salvador Dalí collection.

Even before its renovation and expansion, the acclaimed art museum had long been considered a source of pride for Sacramento. For years, collections from all over the world had been displayed in the old Victorian built in 1872, but now most art pieces were displayed in the modern pavilion that had been constructed next door. She'd been working toward this for the past five years: her first private showing in a major gallery. All the more reason to keep her wits about her.

The idea of leaving her tidy, comfortable world didn't cause as much trepidation as it might have last week. Yes, this was her place where everything was in her control. But out there? She resisted the urge to look out the window. Well, the other night was the perfect example of what happened out there, but beyond that, she could only imagine what inspiration she might find. She needed to embrace the opportunity.

Greta tossed her phone down and headed back to

her stool and resituated herself with her glasses. Her view caught on the window across the street as she angled the glasses at the third floor. She blinked against the sunny glare on the glass and turned her head away to get rid of the spots from her eyes. When she looked again, for the second time she found two men standing in the office in question.

One guy was a uniformed security guard she'd noticed earlier and the other...

Greta gasped and nearly dropped the glasses. "Jack."

Except he wasn't smiling. Not one little bit.

Chapter 3

Greta Renault might be many things, Jack thought. Beautiful, interesting, eccentric. One thing she was not, he realized as he caught her peering at him through what he suspected were binoculars, was stealthy. What in the world was she doing?

"Pretty great view, right?"

"Stunning." Jack turned away from the window as Fritz approached. He cleared his throat. "Love the historic buildings in this part of town." He took in every inch of the office space he could. As he was not here officially, he couldn't very well pull out his cell phone and start snapping pictures. But he could appraise and determine if there was cause to come back. It was a crossed line, but one he could live with if it meant getting to the bottom of this.

The pale green walls were no doubt an effort to evoke a sense of calm, but seeing the unfinished chaos of the office, that was a long way off. Long, thin boxes held what he could only assume were framed art pieces awaiting to be assigned a wall. A large clear plastic tarp had been whipped haphazardly over what looked to be an antique desk large enough even Napoleon wouldn't have a complex. Giant rolls of carpet sat against the wall like drunken guardsmen. The glass element extended beyond the windows and around the room as floating shelves, no doubt to display Fremont's countless awards and accolades waiting to be unpacked. The only other furniture at this time was a small circular table in the front corner along with two metal folding chairs. Cheap by comparison. They didn't quite fit.

"Mr. Fremont picked this office specifically," Fritz told him as if talking like a proud father. "He says he can see the entirety of the city from the rooftop garden."

"Your boss does seem to always have his eye on the prize," Jack agreed. "Has he been out of town long?"

"A few days," Fritz wandered over to the side counter where a pod coffee maker had already been set up. "You want?"

"Sure. Whatever you've got." Jack pinned his attention to the cement floor as he wandered the perimeter of the room. If this was where Greta had seen Fremont murder his victim, there should be some indication. Dead bodies were messy, whatever the cause of death and yet, try as he might, he didn't see any indication one had been in this room.

Jack crouched, set his cell on the floor to check for dampness. Dry as Death Valley. He took a deep breath, smelling for any hints of bleach or industrial cleaner. Nope. Nothing there, either. Just that stomach-churning stench of new construction and paint.

"You drop something?" Fritz asked.

"Yeah, my cell." Jack picked it up and accepted the paper cup. "Seems like this place will be up and running pretty soon."

"By the end of the month, if all goes according to plan," Fritz said. "We're getting the security cameras hooked up this week. The renovations have been done in record time, only six months, but when Mr. Fremont sets his mind to something... Hey, this is all the boring stuff. The rooftop garden is something out of a magazine. He's even growing fresh vegetables and herbs up there for the organic restaurant."

"The guy's almost too good to be true." Jack started to follow Fritz out, then something glinted under the table. "Oh, hang on." He patted his jacket. "I think I dropped my glasses, too. Sometimes I'm afraid I left half my brain on that operating table," he joked.

"You're lucky to be alive," Fritz called over his shoulder as he held open the door. "I heard that bullet missed your heart by nothing."

"A little more than nothing, thankfully." Jack backtracked to the table, bent down and looked at the piece of round, recognizable glass.

"Find what you were looking for?"

"I sure did." Jack angled his phone to snap a picture. Greta had said the supposed victim had been wearing round-rimmed glasses. It wasn't solid evidence of a crime. Not by a long shot, but it backed up part of her story. As much as he wanted to retrieve the lens, he had to leave it where it was. He stood and followed Fritz to the elevator just as the doors dinged open.

"Afternoon, Fritz."

"Mr. Fremont." Fritz sucked in about an inch of gut and straightened his spine as Jack skidded to a halt beside him. "Good to have you back, sir. I was just showing one of my former colleagues around the place. Detective Jack McTavish, Doyle Fremont."

Jack had seen enough photographs of Fremont to have recognized him without an introduction. The camera loved the guy, as did the papers, both legit news and tabloid. Always with the gregarious smile and generous attitude, Fremont had earned his reputation as one of the good guys by funding local and national charitable causes and promoting his reputation as being approachable, not to mention carefree and single. Jack had often heard of the man's so-called legendary charisma, much like powerful politicians or A-list Hollywood celebrities who drew in similar individuals like a gravitational force. To even consider this man a murderer should be enough to end his career.

"McTavish." Fremont offered a well-manicured hand, which Jack accepted. "I'm familiar with that name. Aren't you the detective who was shot last year protecting Dr. Allie Hollister?"

"That's me." That really was going to be the epithet on his tombstone, wasn't it? "Except it's Dr. Kellan these days."

"That's right. I'd heard she got married recently. To a former firefighter, if I remember correctly. Come on in while I drop this off." He hefted the soft-sided leather case and jerked his head. "Fritz, you, too."

"Actually, sir, I need to check on the boys downstairs, if you don't mind?"

"Of course not." Fremont offered an understanding smile that brightened his already wide brown eyes. "That's why I hired you. Top of your game. That's what I'm counting on. Detective, please. Join me while you finish your coffee."

Why did that sound more like an order than a request?

"The benefits are great," Fritz told Jack under his breath as he stepped into the elevator. "And you won't get shot in the heart."

Jack gave him a nod of acknowledgment as the doors slid closed.

"What brings you by, Detective?" Doyle Fremont's casual tone didn't quite ring true, but for now Jack was willing to chalk that up to his own radar being off.

"Curiosity." Jack returned to the office, leaned against the wall as he watched Fremont settle behind his polished redwood desk. He sipped his coffee, taking in the man's pristine image of professionalism. Even in casual dark slacks and crisp polo shirt, the adaptability was on display. The man could command a boardroom as easily as he could a boat deck. He matched Jack in height and stature and moved with a casual confidence that came with success. Again, Jack understood the guy's appeal, but was Jack's distrust genuine or influenced by a certain blonde artist across the street? "I'm exploring other employment options," Jack said. May as well stick with the one lie he'd already told today.

"Really?" Doyle flipped the plastic tarp off the intricately carved wooden desk and looked Jack directly in the eye as he wrapped it up and shoved it in the trash can. "After all your hard work to get back on the force, you're thinking of walking away? I'm not sure I buy that."

Jack sipped more coffee. So Fremont knew more about him than just his name. "No?"

"No." Doyle took a seat and gestured for Jack to do the same.

Jack grabbed one of the metal chairs and dragged it over, hoping, praying that Greta had stopped playing spy and put the ridiculous glasses away.

"You know what I think?" Fremont asked as Jack crossed an ankle over one knee.

"Not a clue."

"I think someone sent you here to check up on me."

Jack kept his eyes steady on Fremont's. "Who would have sent me?"

Whether Fremont meant to or not, his dark gaze flickered lightning quick over Jack's shoulder. The hairs on the back of Jack's neck leaped to attention. There was only one thing in that line of sight. Greta's loft.

"I'm being paranoid, I'm sure." Fremont returned his focus to Jack and leaned back in his expensive leather chair. "If I had to guess, I'd say the mayor might be worried I'm going to run against him in the next election."

"And if I had to, I'd say you're guessing up the wrong tree." Because he suspected it would annoy Fremont, Jack mirrored the man's posture, appearing to shrug off any suspicion.

"Maybe a bigger tree, then? The governor?"

"You golf with his lieutenant," Jack reminded him as he began to understand the rules of the game. If Fremont thought he could wind Jack around his finger, he clearly didn't know him at all. Jack had spent almost a decade as a cop in Chicago. He'd gone up against men ten times as ruthless as Doyle Fremont and lived to tell about it. A familiar twinge of guilt struck him between the ribs. Was that why he was so determined to believe Greta even when what she said made no sense? Jack wondered if he was trying to make up for mistakes he'd made in the past.

"I'm thinking you'd already know if someone had you in their sights, Mr. Fremont. I'd bet most people find it difficult to keep secrets around you."

"Doyle, please. And you'd be right. Secrets are a passion of mine." His smile would have frozen water. "They're powerful. It's amazing what people will do to keep them. They run. They hide. They try to pretend to be someone they're not. Pushing their buttons, holding those secrets over them, it's a kind of addiction, but one I'm not going to apologize for. It's given me a rather ruthless reputation that has made aspects of my business far easier. A reputation I'm sure you disapprove of."

"I'm not sure why my approval should mean anything. But it does beg the question. What would you do—" Jack asked because it would have been rude not to walk through the door Doyle had opened "—to keep your secrets?"

"You must not listen to rumors, Detective." Doyle smiled, but for the first time, the humor didn't quite reach his eyes. "I don't have any secrets. I am that rare open book who will answer any question at any time. But the same can't be said for others." He sat forward, folded his hands on top of the desk and pinned Jack with a look Jack suspected had scared off more than a few business rivals. "Whatever curiosity brought you here, Detective McTavish—"

"Jack, please."

"Jack it is." Impatience flashed across his normally controlled features. "Whatever curiosity brought you by, I hope it's been quieted. I can assure you, there's nothing here for you to find."

"At least, not anymore, right?" Jack got to his feet and offered his hand. "Appreciate your time, Doyle. I'll see myself out." As he strode off, he put a mental check next to the name Doyle Fremont. He'd be seeing him again. And soon.

"What on earth is he doing there?" Excitement pounded through Greta as she watched Jack bend down to examine the floor. She bit her lip. My, but he was beautiful. She shook her head in an attempt to clear it. "Did he find something?" Was it possible…

Her heart thudded as Jack stood and followed the security guard out of the office. Hope took a tiny bounce inside her as she lowered the opera glasses. Maybe she wasn't as alone in this as she thought. Why else would he be over at Doyle Fremont's office? Unless he was feeling guilty about how his deputy had treated her the other night.

She looked down at Cerberus, unwilling to admit out loud even to her oblivious cat, that she didn't like the idea of Detective McTavish thinking she was—what was it Deputy Bowman had called her?—*kooky*.

Disappointment, all too familiar to her, clanged inside her like a forgotten, rusted church bell. She'd been called worse over the years. A lot worse, but she'd learned a long time ago to shake those comments off. Unless they had a connection to a detective with kind eyes and a wounded soul.

Her back ached, reminding her she'd spent far too much time hunched over waiting for…whatever was going to happen across the street. What did she think would happen? That Doyle Fremont was going to wave to her this time? Point to wherever he'd hidden the body? She shivered. He wasn't that stupid. Or careless.

And yet she'd seen him.

She lifted the glasses again, did another scan of Doyle's office. Deputy Bowman's question about how the man with the birthmark had been killed gnawed at her, which had her chewing on her lip. She hadn't seen a gun. Or a weapon of any kind. She could only remember that Fremont had moved like a rattler, coiled to strike. A fast movement, so quick it was imperceptible to her frantic mind trying to grab hold of every detail. Searching her memory wasn't doing her any good. Staring at the window for endless hours wasn't helping, either.

"I need to get this on paper." If there was one thing that had always grounded her, it was putting a pen or pencil in her hand. What she'd seen that night had been playing over and over in her head. She may as well commit it to paper, right?

She was climbing off her stool when a flash of movement in the office across the street caught her eye. She gasped, kicked the stool back and dived for cover. She inched out, just enough to angle the glasses at the window.

Doyle Fremont was back.

Looking at him, in his neat, casual clothes, one would never have guessed he'd killed someone. Greta shivered.

She dialed the focus on the glasses to see if she could zoom closer, but they only blurred. She was asking far too much of the antique device. She struggled to find a hint of guilt, any hesitation or motion of self-doubt indicating he'd made a mistake in the actions he'd taken, but he showed none. He moved with purpose and grace, dropping his briefcase onto the chair behind what she assumed was a desk, his lips moving as he seemed to be speaking to someone out in the hall.

Someone who soon joined Doyle in his office.

"Jack." What was he still doing there? She thought he'd left. Why hadn't he left? And why were they chatting as if they were lifelong friends? All the years she'd spent alone, observing other people go about their lives, she really should have taken up lipreading. And as much as she knew she should keep her focus on Fremont, her attention kept drifting to Jack right up to when he left.

That's when she should have looked away, but she didn't. She angled the glasses back to Fremont where he sat at his desk, leaning back in his chair, a finger pressed against his lips as he appeared to stare blankly ahead.

Chills erupted on the back of her neck. She scooted back as Fremont got to his feet, walked around his desk and stopped at the window. His gaze never wavered as he skimmed the line of her loft, back and forth. Back and forth.

Her heart thudded in her ears. She didn't dare move, didn't dare breathe for fear of fluttering the thin curtain bunched near her face. Could he see her? Or was he just playing some kind of game to entertain himself?

She yelped as Cerberus wound himself around her bare feet again. "Don't do that, Cerb. I'm scaring myself enough. I don't need help." She picked up the cat to nuzzle his fur, wishing not for the first time she could turn back the clock. If only she'd ignored what had happened, what she saw, then nothing in her life would have changed.

Instead, now, she was left to wonder and worry about which side of her sanity she'd landed on.

The intercom buzzed. Greta jumped, and her heart just about exploded in her chest. She stood there, blinking, barely breathing as her mind raced. To be safe, she returned to the window, leaned over just enough to peer back into Fremont's office. Doyle Fremont was still there. The intercom buzzed again. She scrubbed her damp palms hard against her bare thighs and walked to the door. Her hands shook as she pressed the button to activate the front-door camera. She sagged against the wall, half laughing and relieved to see the detective.

She buzzed him in and stood waiting behind the closed door until she heard the stair door creak open. Only then did she open her own door, but only by a crack. She tried not to notice how the blue of his shirt made his eyes glint, or how just the sight of him made her feel better. But she did notice. Both. She also noticed he was more than slightly out of breath, despite trying to hide the fact. "Detective."

"Are you trying to get yourself killed?"

His words sliced straight through her. "Excuse me?"

"What were you thinking spying on him like that?"

He braced his hands on either side of the frame and glared at her. "You may as well be holding up a sign that says *Here I am. Come and get me.*"

Whatever gentleness and understanding had been in his voice the last time they'd spoken had completely evaporated with the steam coming out of his ears. Anger sparked in his blue eyes, like tiny orange flames erupting in the ocean. Fascination tempered her offense as her fingers itched for her brush, a pencil, her notepad. "I beg your pardon."

"Don't. Just don't, Greta." She caught a glimmer beneath the anger, beneath the irritation. Was it...concern? Was he worried about her? Something odd and light fluttered in her chest. "You need to stay out of this from here on. You need to stay away from Doyle Fremont."

"Why?" Her chin inched up, her fingers tightening around the edge of the door.

"Don't do that, either."

"Do what?" She frowned.

"Hold that door between us like it's some kind of shield. I'm not going to hurt you."

She gave him a smile that made her cheeks ache. "Maybe I'm trying to protect you from the kook who lives here." Snark wasn't her forte, but the flash of embarrassment that crossed over his handsome features boosted her confidence. "That is what your partner called me, isn't it? Kooky?"

"He did." That he didn't try to deny it earned him points, but the confirmation struck hard, nonetheless. He rubbed a hand against his chest. "I apologize for that. Bowie's experience with the more eccentric residents of our city needs to be expanded. And better tolerated. He could probably also do with a new thesaurus."

Her lips twitched at the unexpected joke. "Do you agree with him?"

"That you're kooky? I wouldn't say so, although spying on a man you're convinced killed someone doesn't seem like the safest of moves. How about I reserve judgment?"

A man you're convinced... She could have stepped into the verbal trap he'd set, a trap he'd baited with a dimple-revealing smile that had her stomach doing somersaults. But rather than taking that step forward, she took one back. And opened the door wider. "How about we have this discussion over a cup of tea."

He blinked. As expected, she'd caught him off guard. "I'm sorry?"

"Tea," she said slowly. "It looks like you could use some. I'm sorry, I don't have any coffee. I know you prefer it."

"How do you know?" He straightened, but hesitated, appeared a bit unsure of what to do next.

"Because you were slugging it down the other night when you were here. Don't get me wrong, I love the smell of strong brewed espresso, but the caffeine wreaks havoc on your nerves, and I don't need shaky hands. So let's do tea." When he came forward, she stopped him with a hand on his chest. Her fingers immediately warmed as they pressed into him. A blood-zinging buzz hummed through her as she curled her fingers under and into the soft fabric of his shirt. She couldn't have let go of him if she'd wanted to. And she didn't want to.

"I thought you were going to let me in."

She lifted her chin, looked into his eyes that drew her in like breath. She wanted to draw him. She wanted to just look at him and let her mind fly. But now, more than anything, more than she should, she wanted something completely wrong, something she'd never wanted before in her life. She wanted...

She stepped forward, slipped her hand up and around to his neck and drew him to her, covered his mouth with hers. She could feel his surprise, taste it on her lips as she moved her mouth, angled her head and deepened the kiss. A surge of energy flashed through her as she felt his hand skim down her side to rest on the swell of her hip. She barely had time to process the skin-tingling sensation before he moved in, pulling her tight against him. Whatever control she thought she had slipped away as he took over, his tongue sweeping through her mouth, tangling with hers, painting an image in her mind of what their bodies could do together.

That thought was enough to prompt reason to return. She broke off the kiss but didn't stop touching him, couldn't stop herself from tangling her fingers in his hair. "I can't believe I just did that." Every nerve ending in her body was sparking like a downed electrical wire.

"That makes two of us. Please tell me you wouldn't have done that if Bowie rang the bell," Jack murmured.

She loved how he made her smile. "I'm sure that was completely inappropriate, so if I should apologize—"

He kissed her again. A short kiss, barely a brush of mouth over mouth, but it was enough to have her wanting more. Enough to prove she hadn't been out of line.

"I have just one question before you come in." She

pressed her lips together to retain the taste of him as she held back a sigh.

"Just one?"

Oh, yeah. She was in serious trouble with this man. And the timing couldn't be worse. "What are you really doing here? It can't be because you caught me playing peekaboo with a serious bad guy over there."

"Actually, it can."

"It can?" She frowned, not understanding even as she dared to hope. She stepped back and lowered her arms. "Why?"

"Because." He seemed unable to resist. He reached up a hand and brushed a finger down the side of her face and spoke the three words that made her heart soar. "I believe you."

The offer of tea couldn't have come at a better time, Jack thought as he wandered her apartment. No doubt the lack of sleep, more than a day's worth of coffee before noon and a truckload of self-doubt had done a number on his system. Why else would he have kissed her back like that?

Inappropriate. Completely and utterly so. It wasn't just that it could compromise any case, but it was just unprofessional. Not that he'd started it, but he was more than willing to keep up with Greta, who might just have succeeded in blowing the top of his head off. He groaned, closed his eyes and took a deep breath. What on earth was he thinking? Noticing, accepting that Greta Renault was a fall-to-his-knees knockout was one thing. Acting on it? Discovering she was so much more? The last thing he needed was another complication when it came to his job.

At least this type of complication.

Getting involved with a witness was a serious breach of conduct, and right now, he couldn't afford even a minor infraction. And there was nothing minor about Greta Renault.

His lungs ached as if he'd climbed a dozen flights of stairs rather than three. If that was the afterburn of kissing Greta, there were worse consequences, he supposed. That said, his poor treadmill was going to quit after the workout he'd be giving it starting tonight. How else was he going to burn off this…energy?

Not, he told himself, by finishing what she'd started. Maybe once the case was over he could pursue things, but mixing mind-blowing pleasure with business was only going to get them both in serious trouble.

The intoxicating scent of jasmine drifted through her apartment. It hadn't taken him long to realize her hair and skin smelled like the exotic flower. While she was in the kitchen, he resisted the temptation to drop onto the sofa. Instead, he explored the expanse of windows overlooking Fremont's building next door.

He could see where she'd had a clear view, and given the sparse furnishings in Fremont's office, she wouldn't have had any issues distinguishing figures either in the light or dark. And that, Jack realized as he stepped back, was part of what bothered him. That office in particular was such an open space; there was virtually nothing private about it, even if you thought you might be alone. And, according to Fritz, there were always at least two security officers patrolling the building. It would have taken pretty meticulous planning on Fremont's part to have returned to Sacramento—about a six-hour drive from LA—when he should have been attending an event, kill someone, then get rid of all of the evidence without leaving any trace other than a convenient glasses lens behind.

"The whole thing doesn't make sense."

While he might not be able to puzzle out the mystery that was Doyle Fremont, he could, hopefully, attempt to gain some insight into his witness. And there was no better way to do that than to browse the only collection of items she had on display: her books. And she did have a lot of them: enough that they filled the shelves stretching nearly around the entire outline of the living room.

The art books didn't surprise him. She had an extensive collection of detailed coffee-table books on dozens of artists, including a few he hadn't heard of. He drew his fingers along the spines, making mental notes before continuing his search.

Interesting. Only the first column of shelves had been dedicated to art, but these others…all of these others held various copies and editions of medical and psychology texts. Pharmaceutical encyclopedias. He trailed his fingers over writers' books on mental disorders and diseases, multiple years' worth of the DSM. Psychosis seemed a favorite topic of hers, as did dissociative disorders. Manic depression, schizophrenia… The subjects just went on and on. And nowhere, in this entire display of texts and written word, did he see anything indicating Greta's personality.

He leaned on the back of the sofa, scanning the

shelves yet again for any photographs, trinkets, knick-knacks he might have missed, but there were only books. Not even pictures of her art shows or even her artwork. All of that seemed confined to her studio, a studio he now realized he'd like to take a more extensive look through.

If the medical texts didn't confuse him, her taste in literature certainly did. *Metamorphosis* by Kafka seemed a particular favorite. She had multiple copies, some of which had extensive handwritten notes and highlighted passages. He did find a few mysteries thrown in, but they, too, dealt with the psychological. The science fiction selections focused on the mind, its power and its flaws. He'd never been so relieved to find a good selection of romance novels, but again, these leaned toward romantic suspense that dug deep into the psychological aspects of the villains of the stories.

"Did she get a psych degree on the side?" He'd always said he enjoyed a bit of mystery when it came to women, but maybe this was taking things a bit too far? Even her DVD selection seemed biased toward crime, noir and psychology, with a collector's edition of every Hitchcock movie, along with some cult classics he'd never gotten around to viewing. One movie in particular seemed to be a favorite as she had multiple versions, including the twenty-fifth anniversary edition, a bootlegged director's cut and foreign editions. "*Midnight Witness*. Huh." He pulled it free to scan the summary.

Mew.

Jack glanced over his shoulder in time to see Cerberus leap onto the stool at the edge of the curtains.

As if reading his thoughts, Cerberus stopped licking

his paw and stared Jack right in the eye. They blinked at the same time, a draw, and, if he let himself think on it too long, Jack wondered if the cat had really smirked.

"Tea's brewing." Greta's soft voice had him breaking contact with Cerberus. "It takes a while. Why don't you sit down before you fall over?"

"Before I…" He set the DVD case in its spot. Whatever he was going to say next evaporated as she walked over and, with one effortless move, slid his jacket off his shoulders and draped it over the back of a chair. "Um." His face went hot when her hands came up and unknotted his tie. What would she go after next?

"I think we're past you feeling shy around me." She whipped the tie off and led him over to sit down. "And don't be such a man. You're struggling. Sitting will help. And so will the tea. African Nectar blend. It's what I drink when I'm feeling stressed and out of sorts."

"I'm not stressed." At least not in the way she might think. But she was already flitting back into the kitchen as if the kiss had never happened. When she returned, she had the oversize notepad he recognized, along with a collection of various pencils. He glanced around, wondering if this was one of those hidden camera shows everyone was so obsessed with. Why did everything within these walls feel just a bit off? "Greta—"

"Relax now. Tea soon. Talk later." She curled up in the opposite end of the sofa, reached behind her for a remote control and clicked on the fireplace. The flames burst to life in perfect blue-tipped orange and immediately sent the aroma of burning wood into the room. If he didn't know better, he'd think she was trying to passive-aggressively seduce him.

She flicked her gaze to his, offered a quick smile, but no offer of conversation. He shifted around, rested an arm along the back of the sofa so his stretched-out fingers almost reached her shoulder. That bare skin of hers, was it as soft as it seemed? As soft as her cheek had been? As supple as her lips?

"What are you doing?" he asked as she focused all her attention on her sketchpad.

"Now that I know you believe me, I assume you need a statement." Her hand started moving in the same way it had the night she met him, lightning quick over the paper. "I do images, not words. Those can come later. Once these are…" She trailed off, her whisper-soft voice fading as the warmth of the fire embraced him, and she fell back into the world at the tip of her pencil.

"You didn't put any kind of hallucinogen in that fireplace, did you?" Jack tried to joke as his eyes went heavy.

"Reality gives me enough to deal with. I don't need help in that area."

He noticed her expression barely flickered as she said it. A face that he now realized he'd seen before, when he'd spent endless hours staring into that painting of hers. But that wasn't possible. The figure in his painting didn't have a face.

At least not before he'd met Greta. Now she would.

"You said you believe me." Greta's statement had him pulling out of a haze of attraction that began to buzz through him.

"I did. I do."

"But you didn't." Greta pinned him with those amazing, eerie gray eyes of hers. "Did you? Please don't tell me kissing you made you feel obligated to make some false confession. If you don't believe me—"

"The thought crossed my mind," he teased, then he continued. "I believed you believed what you saw actually happened. That was enough to make me do some poking around." Was that enough to keep him from getting kicked out of her loft for a second time? He liked it here, the space, the decor. Liked her. Minimalist yet practical and comfortable, both the dwelling and its resident. And not because of how she'd greeted him. He longed to uncover why he found no knickknacks, no framed photographs of friends or even family. Not even a speck of dust seemed to have settled in for an extended stay, while Jack should probably start charging the dust bunnies in his house rent.

"And now?"

"And now what?" Jack wondered how anyone's voice could sound as soft as sable.

"What's changed that you believe me now?"

"I met Doyle Fremont." He waited, focusing on the slow beat of his heart as her hand stilled. "He's a cool son of a…" Jack cleared his throat. "He's a cold customer," he corrected himself. "Not sure I've met anyone frostier." He'd read it in Fremont's eyes as he'd sat across from him. Almost as if they were playing some kind of game, and only Fremont knew the rules. Little did he know he'd triggered Jack's suspicion. "It's not out of the realm of possibility he killed someone."

"He did." She didn't look away from her pad. If anything, her pencil strokes became stronger, harder. Went faster. "I don't know how without a knife or a gun, but he did it."

"If he did, we'll prove it." If only it were that simple. Without evidence, without a body...

Now she smiled. "Yes, we will."

"We as in the police," he clarified when he saw the unrestrained interest in her gaze. No way was he letting her anywhere closer to this investigation. It might even be better if she got out of town for a while, holed up someplace no one knew about while he investigated whether one of the richest men in the country had committed cold-blooded murder. "While I can appreciate your enthusiasm—" he gestured to the stool and ridiculous enameled binoculars "—I'm going to make a few suggestions."

"I ordered a new pair of binoculars. And I'm thinking about getting heavier curtains." She tapped a fingernail against her teeth.

New binoc... Jack's head pounded against the surge of frustration, but he kept his voice controlled. Barely. "How about you stop looking altogether?"

There went that eyebrow again. Pale, considered and angular as she aimed a look at him. She really could look determined when she wanted to. "No."

"You called me. Well, you called the police," he corrected as he searched for a way around her argument. "You wanted us to look into what you witnessed. So let us. Me. Not we." He pointed between them. "We as in me as in the police pursue this."

Her lips curved. "I never knew pronoun confusion could be so entertaining."

"I'm not trying to be entertaining, Greta." Did she not take this seriously? The residual fog of attraction dissipated, and he slipped back into cop mode. He knew

how ruthless people could be. He knew the lengths
they'd go to, to silence those who went against them.
His hands had been covered in the blood of the after-
math once. He was not going to let it happen to Greta.
"I spent five minutes with that guy, and I can tell you
something is off with him. I don't want him shifting
his focus on to you. Not any more than it already is."

Greta bit her lip and winced, turned her attention
back on her drawings.

"What?" Jack demanded as gently as he could manage.

"I think he saw me watching him earlier." Greta
shrugged. "Just after you left. I can't be sure, but—"

Jack swore as a timer dinged in the kitchen.

"That's your tea." She uncurled from the sofa and
set her pad between them. "Here. I'll get the tray. You
can start looking through these and get your notes organized." She ripped off an oversize sheet of paper and
handed it over. "Or jotted down. Or whatever it is you
Columbos do."

"Columbos?" Jack suspected he was going to be in
a constant state of confusion around this woman. She
flitted from subject to subject like a hummingbird on
a nectar high.

"I like old TV shows sometimes. Old movies, too.
Too dated?" She stopped, braced paint-spattered fingers
against the wall into the kitchen. Jean shorts that fit her
like a second skin revealed the curves that had been hidden behind silk the other night. Curves that could keep
a man's hands entertained for a lifetime if he ever got
bored with those endless legs. The bright yellow of her
tank was like a shock of sunlight in the darkness, much

like the woman wearing it. She wasn't small or delicate or any of the things he normally found appealing in a woman. She was full-bodied and graceful and… Jack blew out an unexpected breath…tempting as a glass of smooth whiskey after a long, trying day.

"Never too dated for Columbo." How was she to know the classic TV detective was one of his earliest inspirations? He used to drive his sister, Ashley, nuts racing around his house in a thrift-store beige trench coat, chewing on a fake cigar while he interrogated everything from the family dog to their mother's houseplants.

He had no idea if Greta heard him as she disappeared into the depths of the kitchen to rattle around while he lifted the paper she'd drawn on. His blood ran cold, and the chill couldn't be tempered by his admiration of her skill as he moved on to the sketchpad. In the few short minutes since he arrived, she'd casually sketched out four images, almost like a comic strip, each of which clearly depicted a violent scene, ending with Doyle Fremont standing over the body of a large man, his eyes open as he stared at the ceiling.

"If you ever get bored with your artwork, you could have a second career as a sketch artist," Jack said when she returned in an attempt to keep the mood light. It hadn't escaped his notice that beyond the figures and the arrangement of the sparse furniture and surroundings, the same elements often found in her paintings loomed large. A sense of foreboding, of invasion or attack. Just hovering beyond the line of reality and reason. His eyes drooped and despite his determination not to, he slid down on the sofa and leaned his head back.

Control evaporated as he blinked, slowly, slower...and sank into the welcoming, warm darkness.

"I think you'll like this tea." Greta carried a brass tray laden with a steaming teapot, mugs and a plate of macadamia-nut cookies. Her assistant Jessie kept Greta supplied in the sweet treats. "It has rose and..." Greta stopped shy of the sofa, a bubble of surprise popping in her chest. "Oh."

If she'd ever seen a more delightful sight than that of Jack McTavish sound asleep on her sofa, she couldn't recall. The lines of him, strong, long, determined to hold on to control even as he drifted in sleep spoke to the deepest part of her. That he felt comfortable enough in her home to let himself go warmed her in a way she'd never felt before, from her tingling fingertips to her bare, paint-splattered toes. Not, she mused, unlike how she felt kissing him.

His face relaxed, the lines around his eyes erased as he let go of this world and slipped into another, another she'd never be able to follow him into. Silly, she told herself, even as she imagined him taking her hand and leading her through a foggy maze of sunshine and roses, away from the darkness that always seemed to loom around her. Light, she thought as she inclined her head and smiled down at him. He was like a light shining at the end of an endless, meandering tunnel. A tunnel she couldn't let herself fall into.

She set the tray down on the coffee table, careful not to make any noise. She poured herself a cup, then retrieved a weighted blanket from the hall closet. He didn't move as she draped it around him, didn't stir as she retook her seat at the other end of the sofa where she sipped her tea and returned to her sketches.

It was, she realized, the most settled she'd felt, not just in the last few hours but in a good long while. Something about Jack's presence calmed her, focused her, much as it had in her studio when she'd painted him. Now, with her feet curled up inches from him, toes scrunching into the soft fabric of the sofa, she dropped deeper into memory and etched out the details of the scene she'd seen from the window.

The gas fire crackled and burned, taking with it each moment as she lost herself. Not one to need a clock with Cerberus around, she didn't surface until the cat leaped up next to her, nudged the back of her hand with his head, then slinked cautiously over to Jack.

It occurred to her she should stop the feline from exploring their visitor, but how someone reacted to her beloved cat, or how Cerberus reacted to them, was a test nature had put in place at the beginning of time. When he began to purr and paw Jack's lap, Greta couldn't be certain if it was the soft gray fabric of the blanket or the appeal of the man that had the cat curling up and resting his head against the arm of the sofa.

A giggle erupted from inside her before she could stop it. She covered her mouth as Jack stirred, his brow furrowing before he awoke completely, as if trying to decipher where he was.

"Hi." She rested her cheek in her hand and smiled at him.

"Hey." That furrow became a full-on frown. He lifted an arm, only to find it trapped beneath the blanket. "Wow. Did I fall asleep? Oh, hi there." He tipped his chin down and looked at Cerberus. "Nice kitty." He rested his hand on the cat's fur as confusion settled on his face. "I'm sorry. That's never happened before."

"Falling asleep or attracting cats?" Greta pulled her feet in under her, genuinely interested in the answer.

"Uh, both. Sleep hasn't exactly been a friend lately. Um…" He lifted the edge of the blanket. "Is this thing magic or something?"

"Or something. Works great, doesn't it? I have a few all over the loft. I don't sleep much. Insomnia. But I know I need to, so it helps." She leaned over and poured him some tea, disappointed that it had gone cold. She looked out the window, saw that the sun had shifted significantly. "I guess maybe I should have awakened you as it's later than I realized. We both got a bit lost."

He extricated his hand from under both blanket and cat. "Oh, wow. It's after four. I really zonked out." He tried to move. Cerberus glared at him. "I'll wait a bit. Thanks." He accepted the cold tea and sipped.

"What do you think?"

"I think it tastes like a mouthful of roses. Not that I'd know," he added with a quick smile. His cheeks carried color now, healthy color that had her breathing a bit easier. He hadn't looked particularly well when he'd first turned up. Personally, she'd love to take credit for that healthy color in his cheeks, but she wasn't quite that arrogant.

"Have some cookies."

"Cookies?" His stomach growled. "Yeah, sure." He snagged one, bit in and his eyes lit up. "You bake, too?"

"Not even a little. I'm too easily distracted. Baking takes attention." She nibbled on her own cookie. "My assistant does, though. And cooks like a dream. She's studying to be a personal chef and caterer at CSUS, and lucky me, I'm her test subject."

"What's her name?" Jack asked and fumbled for his phone. His frown returned when he looked at the screen, but he tucked it away and pulled out a notebook instead. "For my Columbo file. I'm still old-school."

"Ah." There was so much to be said for respecting the past. Greta found herself liking him more with each passing moment. "Her name is Jessie Jeffries. I know." Greta grinned at his expression. "She sounds like a comic book character, doesn't she?"

"Something like that. She come here often?"

"A couple of times a week, whenever she doesn't have classes. She's due here tomorrow, actually. Once your appetite is back, she'll have whipped me up some of her miraculous mac and cheese to stash in the freezer. It's my personal favorite."

"That's a pretty tempting offer." He hesitated, hand tightening around his pen. "What makes you think I don't have an appetite?"

"Your jacket doesn't fit right. The shirt, either." She pointed to his button-down. "They're too big. I'm not judging. But if I were, I'd say I doubt you had a reason to lose weight. So I guess some personal issues came up?"

"Something like that." He shifted on the sofa, didn't look at her.

Something in his voice made her heart hurt. If she had to, she'd guess a woman was behind that tone. "She's not worth it."

"Who's not worth what?"

"Whoever broke your heart. Sent you spiraling."
Struggling.

"It wasn't a woman. It was a bullet."

"Oh." Not something she anticipated hearing. "I'm sorry."

He shrugged. "It was almost a year ago. Your 9-1-1 call was my first when I got back to the job. So, yeah. Still adjusting."

He said *bullet* so casually, she thought for sure she'd misheard. How interesting, that he could speak more openly about nearly being killed than he could about a woman from his past. Dozens of questions popped into her mind, but because she couldn't chance the conversation turning to her, she choked down her curiosity and swallowed the sympathy. "I'm glad you're doing better."

"Thanks." He flicked her a tight smile before he set his cup down and scooped Cerberus off his lap with unexpected finesse before he got to his feet. She watched, amused as he struggled to fold the blanket.

"You do that a lot." She pointed her half-eaten cookie at him. "It's like you've got a separate conversation going on in your head that you don't want anyone else to know about. I understand if you don't want to talk about it. I was just making conversation."

"I think we can find something else to talk about other than me failing superhero school with my inability to stop a bullet. How about you tell me why you've moved around so much all these years? Six states in seven years. That's…restless. Where's your family? Your parents? Siblings?"

The panic she'd expected descended instantly. Cold, icy panic that nearly had her teeth chattering. He'd looked into her past. The question was, how far? She managed to keep calm as the peace surrounding them disappeared. She smiled but remained silent.

"That's what I thought," Jack said. "So. Doyle Fremont."

"Yes. Doyle Fremont." As much as she regretted uttering a word about what she'd seen, if she hadn't, Jack McTavish wouldn't be standing in her living room folding a blanket. And that, she knew, especially now that she'd kissed him, would have been a shame. She could already feel those locked spaces in her mind opening, expanding. For the first time in a long time, she was anxious to get back to work.

"The accusation you've made against Fremont isn't anything to joke about." The man who had been sleeping on her sofa disappeared behind the tense, suspicious face of the cop.

"I know." She flinched. "But talking with you about anything else is more fun. And just a bit less scary." She shouldn't be pushing him about his personal life, not when she didn't want him within an inch of her own.

"Only a bit?"

Clever, she thought. "You found something in his office, didn't you? Something beyond your impression of Fremont helped convince you I wasn't imagining things. That's really why you're here."

"Yes." He picked up his tea and drank deeply, surprising, it seemed, both of them. "I don't suppose you're interested in taking a vacation, getting out of town for a while."

"No." If she'd had any doubts that he believed her, they vanished with that suggestion. What she'd seen in his eyes earlier had been true. He was worried. "Even if I wanted to, I have a show in a few weeks and a ton of work to do before then. So—" she pointed behind her without looking away from him "—we'll compromise. I'm definitely going with the heavier curtains." She popped the last of her cookie in her mouth and picked up her tea. She sipped, swallowed and considered him. "So what do we do next?"

Jack choked on his tea. "By we you mean—"

"You and me." She snapped her teeth through a second cookie and grinned. "You don't really expect me to stop now that I'm invested? I'm your only witness, Detective. That means you're stuck with me. No matter how confused your pronouns were earlier."

"Uh…" He pinched the bridge of his nose and squeezed his eyes shut. "That's not the way things work, Greta. This is my job. I will take care of it."

Had a man's irritation ever been so utterly appealing? No way was he going to investigate this without her. She couldn't allow it, not with what she had at stake. "I'm not going to let this go, Jack. I can't. Not until I get to the truth." Because she needed to know, with 100 percent certainty, that what she'd seen had actually happened, no matter the consequences.

Chapter 4

Back at the station, Jack exited the elevator right before the end of shift, eyes glued to the screen of his cell phone as he enlarged and reangled the image he'd taken in Doyle Fremont's office. Too bad his phone didn't have a filter to lift fingerprints off a stationary object. But there was no mistaking the round piece of glass was a lens that had popped out of a pair of glasses.

"Where have you been?" Bowie's conspiratorial whisper was Jack's only warning the deputy was nearby, lurking, as if waiting to pounce on him the second he got back.

"Working." Did sipping tea, eating cookies and kissing a witness count as work? His lips twitched. "Why?" To say he'd gotten a burst of energy at Greta's was an understatement. That nap had been the first time in months he hadn't had the dreams. He actually felt… good. Or he had until she'd announced she expected to be part of the active investigation. As if…

"McTavish!" Lt. Santos bellowed from the other end of the Major Crimes department.

The unassuming cop who had served as Jack's boss since Jack had transferred from Chicago stood outside his office, looking at him with an expression that would have put a laser beam to shame. "My office. Now!"

While the rest of the department fell into an uneasy silence—their lieutenant was one of the coolest and most controlled cops around—Jack took his boss's order as confirmation he'd made the right choice when it came to where he'd spent most of his day.

"What did you do? Working on what? We haven't had more than a D and D and a burglary." Bowie tagged behind him like a puppy seeking attention. "Are you working on that call from the other night? I thought we were partners on that."

"I thought we were, as well." Jack stopped at his desk long enough to stash his sidearm and slip out of his jacket. "I didn't think you were interested in following up on what a kook had to say."

Bowie straightened, his normally easygoing expression shifting into uncertainty. "Sir?"

"We protect and serve, Bowie. Everyone. We don't get to pick and choose who is worthy of our attention. And we certainly don't suggest they're mentally unbalanced within earshot without at least looking into things. Nor do we turn them into a sideshow within these walls." He smacked his drawer closed. "Disrespect a witness again around me and I'll put you on report."

"Sir." Bowie's jaw locked as his eyes hardened. "I was just—"

"You were trying to make an impression. You made one. Just not a great one, at least not with me." He caught sight of Lt. Santos returning to his office. "We can talk about this later, but I'm disappointed in you, Bowie." He knew it was a slap. A big one. And maybe Jack was overreacting. But he had eyes, and he'd seen the pain Greta had attempted to hide behind a forced and amused smile. The urge to protect her felt so primal, even before he'd kissed her, had felt so overwhelming, he wondered if the instinct was coded into his DNA. While he knew he needed to pull that under control, that didn't stop him from being frustrated with his friend and fellow officer.

"What have you gotten yourself into, Jack?" Lt. Santos closed the door behind Jack as if sealing them in a cone of silence. His boss stood a good foot shorter than Jack, and Santos's youthful appearance was part of the reason he'd had a long, successful history with gang undercover work. But that same tenacity and cool-headedness was also what made the officers under his command all but quiver in their comfortable shoes even as they worshipped at his feet. "You want to tell me why I've got the chief calling me to ask why you're interrogating Doyle Fremont as if he's some kind of suspect?"

Well, well, well. He must have spooked him after all. "Fremont called the chief?"

"No. He called the mayor who called the chief. And then his lawyer called all of us. A lawyer we can both assume makes more money in an hour than the two of us make in a year. The word *libel* was thrown around multiple times."

"Huh." All the confidence Jack lost these last months surged back. "That didn't take long." What an overreaction for someone who claimed to be an open book.

"What didn't take long? I don't like being sideswiped, Jack. Especially by my boss. Sit. Explain." Santos pointed a sharp finger at one of the two chairs on the other side of his desk.

"Can I have some coffee?" Jack stared longingly at the personal pod coffee machine on top of his lieutenant's desk. He might have appreciated the flavors in the tea Greta had served him, but what he needed was a serious caffeine jolt.

"No. I've read your medical report, Jack, remember? You're supposed to be off caffeine."

So much for coffee to go with the leftover cookies he'd stuck in his pockets on his way out of Greta's loft.

"What's going on?" Lt. Santos leaned back in his chair. The anger Jack had seen in his eyes moments before faded behind concern. "You aren't reckless. Or careless. You don't go asking for a personal tour of a private business without cause while on duty. Or without a warrant. And you certainly don't interrogate citizens like Doyle Fremont like a common criminal. So, I'll ask again. What have you gotten yourself into?"

"Citizens like Doyle Fremont?" Jack echoed and crossed an ankle over one knee. "You make that sound as if he's entitled to special treatment. Don't tell me. He's made substantial donations to the Widows and Orphans Fund."

"Does this seem like a good time for witty comebacks?"

In Jack's experience it was always time, but he knew when he was pushing his luck. "Fremont's dirty."

Lt. Santos blinked his dark eyes, the only sign he'd even heard Jack speak. "That's a blanket statement if I ever heard one. Elaborate, please."

"It's the call you sent me and Bowie out on my first night back."

"That nuisance call? I thought some old lady had a nightmare?"

Some old lady? Jack frowned. "Bowie didn't turn in his report?"

"It's right here." Santos plucked a file off the top of his inbox. "I haven't had a chance to look at it yet. What was this woman's name again?" He turned to his computer and started typing.

"Greta. Greta Renault."

"Greta Renault." Santos's fingers seemed to freeze over the keyboard after typing in her name. "Definitely not an old lady."

No, Jack thought. She wasn't. "Is that why I was sent out there? Because you all thought it was a throwaway case?"

"I thought it was a way to gently ease you back in," Santos said without a hint of apology in his voice. "You've had a rough go of things, Jack. I didn't want you in over your head your first case back, especially since Cole's still on vacation. Not with—"

"Not with all the higher-ups' eyes on me." Because the opportunity had presented itself, he figured he had nothing to lose. To say he'd been encouraged to retire rather than return to the job was an understatement. They didn't see him as a cop anymore. They saw him as a liability.

"Your shooting and fallout from the Mina Goodale case exposed a lot of holes in various government agencies, and they're all pretty much blaming each other. On the one hand, what happened will trigger important changes. On the other—" Santos cringed "—you didn't make many friends."

"How selfish of me to get shot." He didn't even try to hide the bitterness in his voice. Times like this he wondered why he hadn't taken the early retirement that had been offered. He didn't want anyone's sympathy, and he sure didn't need it. He already blamed himself enough; he didn't appreciate the politicos piling on.

Lt. Santos looked at Jack long and hard enough to leave him wanting to squirm. Finally, he asked, "Are you certain about Fremont?"

Certain? Could anyone ever be certain about anything? He couldn't shake what Ashley had told him, that his instincts might not be as sharp as they once were. That it would take a while to get back to the top of his game. Even so… "Yes."

"And you're willing to take this all the way? Even if it blows up in your face?"

He thought immediately of Greta, of the disappointment-glazed grief he'd seen in her eyes the other night. And it was that, even more than the determined declaration she'd made about proving Fremont guilty on her own, that had him nodding. "Yes."

"Okay." Santos nodded. "Then I'm going to make an off-the-record suggestion you're not going to like."

"Because this conversation has been going so well so far."

Santos ignored the quip. "If you have something on Fremont, you need to tie off every possible thread he can pull loose. You start digging, you dig fast and you dig deep. Most of all, you need to be careful. Invisible careful."

Having never heard his boss use that term before, he wasn't entirely sure where this was going.

"Fill me in, Jack. Tell me about the case, everything you know so far. All of it, so I know what's coming at us. Tell me about Fremont and—" Santos pointed to his screen "—Greta Renault."

"We should probably bring in Bowie to hear the full explanation."

"You sure?"

"Yeah."

Less than a half hour later, Jack was finishing his coffee while he and Bowie meticulously went through the events of visiting Greta Renault, after which Jack continued the story with his visit to Fremont's office and a kiss-and-nap-redacted version of his follow-up with Greta.

"You didn't take Deputy Bowman with you today," Santos observed as Bowie stood at attention by the door. "At ease before you sprain something, Deputy."

"Sir."

Jack shook his head. "Because it wasn't official." It made sense even if it wasn't the truth. "And no offense, kid, but even in plain clothes, you look like a cop."

"None taken. Sir."

Santos's eyebrows lifted. Silently, Jack sighed. He

shouldn't have jumped down Bowie's throat. He was going to be paying for his misjudgment of his stand-in partner for quite some time.

"Greta Renault claims to have seen Doyle Fremont murder someone," Jack said. "Before we have her come in to make a formal statement and have the media crawling all over it, I wanted to check Fremont's offices out. See if anything she said she saw actually fit." Jack noted a flicker of recognition on Bowie's face out of the corner of his eye. "As much as I didn't want to admit it at the time, there was a part of me that didn't quite believe her. She's…" Bowie straightened. Jack continued, "Different. Eccentric. And could, to some people, come across as—"

"Kooky?" Santos finished for him. He frowned and leaned his arms on his desk. "Deputy Bowman's voice carries at times."

Bowie seemed to sag a bit, surrendering to Jack's dressing-down.

"So, to be sure," Jack said steering them back on topic, "I took a look around the place."

"Without a search warrant."

"Yes, sir." He wanted to argue he had probable cause, but he didn't. "As I said, nothing official."

"I'm assuming that won't happen again?"

"No, sir," Jack assured him.

"So? Did you find something, or was it just speaking with Mr. Fremont that had him calling in the cavalry?" Santos asked.

Bowie's stiff spine relaxed as his eyes flashed with interest. "You spoke with Doyle Fremont?"

"I didn't plan to," Jack explained. "He arrived at the

complex just as I was leaving. And he invited me to stay a bit and talk. Which I did because I was curious. Because I found this." Jack pulled out his phone, clicked it on and set it screen up on the desk. Both Bowie and Santos leaned over to look at the image on his phone. "It's a lens from a pair of glasses. Identical to the glasses Miss Renault described in her account." He reached into his inside jacket pocket and pulled out the folded up drawing Greta had handed him on his way out of her apartment. The storyboard illustrations of the crime she witnessed right there, in black and white. "She drew the lens. It's exactly what I found under the table."

Bowie frowned. "She's telling the truth?"

"We can't say that definitively. Not based on a single piece of glass." Even if it had been enough to convince him. "Or we couldn't." Jack looked at his boss. "I suspected before I got back, but knowing that Fremont's been complaining about my visit? There's something here. I spooked him, which means he's hiding something. I can feel it." And even though his feelings and intuition were a bit off-kilter these days, he still had enough faith left in himself to go with his gut. And if they could prove Doyle Fremont was a killer, he wouldn't have to worry about anyone questioning his judgment for a good long time. "Something went down in that office the other night. Let me see what I can turn up off the record."

"A body would be nice." Santos brought a hand to his lips and tapped his fingers. "Fremont is connected, incestuously connected, to just about every politician in this state if you ask me. If word gets out we're investigating him—"

"It won't," Jack promised. "I won't let it."

Santos smirked. "I wouldn't go playing chicken with Doyle Fremont if I were you. You have some leeway as I've been told Fremont is heading back out of town for at least a week, but keep in mind, these days just the hint of police corruption or a detective with a vendetta is going to end more than just your career, Jack. It'll take all of us down."

"I know." Which was why he'd be keeping a very close eye on Greta. He couldn't risk her going off on her own and wreaking havoc with Jack's and his friends' careers. But he couldn't walk away from Greta, from his witness. He'd done that once before and it had cost someone her life.

Santos didn't look pleased, but there was the hint of a gleam in his eyes. "Okay. You have until Fremont is back in town. If nothing pops by then, I'm pulling the plug. In the meantime, I'll throw you some less consequential cases to keep up appearances, but cover your sixes. Both of you. You keep this far off the official radar until we're solid as cement." He pointed at each of them. "Fremont isn't just a big fish, he's a shark. One that a lot of people are going to want to keep swimming." Santos waited until Bowie left. "Jack?"

"Sir?"

"That invisibility idea we spoke of earlier? Might I recommend someone with an outside connection to the DA's office lend a hand? We've had some success in that area before. Your choice, of course. But that's how I would handle things."

"Right." Jack would have made a longshoreman blush with the string of curses that slipped loose after he closed the door. There was only one PI they both knew they could trust, one who was capable of being stealthy and discreet. And he was about the last man he wanted to talk to.

"Earth to Jack. Hello!" Ashley waved a hand in front of his face before she snapped her fingers. "I know I'm not the most fascinating dinner companion, but you could at least grunt when I pause for a response. Especially since you messed up my sushi order last time."

"Huh?" Jack pulled himself out of the trance-inducing bass of classic rock beating gently out of the overhead speakers at the Brass Eagle. The downtown pub served mostly active and former military, but in recent months more than a few cops had begun to hang out here as well, much to the owner's annoyance. Vince Sutton wasn't the biggest fan of the police, but he was a fan of staying in business, so Jack and Cole putting out the word meant it all worked out. "Sorry, Ash. What did you say?"

His sister rolled her eyes and sighed. "I said that next week I plan to add a pair of snow boots to my Tinker Bell costume for when I walk through the Railroad Museum in Old Sac." Ashley peered over the rim of her wineglass with something akin to sibling annoyance. "What do you think? Pink or turquoise sequins? I'm leaning toward turquoise—"

"Point taken." Jack held up his hands, abandoning the beer bottle he'd been nursing for the past half hour. "Sorry." Despite his need to speak to the bar's owner tonight, it was Greta Renault who occupied most of his thoughts. While falling asleep on her couch had mortified him, it hadn't seemed to phase her one bit. Neither had their ensuing conversation that left him feeling more than a bit uneasy about how the next few days were going to play out. He found her distracting. Utterly and completely, but also captivating and he was curious to know more, to know everything about her. He felt his lips curve as he remembered how easily off track she could get. One of those delightful quirks he found endearing. It hadn't hurt that she could kiss a man into unexpected submission. He really, really didn't need this. But want? That was another story. "Long day at work," he finally said.

"Too long." Ashley nodded. "I guess we both got hit with the work-til-we-drop gene. Are you even going to toast to celebrate with me?"

"Celebrate what?" Too late, he realized what he'd said. Ashley's eyes narrowed in the same way they had when they were kids and she was about to throw one heck of a temper tantrum. "Sorry! Kidding." Kind of. "Of course we are going to celebrate. Congratulations to the newest doctor on the Folsom General staff." He clinked his bottle against her glass and scooted the bowl of sweet and spicy pretzels in front of her. "Dinner's on me."

"Darn right it is," Ashley grumbled with a good-natured smirk. "I've been catering to you long enough. You do okay today? Chest hurt? Breathing even? I know you still aren't sleeping very much. It's like living with a very large, insomniac rat rustling through the house every night."

"Jeez, Ash." How he loved having it spelled out for

him. "I'm fine. You want to perform an exam right here on the table?"

"Ugh." She shuddered. "No. I just want to make sure my big brother is taking care of himself. How many coffees did you drink today?"

"None."

"Liar. You forget I know your tell." She poked her index finger between his eyes in such a way that he laughed. "If you managed under five, I'll be happy."

"Oh, well then. Three. And one decaf. And one tea."

"Tea?" Ashley's naturally long lashes fluttered. "Ooh la! Drinking tea now, are we?" She rested her chin in her hand. "Who's the girl?"

"Seriously?" But Jack didn't look at her. He busied himself scanning the area behind the bar. "Why do you always think there's a girl? There is no girl."

She popped a pretzel in her mouth. "Uh-huh. Right. And uh-uh." She pushed the bowl away, slapped her hands together to dust them off. "Don't put things like that in front of me. They're addictive."

"There are worse things to be addicted to," Jack teased around the pride bursting through him. His sister was off-the-charts smart and had focused that intelligence brilliantly through life. An accomplished emergency-room trauma doctor and a woman who had jumped three grades in grammar school, his baby sister had graduated from high school nearly two years before he did. One reason he was more than used to his ego being kicked around like a hacky sack. "Have we reached the part of our relationship where you're going to tell me what happened between you and Adam?"

Ashley paused, her glass halfway to her lips. "I didn't

think dinner included a therapy session about my ex-husband."

"It doesn't. It's just…you're amazing, Ash. Successful. Funny. Pretty. Smarter than I can ever hope to be, but sometimes I wonder if there's a reason you haven't started dating yet. It's been over a year, right?"

"Long enough for him to have gotten remarried to some postpubescent Bitsy… Bunny… Boopsie? Who can remember her name?" Her eyes glinted in a way that told Jack she remembered perfectly. She plucked up another pretzel and munched it with the force of Godzilla attacking a city. "They had a baby last month. A boy. Phoebus. Poor kid. Sounds like a name for a depressed beagle. Funny how it was never the right time to have a baby when I was married to Adam." She cleared her throat as if had become clogged with tears.

Jack pushed away the loathing of his former brother-in-law along with sympathy he knew Ashley would throw back in his face. As dedicated as she was to her career, he knew the one thing his sister had always wanted more than anything was a family of her own, but her unexpected whirlwind marriage to an undercover cop had worked against her. To say her life had become unstable was an understatement. She'd spent most every shift in the ER wondering if they were going to wheel in her husband. "You should get married again."

"Oh, what a great idea." She gave him a slow clap. "Actually. I shouldn't. I'm out." This time she ate two pretzels before she waved a dismissive hand but didn't quite manage to hide the flash of pain in her eyes. "And you can stop deflecting from the real reason we came here for dinner. Get on with it already."

"I can't," he admitted, giving up on the subject. For now. "Not until…well, now." Vince Sutton emerged from the door leading up to the second-floor offices. His laser-beam gaze circled the room and landed square on Jack. Given Jack hadn't stepped foot in this place since he'd been shot, he could pretty much guess what was going through the former Marine's head.

"Great. So, we can order? Hey, Vince." Ashley beamed up at him as Vince approached the table.

"Well, this is a surprise. Ashley. Good to see you." He rested a gentle hand on her shoulder and squeezed, his gold wedding band glinting in the dim light. The genuine affection Vince, Cole Delaney, and Max Kellan had shown his sister since she'd arrived in town had made Jack realize just how lucky he was to have friends like them. They and their wives had welcomed Ashley into their circle as if she was family because, to them, just like Jack, she was. "Special occasion?"

"It is for me. I got the job." Ashley grinned and emptied her wineglass. "I am most definitely celebrating with the rarest and biggest burger you've got. And those sweet potato fries you make."

"You got it. Congratulations." Vince motioned for her to scoot over, and he dropped onto the padded booth bench beside her. "Dinner's on the house. It'll be nice to have a doctor in the family. Well, another one. One who doesn't dive into your head every time I see her."

"Allie only surface dives." Ashley laughed. "But true, I am more the stitch-them-up and move-them-out kind of doctor."

"So, what brings you by?" Vince honed his attention on Jack. "Not that I'm not buying the celebration excuse."

"You're not? But that was so believable!" Ashley whined like a five-year-old and pouted.

Jack's lips twitched. How was it Ashley described Vince? A cross between an action star and a purring tiger. The movie-star reference he got in spite of the scars and close-cropped military hair on the former Marine. But the tiger? He couldn't ever remember hearing Vince purr. Growl sure, but purr?

"What's going on?" Vince asked him.

"I need your help." Jack swallowed his reluctance. His LT was right. They needed to keep this low key. If the wrong person got wind of Jack's investigation...

"I will take this as my cue to visit the ladies' room." Ashley shooed Vince out of her way. "I'll take my time. You still have that pinball machine in the back room?"

"Jason got a new high score last week," Vince said, a proud smile spreading across his big-brother face as he reached into his pocket and handed her some quarters. "See if you can beat it."

"Consider him toast."

"Must be pretty bad for you to come to me," Vince said once Ashley left. "What's up?"

Jack found it difficult to meet the other man's eyes. "I have this case—" He broke off as Vince leaned forward to peer out the front window.

"Huh."

"What?" Jack joined in searching the dark sky and passing headlights. "Did you see something?"

"Just checking to see if hell's frozen over."

"Ha. Funny." But the joke made him smile. "You know who Doyle Fremont is, right?"

Vince's brow arched.

"Right. Who doesn't?" Jack wished this was easier. "I'm working something that looks like it involves him, but given his connections—"

"You need to do a deep dive without alerting anyone," Vince finished.

"I hate asking."

"I imagine you do." Vince popped a pretzel in his mouth. "Fill me in."

"You'll do it?"

"Fill me in," Vince repeated. "Then we'll figure out the details."

Jack did as Vince requested, finishing with, "Greta says he's seen her a couple of times now, and while she isn't acting like it worries her, it worries me." Massive understatement. "It worries me a lot."

"Fremont should worry you." Vince munched a peanut. "Rumor has it he isn't just politically connected, he's *connected* connected."

"He's mobbed up?" Jack sank back against the booth. Now, that did surprise him. But then, Vince and he worked in varying circles, and you never knew who you were getting involved with on the other side of the table. "That doesn't really align with his political aspirations, does it?"

"Probably more than it should." Vince shrugged. "Can't prove it, of course, at least not yet. Haven't had cause to find out, really. But I've worked enough cases where I've heard his name. What about your witness?"

"Greta?"

Vince's steely stare barely flickered. "Yes, Greta. Have you looked into her background? You sure she's reliable?"

"Meaning am I sure she's not trying to lead me around by the nose?"

Vince slapped his hands clean. "You wouldn't be the first to get his nose caught in something he shouldn't. A pretty face is a nice distraction."

"How do you know she has a—"

"You just told me. Please tell me you're coming back to play poker with us, because your tells are all over the place."

"It's already on my social calendar," Jack assured him. But Vince did raise a good point. He'd be lying if he said he didn't have an odd, niggling feeling something wasn't quite right with Greta. And if that something could whip around and bite him, he needed to know. He wasn't normally one to assume, but she hadn't seemed particularly forthcoming with personal details so far. What would it hurt to have Vince take a peek? "Would you mind taking a look?"

"Give me everything you have on her before you leave," Vince said. "I take it you'd like this to remain between us. No, shall we say, prosecutorial involvement?"

"That would probably be for the best." The last thing he needed was to pull Simone Armstrong-Sutton and thus the DA's office into this mess of a case until it was a slam dunk. "That work for you?"

"Simone doesn't ask about my clients." Vince shrugged. "Not that you are one. You're a friend, which means this is on me."

A bit of admiration sneaked in under the discomfort he'd been pushing aside for a while. Far be it from him to ignore an opportunity to clear the air. "About Simone—"

Both of Vince's eyebrows went up this time. "What about her?"

"When she and I were, well, seeing each other."

Vince's expression didn't flicker.

"Look, it wasn't serious between us. Not really." Suddenly Jack was back in high school having to confess to the star quarterback that he'd been dating the head cheerleader behind his back. "I mean we never…well, I mean, you know."

"Yeah. I know." Vince grinned as if he was actually getting a kick out of the conversation. "Even if it had been otherwise, that's none of my business. Simone's easy to fall for. And she's not easy to get over. Case in point, I've now married her twice." As a man not prone to obvious emotion, Jack was surprised by the understanding glint in Vince's eye. "This discussion is long overdue, Jack. There's nothing to worry about between you and me. If anything, I'm glad that for a while she dated a really good guy."

"Made her see what she was missing, huh?" Jack joked.

"You know she'd dress you down for talking about yourself that way. So, allow me to channel my prosecutor wife." He cleared his throat and resettled in his seat. "There is someone out there, perfect for you, Jack McTavish. You just have to be ready for her when she arrives."

Jack couldn't help it. He laughed. Because the only image caught in his mind at the mere mention of a woman was Greta Renault with her starry blue eyes, to-die-for legs and a smile that could power a small city.

"You do sound a bit like Simone," Jack teased.

"I've been practicing. So. Your problem? Doyle Fremont and Greta Renault? I assume you want to do this fast?"

"Fast and quiet."

Vince just stared at him. "It's what I do."

"Then, yeah. Whatever you can dig up, I need to know."

Chapter 5

"Sorry I'm late."

Greta shielded her eyes against the morning sun as Yvette Konstinopolis hurried down the path toward their usual park bench in Cesar Chavez Plaza. The cultural and natural oasis in the heart of midtown was one of the few places Greta felt comfortable and, for want of a better term, safe.

In the summer months, the park was home to food-truck events and farmers' markets and was a venue for concerts, but today the park was mostly empty, save for the early coffee drinkers and joggers making their way around the flora-rich haven. "No problem." Greta offered her friend one of the paper cups from the nearby café. "You're working today?"

"Sadly, yes." Yvette tugged at the hem of her tailored, waist-length suit jacket like a navy officer and shifted on needle-thin heels that should have left track marks in the cement. Polished and poised, Yvette's dazzling warmth was only dimmed by the three-karat diamond wedding set sparkling on her finger. With a mere look, Yvette loosened that knot of unease that had formed inside Greta ever since the tragic moment at the window. Beneath that elegant facade of Yvette's lived a woman who thrived on chaos and the unexpected, which was no doubt why they made such good friends. As long as Greta had known her, there wasn't anything that threw Yvette off her game. And she'd had a lot of practice with Greta. "But I have plenty of time before I have to be in the office. Besides—" she set her bag down, accepted the cup and drank with a sigh of relief "—you need to fill me in on what's going on."

"Going on?" Greta cringed as she glanced away, pretending to be interested in the cluster of trees nearby.

"Other than your loquacious *I'm fine* texts, you haven't returned my calls." Yvette knocked her shoulder against Greta just like she had when they were teenagers. "I figured I'd better check in and make sure you were still alive." Greta didn't realize she'd winced until Yvette's amber eyes sharpened. "I knew it. Something's going on. What is it? Why haven't you returned my calls?"

"I've been busy. Trying to finish up the pieces for the show?"

"Uh-huh." Yvette's tone let Greta know she wasn't getting off that easy. "And?"

"And—" Greta shrugged "—there might have been a little something that happened with the police." Greta sipped at the mint tea she'd ordered and wished she'd given into temptation and bought one of the homemade pastries offered in the café.

When she dared sneak a look at her friend, she found Yvette watching her with that familiar, patient, *what am I going to do with you* expression. "It's nothing, really," Greta rushed on. "I was up late a few nights ago and witnessed an altercation across the street. I called the police to report it, a detective came by, asked me a few questions." She tilted her head. "Just threw me off a bit. Sorry I didn't call back."

"An altercation?" Yvette shifted around so she could see her better. "You're out of practice. You used to lie better. What happened? What did you see?"

"It's fine, Yvette. They're looking into it."

"They as in…?"

"The police." Given Yvette's position as the mayor's number-two PR person, and considering the bad guy involved, aka Doyle Fremont, telling Yvette any more would only place her friend in a precarious professional position. The further Yvette stayed out of this, the better. "It's nice of you to check in on me, but everything's—"

"If you say *fine* one more time I'm going to strangle you with a tea bag." She tapped a finger against Greta's cup and the thin white thread and tag dangling free. "Now I know there's something wrong. You never use tea bags. You bring your own."

The long-running joke of Greta's abhorrence for tea bags versus fresh tea leaves had Yvette's direct gaze softening with concern.

"I'm okay, Yvette. Really."

Yvette frowned. "It must have been pretty bad for you to even think about calling the police."

"It was…disturbing." Yet in a way, illuminating. "I didn't even stop to consider anything. It just happened. Then a couple of detectives came around to ask me some questions."

"That must have brought up bad memories."

"It did." Greta forced a smile. "I'm working through them." Now, that wasn't a lie. But she wasn't about to tell Yvette she'd begun hearing the ghost again; seeing the flashes of white and silver, the figure who had become a part of her life all those years ago. It was stress, she'd told herself. Stress that had her caught between lying awake for hours and finding herself in different parts of the loft when she woke up.

"You're alone too much," Yvette said. "I thought once you moved here, we'd be able to spend more time together. That's my fault. I'm sorry. With Richard's business failing and the legal fallout—"

"Richard is your husband and deserves your attention," Greta said not for the first time. "And you did enough, helping me buy my building, getting me moved in. Being able to walk through that front door, having everything in place and organized from day one was what I needed. But I'm a grown woman, remember? And you have your own life now. I don't need my best friend watching out for me anymore."

"I will always watch out for you." Yvette reached out and covered Greta's hand with hers. "But answer me one question."

Greta sighed. "Fine. One question."

"Who'd they send? What's the detective's name?"

"Jack."

Yvette blinked, clearly waiting for more information. "Jack McTavish."

"Oh." Yvette's eyes went wide. "Well, okay then." Yvette's face split into a wide, teasing grin and she circled a finger in front of Greta's face. "I haven't seen that look on you in years. No. Scratch that. I've never seen it. And you called him Jack. You're blushing! There's pink on your cheeks, and it isn't paint smudges."

"It's the sunshine." Greta resisted the urge to cover her cheeks. "I want a cookie. Do you want a cookie?" She started to stand, but Yvette stopped her, tugged her back onto the bench. "You don't want one?"

"Carbs and a nonelastic waistband don't mix. You're changing the subject." Yvette tapped a red-polished finger against her lips, considering. "Jack McTavish, huh? You've got excellent taste, Greta. He's a good guy."

"I don't have any…" Um. Well, that wasn't true. She had kissed him, hadn't she? It wasn't often her impulses got the better of her, but hearing those words, knowing he believed her, had emptied her brain of everything other than desire and gratitude. Oh, who was she kidding? She'd kissed him because she'd wanted to. She still wanted to. "And how do you know he's a good guy?" She remembered thinking Jack had recently been hung up on a woman, but it couldn't have been… "You and he didn't—"

"Honey, please." Yvette waved off her concern. "I've been a one-man woman ever since I laid eyes on my husband. And if you're asking the question, I'd say you're poised to take the fall yourself."

"Don't be silly." Greta's stomach clutched.

She didn't want to fall, not for Jack, not for any man. Greta lived every day with a sense that did not allow for anything close to permanence. She bit her lip, regret weighing heavy on her chest. No matter how much she might find herself thinking about it. Wanting it. Wanting him. And she had thought about it. Quite a lot since meeting Jack. "He's a friend, nothing more." As if friends kissed like that.

"He's also a straight-up hero." Yvette sipped more coffee. "Yummy. The coffee and the man."

She'd get no arguments from Greta. "He mentioned he'd been shot. I don't remember hearing about it at the time, though. Was I here?"

"You were getting that piece for the Mondavi Center finished," Yvette told her. "By the time you came up for air, he was on his way to a full recovery. He has a really good reputation in the department, if that's what's worrying you. And between you and me, he could have cashed in big-time from the city over what happened, but he didn't. He's a decent guy, Greta. Reliable. Dedicated. He won't hesitate to put himself between someone he cares about and danger. Also makes for great press. He hit the front page of a lot of papers. Didn't hurt he helped close a cold case from two decades ago."

Greta gave her friend a quick smile. She knew what Yvette was telling her. That Jack McTavish was the kind of man she could trust with the truth about her past, about who she was. About…everything.

"The fact you don't seem to want to talk about him gives me hope," Yvette teased.

Jack didn't strike her as the kind of man who relished or even enjoyed the spotlight. But maybe she was wrong.

She didn't know much about him, only how she reacted whenever she was around him. All she wanted to do was burrow under the covers with him and never come up for air. He made her feel alive, made her feel as if anything was possible as long as he was by her side. But that was the stuff of fairy tales, and Greta, more than anyone else, knew fairy tales were nothing but fiction.

"Well, whatever happens with you and Jack, it's good to see you with a spark of interest," Yvette announced. "I was sure your pilot light had gone out on that particular stove. This will ease my mind a bit."

"That was the goal," Greta muttered. "So, now that you've done your drive-by check—"

"I also wanted to find out if you needed a hand with the opening."

"I have a meeting there tomorrow, but I think I've got everything covered."

"Look at you, taking charge of your own career. Impressive." Yvette gathered up her bag. "You have all your paintings done?"

"Uh-huh."

This time they both knew she was lying, but Yvette didn't say anything. "Do me a favor and enjoy the sun for a while, okay? And go get that cookie. I'm here if you need backup. Speaking of, don't forget to add a plus-one to the opening. You know, in case you want to bring anyone special."

"Jack and I are just friends," Greta repeated even as her heart skipped a beat.

"I've called every hospital in a two-hundred-mile radius." Bowie hung up the phone and sagged back in his chair as Jack glanced up from his monitor. "No one matching the description of our supposed murder victim pops up in their records."

Not surprising, Jack thought, considering they were looking for a dead man. "What about the morgues?"

"Nothing there, either." Bowie pressed his fingers to his temple. "If Fremont is as smart as you think he is, he knew what he was doing hiding the body. I always thought detective work was supposed to be more glamorous than patrol."

"Don't know where you got that idea," Jack muttered. The tension between them had been gradually dissipating since they'd left the LT's office the day before, and they'd fallen back into routine. A sketchy few hours of sleep last night hadn't hurt, either. But the morning hadn't been particularly rewarding other than the oversize apple fritter Jack scarfed down for breakfast.

"What are you looking at?" Bowie stood up, let out what sounded like a muted yowl of pain and pressed his hands into the base of his spine. "I'm going to need a chiropractor by the time Cole gets back. What's that?"

Jack leaned back in his chair. "From what Greta said, Fremont and our mystery man knew each other. It only makes sense. So I'm going through every photograph of Fremont online to see if our dead guy shows up." He'd also scanned through Fremont's social media pages, both personal and business related.

He now knew Fremont preferred imported wines, preferably white, and designer suits, and apparently had a set of cuff links he wore whenever he made a deal. He was also an expert in Krav Maga, a hybrid of physical combat and martial arts. He owned several boats, including one yacht he kept docked in Florida. Jack had made a quick note of each of the names. Given Sacramento and the northern valley's vast waterways, it would be an easy way to dispose of a body. The delta could keep secrets buried for years, but he didn't have years. Which was why he'd called his friend Darcy Ford who worked with DART, the local water-rescue unit. Just to have her keep an ear open and an eye out for their victim.

Bowie sat on the edge of Jack's desk. "I really hate to bring this up," he said as he popped a knuckle. "Believe me, I do, but are you really sure searching for this guy is the right way to go? I mean, if Fremont did kill someone, how did he get the body out of the office? And if he did manage that, it stands to reason, at least to me, that he'd know where to stash the guy so he wouldn't be found."

"And that would be one reason I didn't sleep very well last night." Jack purposely kept his attention pinned on his computer. He didn't need to see the doubt rising again in Bowie's eyes. But there might be another tactic they could take. Vince had mentioned something about Doyle possibly being involved with organized crime. That could be a thread worth pulling.

"What?" Bowie asked.

"What what?" Jack echoed.

"I know that look. You're thinking something you shouldn't be."

"I'm thinking this might be a bigger case than we thought. I heard through the grapevine Fremont might be connected to organized crime. I'm wondering if any of our federal friends might be able to give us a hand."

Bowie plucked up the receiver on his desk, but Jack shook his head, gestured for him to hang up. "We want this quiet, remember? I'm thinking maybe an in-person visit might be best. I know he's thinking of retiring, but for now Eamon Quinn is still working at the San Francisco office. You feel like taking the drive and seeing if he can give us some off-the-record help?"

Bowie's chest actually puffed out. "You want me to go? Really?"

No, actually Jack would prefer to go himself, but he didn't like the idea of being that far away from Greta. Professionally speaking of course. "Nothing official," Jack told him. "Your sister's still down there, right? Maybe you can stop in for a visit?" In case anyone noticed a Sac PD deputy asking questions.

"I can do that. Thanks, Jack. For trusting me with this."

"Yeah, well, let's see if we can get a better description of the victim from Greta before you get too excited."

"It docs seem she had no trouble identifying Fremont, but she can't seem to remember what the victim looked like," Bowie said. "Other than body type and the birthmark. Even in the drawing she did, the face is turned away. There aren't any details, except the glasses, to grab hold of." The elevator dinged above the familiar din of the squad room.

"I've been thinking on that," Jack mused. "I might have an idea to solve that problem. Next time I see her—"

"How about now?" Bowie cut him off.

"Huh?" Jack sat up so fast his chair nearly wheeled out from under him.

He barely noticed the uniformed desk sergeant leading her into the squad room. Seeing her here, seeing her anywhere other than in the dim, soft light of her loft, sent his mind spinning. Her thick blond hair was tied back neatly to trail almost to her waist. The forest green wraparound blouse she wore accentuated every curve against the crisp white of her slacks. He couldn't help but skim his gaze down her figure to the less than practical, pointed-toe, spiked heels she wore.

Man, he thought. The woman was a pure knockout.

"I'm going to get some coffee before I step on your tongue." Bowie slipped past him as Jack found himself reaching up to straighten his tie, smooth his hair. The air in the squad room crackled as if a live wire had broken free. Even in his slightly dazed state, he noticed the chatter in the room fade under the searching, albeit uncertain, gaze of Greta Renault.

When she spotted him, she smiled, and he could all but hear her sigh in relief. He sucked in a breath. His entire body sang with the hit of attention. Her smile widened against the flicker of nerves in her eyes. She strode forward, a large handled paper bag in one hand, an art portfolio in the other. He heard the scramble of footsteps behind him, anticipated the stampede to welcome their visitor and moved out into the aisle to greet her.

"Greta." She faced him, sending the scent of jasmine and springtime into the stale office air. So good, he wanted to free her hair, bury his hands, his face, his soul, in that thick, luxurious mane. "This is a nice surprise." He nodded his thanks in the desk sergeant's direction and drew her away. He should have been clearer about needing her to stay away—from the investigation and the station. Every visitor was logged in, which meant he needed to give the curious eyes and stares aimed at them another reason for her visit. He bent down and brushed his lips against her cheek, enjoying her unexpected gasp of surprise. "I thought we decided I'd come to you?" he murmured before he stood up straight.

"You did." Her eyes clouded with confusion as he took hold of her arm and squeezed. "Is now a bad time? I have an appointment at the Camellia in a bit, so I thought I'd save you a trip and drop off the statement I wrote last night and show you the rest of the drawings I finished." She hoisted the portfolio only to have him gently push her hand down.

"No, yeah, that's good. It's fine. Now is..." He glanced around, grateful to see the LT was nowhere to be found. "Now is fine." He pointed toward the coffee room. "We can talk in there."

"Sure." She waved at the people still watching as she trailed behind him. "Hi. Hello."

"I can take that for you." Jack slid his hand down to the handled bag and moved her along before any questions or introductions were thrown their way.

"Oh, right. It's for you." She let out a nervous laugh that brushed featherlight against his heart, and for a moment, he forgot where they were. "I thought maybe after yesterday you could use one."

Curious, he pried open the sides and looked in. He snort-laughed, trying to ignore the pang of affection. "It's a blanket."

"One of the weighted ones like I have. I wasn't sure what color you'd like, but then I saw this blue and, well. It reminded me of your eyes." She shrugged and caught her lower lip between her teeth in a way that had Jack wishing they were anywhere but where they were. "I hope it helps."

He couldn't remember the last time someone had given him a gift that didn't come with a *Get Well Soon* tag attached. "I can't wait to try it. Thank you."

A throat cleared behind him.

"Oh, Officer Bowman." Greta stepped away from Jack. Jack turned and narrowed his eyes in silent warning, but only found a blank expression on his substitute partner's young face.

"Ms. Renault." Bowie set his coffee on the counter and rounded the smattering of tables, hand out. "I wanted to apologize for my behavior the other morning. There's no excuse for the disrespect I showed you, and I hope you'll give me another chance."

Jack had to give the kid credit. He had style.

"Of course." Greta returned the handshake. "Although I have to admit, adding *kooky* to my resume and bio might just do me some good."

Bowie's face went bright red. "That was rude of me."

"When you know better, you do better, right?" Greta said. "Don't let it worry you, Officer. I didn't exactly come across as… Well, I know how I come across. I can be a bit scattered and—" she sighed "—never mind. Oh, no, please stay." Greta caught Bowie's arm when he started to leave. "I could use another pair of eyes."

Bowie looked between Greta's friendly gaze and Jack's irritated expression. Jack made no apologies about wanting to spend time alone with Greta, even in the middle of the station house. And that, he knew, was not a good thing. She pushed him so far off-kilter he forgot what world he was supposed to be inhabiting.

"Happy to." Bowie's grin took up half his face. "And it's Bowie, please. What's in the bag?" He elbowed Jack in the arm as Greta lifted her portfolio onto one of the tables and unzipped it.

"Just a thank-you gift." Greta flashed that brilliant smile at Jack. "For making me feel better the other day," she added when Bowie's eyebrows disappeared under his hairline. "Here's my written statement." She handed Jack the sealed legal envelope. "I assume you need me to sign something official, so just let me know when to come in to do that."

"We'll do that," Jack said as he pocketed the statement. She didn't need to know he didn't plan putting this anywhere near an official file. It was risky enough her name was in the file for the original call and follow-up visit. For now, he planned to keep it limited to that. He'd keep her written statement close, though. At home. Where he knew it would be safe. "So, the drawings?"

"I told you I think in images rather than words, but now that I've got all my thoughts arranged, I can do the latter." She stepped back and motioned to the drawings. "I hope these are all right."

"All right?" Bowie let out a low whistle. "These are amazing."

Jack had to agree. They were incredibly detailed, like reading a graphic novel illustrated by a master. He could see everything she'd told them the first night. "If every witness offered these we'd be out of a job," he said. But he also noticed what Bowie had earlier. In none of these illustrations could he see the victim's face. They went through all the sketches twice, then, on the third time, slowed down as Jack tried to focus on the one element most needed to get a handle on the case: their victim.

He was a large man whose suit was significantly wrinkled. The detail in the drawing was amazing. Jack bent closer to take it all in.

"Rage," Bowie murmured when Greta moved off to explore the coffee and tea offerings. She leaned over the donut box and took a deep breath, sighed and shook her head, as if talking herself out of indulging. "I get it now," he told Jack. "I see it."

"Yeah, but that's not what's worrying me." Jack kept his voice low and flipped to the last page where a solitary Doyle Fremont stood, framed by the window, hands in his pockets, looking directly up at Greta's window. "That does. You see that." He poked a finger against Doyle's illustrated eye, probably a bit harder than necessary. "He knows she saw him. He knows." And even at his most controlled when they'd met, Doyle had been unable to resist gloating with that glance to where the witness had stood.

"Not much he can do about it, though, is there? Not without bringing attention to himself," Bowie kept his voice low. "The smart thing would be to just lie low and do nothing. This almost feels like he's taunting her."

Jack smirked. "Doyle Fremont is not a do-nothing kind of man. He gets off on stuff like this. On knowing people's secrets. On using them to his advantage. He told me that himself. He's like a cat with a new toy."

"Why?" Bowie asked.

"Why does he use them, or why did he tell me?"

"Both."

Good questions. "Because everything to him is a game. Or a puppet show. And he prides himself on being the puppet master." Jack had dealt with men like Fremont before. He knew how they thought, and what they thought was that they didn't care about collateral damage.

Jack straightened and looked at Greta who was flitting about the cabinets exploring and examining their less than stellar offerings. Fremont wouldn't care who got hurt so long as he got what he wanted. The question was, why bother himself with someone like Greta? What endgame was Jack missing?

"Greta?" he called.

"Hmm?" She turned, a box of bagged tea in her hand. "You all do realize that drinking from tea bags makes the tea taste like paper."

"Hadn't really crossed our minds," Jack said. "Did you check the date on the box?"

She flipped the box over. "Oh. Five years ago." Greta laughed, and every cell in Jack's body flickered to life. "Never mind. Do you have more questions for me?"

"In a bit, yes. Bowie and I were wondering something. About your drawings."

"Wondering what?"

"The victim's face," Jack said. "Other than the birthmark, you never show it."

"Don't I?" Her eyes widened, and she joined them, tea box still in her hand. "I could have sworn…hmm." She flipped through the pages. "You're right. It's not there at all, is it? Seems strange I didn't realize that."

"Did you see his face?" Bowie asked.

"Did I—" Greta drew her finger across one of the

images as she considered the question. "I'm sure I did. But I can't seem to remember it now. All I can see is— isn't the mark enough?"

"Maybe. We need to figure out who the victim is before we can figure out why Doyle would have killed him." San Francisco was a long shot. Greta's memory on the other hand...

"Or how he was killed," Bowie added. "I'm still not seeing that answer here."

"The answers have to be in my head," Greta whispered, sounding almost defeated. "I'm so sorry. I thought I gave you everything you needed."

Bowie glanced over her head to Jack, the answer written all over the young deputy's face. Jack gnashed his teeth. He didn't want Greta any more involved in this than she already was, especially given the expression shown in that picture of Doyle Fremont. This wasn't over; he wasn't done. But the only way to keep Greta safe was to push through and dig for answers.

"I know someone who might be able to help."

"You do?" Greta's eyes went wide. "How?"

"That depends. How do you feel about regression therapy?"

Greta's hand covered the leather band on her wrist. Of all the things she thought she'd have to face as a wit- ness to a murder, she didn't think regression therapy was going to be one of them.

Her entire body went cold, as if the past was trying to wrap itself around her again. Lock her in. Suffocate her. Because her art remained her only real safe place, she turned her attention back to her drawings, tried to recapture the power and control she felt while sketching them.

"Regression therapy?" Her voice trembled, and she squeezed her eyes shut, silently willing the room to stop spinning as she forced herself to remain on her feet. "No." The refusal came easy, an automatic defense of the life she'd created for herself. "I'm sorry, but I can't—"

"We have a friend," Jack explained. "Dr. Allie Hollister-Kellan. She's worked with us on quite a few cases and while most of her patients now are vets and first responders dealing with PTSD, I'm pretty sure she'd be up for a favor."

Something about the name sounded familiar. Dr. Allie… "She's the woman you saved. Last year. When you were shot."

"Yeah." There it was again, she noticed. That uncomfortable flinch, as if he didn't like even the slightest reminder of what had happened to him. Which of course he wouldn't. Standing so close to him, she could feel the tension move through Jack's body, turning his occasional gentle touch to one of steel. "So, I guess you could say she owes me one."

"Or ten," Bowie added. "It wouldn't take more than a phone call to get her here."

"Weren't you listening? I said no." Hands shaking, she tried to zip up the portfolio but gave up when the zipper stuck for a third time. "You know what? You keep that. I don't need them anymore anyway. I'm going to go. And I'll…call you. Right, I'll call you, Jack."

She shoved her hand through her wristlet and hurried out of the room. Blood pounded in her ears so hard and so loud she couldn't hear anything above it. What had she been thinking? Her desire to bring a murderer to justice and prove she wasn't making things up had just backfired big-time and in the worst way possible. "What's past is past," she whispered over and over. "It can't hurt me. It can't stop me. Keep the past in the past—"

"Greta." Jack caught up to her at the elevators, just before she bolted for the stairs. "Greta, it's okay to be scared. I would be, knowing I'd seen what you did."

"You're a detective. What could possibly scare…" she trailed off, seeing that haunted expression float across his face. The same expression that sleeping on her sofa yesterday afternoon had started to erase. "I'm sorry. That was thoughtless. I should have chosen my words more carefully."

"As I should have apparently," Jack said. "Look, how about we table the idea of the regression therapy for now. Maybe we can figure out another way for you to remember his face. How about dinner tonight? I know a great sushi place, if you like sushi that is. We can relax a bit, then maybe talk through things again. Maybe jar something loose. And if you still don't want to—"

"I won't." There were some lines she knew she'd never cross. As much as she wanted to prove what she'd seen was real, that she'd witnessed a murder, she couldn't take the chance of opening doors she'd closed long ago. "But I love sushi," she added. For the first time, the idea of hanging out with Jack didn't seem like such a good idea. She'd been nervous about leaving the loft, but knowing she was going to see him tempered her anxiety. To the point she'd looked forward to stepping inside a police station. But now… Now she wasn't so sure this had been a smart move. He'd keep digging, keep pushing, and the more she fought him, the more curious he'd get. She needed to find a balance, keep him close without letting him in. A flirtation was one thing, a few heated kisses and gentle conversations a bit more, but his offer felt so normal. So appropriate. So needed. And she so wanted to be normal. She needed to be. Just once. "Dinner would be nice." Unexpected. Exciting. Terrifying. "I'm not sure how late I'll be at the gallery."

"I'm off in a few hours. I can swing by and get you. I've been meaning to check out the new Dalí exhibit anyway."

Greta's heart sighed, and she leaned toward him. He was a Salvador Dalí fan. There really was a lot to like about the man. From his ability to make people think they were the most important person in the room, to the Star Trek key chain hanging out of his pocket. Maybe Yvette was right. Maybe he would understand…

Which meant maybe she could take the chance. "Okay then," she found herself saying. "It's a date. I'll see you at the gallery in a few hours."

Chapter 6

"I am sure everything will be absolutely lovely." Greta's neck ached from walking beside the tall, slim woman who towered over her like a giraffe. Managing five-inch stilettos was an impossible task in Greta's world—she was barely managing three-inch pumps—but Collette acted as if she was simply walking on a cloud rather than escorting Greta through the section of the gallery currently closed to the public.

"The plans you've made are perfect," Greta went on, having learned from Lyndon's notes that effusive compliments to the event planner were the key to a smooth event. She'd even been able to stay focused. For the most part. It had been nice to have a distraction from Jack's recommended therapy session. "I love the lighting and the flow of the room. It's a good open space."

Collette bowed her head almost in reverence as her arms tightened around the tablet computer she clutched to her chest. "We are truly honored you chose the Camellia for your debut showing, Ms. Renault."

"Greta, please," Greta repeated for what felt like the fifth time. She could hear the murmurings of visitors echoing down the long, wood-floor hallways as they meandered in and around the open exhibitions.

"I appreciated the invitation," Greta said. "The lighting in this part of the pavilion will show off my pieces perfectly." As would the polished dark wood floor and pristine white walls. "Which reminds me, when would you like to pick the pieces up?"

"Next Thursday, I believe." Collette directed piercing brown eyes to her screen. "Yes. That will give us enough time to experiment with the arrangement and have you return to see if there are any changes you'd like to make."

"I'm sure everything you decide on will be fine." In the past three hours, Greta had garnered a new level of respect for Lyndon and the work he'd done on her behalf all these years. Her cheeks ached from smiling so much, and her feet were about ready to abandon her body and race toward anything resembling a hot bath. What had she been thinking by wearing heels? Especially knowing she was going to be on her feet so long. "I have ten works set aside already. I should have another two finished by pickup day." At least she hoped to.

"Excellent." Collette made a note on her pad as they headed toward one of the staircases. "Our invitations went out just a few days ago, and already the response has been quite encouraging, especially from the press.

I would be quite surprised if we didn't have a full house for the event."

"Great." Another smile, and Greta swore she pinched a nerve in her face. "Thank you for meeting with me. I'm sure your time is very limited. Would it be all right if I continued to look around?"

"Take as much time as you'd like." Again, Collette bowed her head in a way that reminded Greta of one of those stiff, animatronic robots. "I hope you'll convey my good thoughts to Mr. Thornwald. You said he still hoped to make the showing?"

"He said he plans to, yes." Greta caught the flash of movement on the other side of one of the partitions. Jack, perhaps, here to pick her up? Or a glitch in a light. Anticipation knotted in her stomach as she finally let herself think about having dinner with him this evening. Mistake or not, she was looking forward to an evening out with Jack McTavish. "I'm going to finish looking at the Dalí exhibit. I didn't quite make it through the entire thing."

"Of course." Collette nodded. "I have a conference call scheduled in just a few moments. Can you find your way back to the main house?"

"Yes, thank you." It took all her patience not to roll her eyes, but then maybe Collette had had issues with other artists' sense of direction? They parted ways, and Greta went to the elevator, making mental notes about the information she needed to pass along to Lyndon. Humming, she found herself thinking of the upcoming evening with Jack.

A date. When was the last time she'd gone on an actual date? Five, maybe six years ago? When she'd been living in Phoenix? Or was it Provo? She couldn't recall. Probably because no man had ever made smoke come out of her ears like Jack did when she'd kissed him.

She heard footsteps behind her, glanced over her shoulder as whoever it was moved out of sight. Odd. She was sure Collette had said no one else was in this section of the pavilion this afternoon.

"Hello?" She leaned back, scanned the hallway behind her, the closest display room. No one there. The overhead lights flickered, the sound of buzzing and popping fluorescents making her cringe. For a long moment, the gallery sat in darkness, bathed only in shadows from the low-hanging sun outside streaming through the sparkling-clean windows. "Collette? Is that you?"

Footsteps drew closer. Sounded heavier.

"Is someone there?"

No answer.

Greta frowned and clutched her purse between her breasts, tapped her foot as she waited for the elevator to arrive. She hit the button again and tried to ignore the chills racing up and down her arms.

"Ridiculous." She slipped trembling fingers around her throat. "You're being ridiculous." She'd done too much today, overloaded her normally confined senses. Had been thrown off-kilter by the very idea of regression therapy. If there was one place she was never going to go back to, it was the past. For a moment, all she wanted was to be back home, lost in her canvas worlds that were utterly and completely in her control.

As a sense of calm began to descend, the overhead lights flickered again. A loud bang exploded behind her just as the elevator doors slid open. She darted inside, punched the lobby button and willed it to move.

A man moved into view, caught between the light and darkness, as the doors began to slide shut. Greta, unable to breathe as her heart seemed stuck between hammering and stopping all together. She thrust her hand out to block the opening. She knew that man.

Big. Hefty. Paunchy. Bald with beady, dark eyes and thick-framed glasses.

Bile rose in her throat. Her mind raced to process what she was seeing. Who she was seeing. But it couldn't be. That man was dead. Doyle Fremont killed him….

She couldn't move. Her feet felt heavy, weighted to the ground as the man turned, just a bit. Just enough for her to see the distinctive wine stain birthmark covering part of his face and neck.

The elevator doors slid closed.

"No! No, wait!" She pounded her hands against the metal. She looked to the panel of buttons, uncertain which would reopen the doors. The gears above her head ground and rumbled as the car descended. She darted into the corner of the car, arms twisted tight around her waist. It wasn't possible. The man was dead. She'd seen him die. Seen him…

What was he doing here? Why here? Why now? Unless…

"Hurry up, hurry up." She had to get out, had to see if she was right. Greta bit her lip, diving for the doors as the elevator stopped.

The seconds ticked in slow motion before the doors slid open once more. A shadow passed in front of her.

She jumped back, covered her mouth with both hands to catch the scream.

The man turned, the relaxed, welcoming expression on his face fading in an instant. "Greta? What's wrong?"

"Jack." Her entire body went limp, relieved once she caught sight of him standing in the lobby. "Did you see him? Did he pass by here?" She scrambled out of the elevator, shoving him aside as she hurried across the ground level toward the stairs. She flew up to the landing, looking for any sign of him, but other than Jack who had followed her, and Collette lost somewhere in the maze of offices upstairs, she saw strangers. The lights were steady. Everything was…normal. She began to tremble. "Did you see him?" she whispered.

"See who?"

Jack walked up beside her, rested a hand on her arm and looked at her with that familiar, gut-twisting, forced-patient expression she'd seen far too often in her life.

"I'm not imagining this." The last word ended on a sob, a sob she'd give anything to control.

"Greta, talk to me." Jack's voice sounded firmer now, as if talking to an errant child. "What's going on?"

"I saw him. Here. He was following me."

"Who? Doyle Fremont?"

She didn't want to say. She couldn't say. Because saying would only mean…

Greta shoved past him and raced back down the stairs, shoved through the front doors onto the street. She looked one way, then the other, scanning the faces of the passersby. She had to be sure, had to know if what she'd seen was real or if…

Was it finally happening? Was she beginning to lose her mind?

"Greta, who did you see?" Jack spoke from behind her in that calm, almost condescending way Officer Bowman had used on her the other night. "Greta—"

"Don't! I saw him. He was here." Her mind raced. Her ankles wobbled in the ridiculous shoes Yvette had convinced her to wear. Swearing, she reached down and slipped them off, leaving them on the sidewalk as she sped down the street toward the historic section of the building. He couldn't have gotten very far. He could even be back inside. Maybe he'd gone up instead of down. Maybe…he had to be here somewhere. She spun in circles. She wasn't going mad. She had seen him. He'd seen her. And there…she froze. Her breath went cold in her chest. She stared across the street to beneath the blinking pedestrian-crossing light.

"Greta." Jack's hands reached out for her.

She tore herself away. Falling, flailing. Horns blared. Tires screeched. She hit the pavement. Hard. Pain blazed up her arm and across her cheek as the world went into slow motion.

Voices exploded around her, concerned, frantic voices, demanding ones. Angry ones. She felt herself being pulled up, first into a sitting position where she found Jack bending over her, hands pressed on either side of her face as he said her name over and over. "Greta. Come on, Greta. Talk to me. You all right?"

"Yes," she finally managed to say and grabbed hold of his wrists. She blinked up at him, touched by the fear and concern she saw in his eyes even as the expression pushed her further inside herself. "I'm okay. Let me up."

A few more voices echoed around her before Jack hauled her up and led her out of the street and over to where she'd dropped her shoes. He scooped them up, and they claimed a small bench in front of the museum.

"Is everything all right?"

Greta nearly groaned. Collette. The last thing she needed was the gallery's curator to see her have one of her meltdowns, let alone the worst she'd had in years.

"I heard the commotion from my office," Collette said. "I have a first aid kit inside. Should I go get it?"

"No." Greta bit her lip as she felt the panic start to build again. Not now. Not here. Not in front of...them. "No, thank you. I'm fine."

"Maybe I should call the police?" Collette offered.

"No need. I'm with the department." Jack pulled out his badge to show her. "I've already spoken with the driver. No harm done on either side. Just an accident."

An accident. Greta looked back to the crosswalk, but the only people there now were ones who had been drawn to the excitement. The man was gone. As if he'd never been there at all. "I'm sorry." Greta pressed a hand against her still-racing heart. "I'm sorry. I thought I saw..."

She caught the look in Jack's eye before he dropped a hand on her uninjured shoulder and squeezed. She needed to stop talking. She squeezed her eyes shut, tried to remember, tried to focus beyond the fear. She'd seen him. She knew she had. And yet...

"I thought I saw an old friend of the family. I've

forgotten his name. Tall, heavy. Has a birthmark on the side of his face? I don't suppose you've seen him?"

"I'm sorry, no," Collette said.

Greta just nodded. Of course she hadn't.

"Greta, you are certain you are all right?" Collette asked and, for the first time in their acquaintance, looked genuinely emotional. "I can call for an ambulance."

"I'm fine, really. Low blood sugar. We're going to dinner, right, Jack?"

"We'll play that by ear," Jack said in a tone she suspected went along with his profession. "Let's get you to the car and talk about it."

"Okay." She let him pull her to her feet. Her head throbbed, a dull ache pounding against her temple. "Oh, wait. Collette?"

"Yes."

"Something I forgot to ask you earlier." Greta cleared her throat. "I know the gallery has a number of sponsors. Is Doyle Fremont one of them?"

Jack's eyes sharpened, and she saw his jaw pulse.

"Mr. Fremont?" Collette's eyes went wide. "Yes, of course. He's one of our biggest contributors this year."

"So, he'll be at the showing," Jack clarified.

"We received his acceptance just yesterday," Collette offered. "Would you like me to provide a list of all those we invited? That would include all our donors, both past and present. I can email them to you right away."

"Yes, thank you." Greta said and winced as her arm began to pound in time to her head.

"You wouldn't happen to know the last time Mr. Fremont was at the gallery, would you?" Jack jumped on her train of thought.

"I believe Mr. Fremont was in just last week to inquire about a possible showing for a friend of his from Los Angeles. He's quite a patron of the arts, as I'm sure you know. His collection is impressively extensive."

"Yes, so I hear," Greta managed. "Thanks."

"Are you certain I can't call for the paramedics?" Collette offered. "You look a bit battered and bruised."

"I'll be fine, thank you."

"I'll make sure she sees someone," Jack promised. "I appreciate your help. I'm parked about a block away," Jack murmured as he wrapped his arm around her waist and escorted her away. "Can you make it?"

"Yes. Jack?" She stopped at the corner, the warm concrete of the sidewalk warming her bare feet. "Jack, I know what you're thinking."

"I don't think you do. Come on, the light's changed."

She walked beside him, trying to process what had happened. It all seemed so silly, so ridiculous. Maybe she was imagining things. Overwrought. Overexerted. Over stimulated. But she knew... Angry tears burned the back of her throat, blurred her vision. What was going on?

"Okay, here we are. In you go." Jack opened the door to his black SUV, helped her inside, but before he closed the door, she held out a hand, gripped his arm. "What?"

"I'm not crazy, Jack." In that moment, she wanted—no, she needed him to believe her. More than she needed to take her next breath.

"Who did you see, Greta?"

She fisted her hand in his jacket until her fingers

went numb. He covered her hand with his. She lifted her gaze, almost afraid of what she'd see on his face when she looked at him. If she told him…would he believe her? Or would he turn his back and walk away? The choice paralyzed her vocal chords. Even if she wanted to tell him—and she did—she couldn't. She needed him. Until she knew for certain, she needed him to believe in her.

Even if she didn't believe in herself.

"It's okay, Greta." He lifted his hand, stroked the backs of his fingers against her cheek and leaned in. He kissed her. A breath of a kiss. Soft. Gentle. Compassionate. And full of a promise she had no business trusting. "We'll talk about it after I get you home."

"Thanks for coming." Jack stepped back to let Ashley into Greta's loft. He motioned to where Greta was pacing back and forth in front of her windows, stopping occasionally to look down at Doyle's office as she chewed on her thumbnail and muttered to herself. "I'm honestly at a loss. You okay? You look frazzled."

"I bet I do. Traffic was horrible and then just outside I nearly got sideswiped by a van speeding out of here like an emergency-room intern given a surprise holiday." Ashley squeezed his arm as she passed. She set her bag down, slipped out of her jacket and handed it to him. "Tell me what happened?"

"From what I saw?" Jack purposely kept his voice low. No matter what he'd said to Greta on the drive home, she hadn't responded, just kept swiping at the tears that trickled down her cheeks. He'd almost gone against her wishes and driven to the emergency room. It was a miracle she wasn't bleeding where she'd knocked her head on the cement when she'd toppled off the curb. "If I had to describe it, it looked like some kind of panic attack. She practically threw herself into the street. Car just missed her. She fell. I lost my hold on her." A sensation he wasn't going to soon forget. "It's her left side, her shoulder mainly. And her head. I'm worried she might have a concussion."

"Okay." Ashley kicked off her shoes and patted his arm. "Hover if you must, but I want to hear from her from here on."

Jack nodded and closed the door. "Understood." One thing he knew was not to get between his sister and a patient. "Greta?" Should he feel this relieved that she turned when he called her name? "This is the doctor I told you about. Ashley Rus—"

"McTavish," Ashley cut him off as she took a seat on the sofa near Greta.

"Right." He should have realized she'd have taken her maiden name back. "Dr. Ashley McTavish."

"McTavish." Greta blinked as if caught in a fog. The concern Jack thought he'd left back at the gallery returned. "Oh, so you two are—?"

"Siblings," Ashley said smoothly. "I used to beat him up regularly when we were growing up."

"Oh." A flicker of a smile curved Greta's lips. "Oh, that's nice to hear."

"It's also a bald-faced lie." Jack stuck his tongue in his cheek at the evil grin his sister shot him. "The beating-up part, at least."

"Greta, have you taken anything since you've been

home? Painkillers? Antidepressants? Any prescriptions?"

"I don't like pills." Greta pressed two fingers into her temple and rubbed, but at least she'd stopped pacing. Instead, she stood barefoot in her living room, the curtains an oddly drab and gothic backdrop.

"That doesn't answer my question. Have you taken anything?" Ashley sat back on the sofa as if they were having a normal conversation. Cerberus leaped down from his bookcase perch to push his head against Ashley's arm. "Hey, there. I've heard about you." She reached over and scratched the cat between his ears. "You freak my brother out, you know that? Which means I'm inclined to like you already." Ashley whipped her hair behind her shoulder. "Now you have two watchdogs." Cerberus made a kind of growling sound, earning smiles from Greta and Ashley. "No offense. Greta, would you mind if I gave you a quick exam? Just to make sure you haven't broken anything?"

"Like my skull?" Greta's strangled laugh scraped against Jack's heart. He didn't think he'd ever seen anyone in so much emotional pain. She looked so confused. So lost. "No, I don't mind." She glanced at Jack. "I promised, didn't I?"

"You did. Thank you."

Ashley flicked a look at Jack, then her bag. Jack took the cue and handed the bag over. Ashley poked and prodded, earned a few flinches of pain from Greta. "Definitely some bumps and bruises. I'm going to want to take a closer look at that shoulder in a minute." She switched on a small penlight and peered into Greta's eyes. "No sign of a concussion, but we'll keep an eye on that. Now about the pills, Greta?"

"Um, yeah." Greta licked her lips and frowned. "I took one when I got home. For anxiety. But that's it." She frowned, as if she wasn't entirely convinced. "I'm not sure they're working. They usually make me foggy and sleepy, but—" she lifted her hands that continued to tremble "—it won't stop."

"Do you mind if I look at your prescription?" Ashley asked.

Greta shrugged. "Go ahead. It's in my medicine cabinet. Master bath, near the right-hand sink."

"Thanks. Jack, I'll be right back." Ashley zipped around the sofa and disappeared down the hall.

"So, you have a sister, and she's a doctor." Greta twisted her legs under her on the sofa and tucked her hands between her knees. It was like watching a turtle pulling into her shell. "That's nice."

"It is most of the time." Because she seemed to need it, he sat on the coffee table so he could stay in eyesight. "She neglects to mention she's younger than me."

Greta's eyebrows arched.

"Yep. She's that smart. Zoomed right ahead of me in school. I went to her high-school graduation before I went to my own."

Greta's smile almost looked real.

"What?" Not that he minded. She was so pretty when she smiled. All he wanted to do was hold her, soothe her, tell her everything was going to be all right. Except he couldn't do that. Not because it was completely inappropriate to become involved with a witness but because he didn't know what or who she'd seen.

"You don't hate that nearly as much as you pretend to," Greta said. "I can see it on your face. You're proud of her."

Jack made a pffth sound and earned another laugh. "What about you? Is there someone I should call? Parents? Brother or sister?"

"No." The curtain dropped back over her eyes. "No, my parents died when I was very young. I have a guardian, an honorary uncle really, but he's in New York. I don't want to bother him with all this. I'll tell him about it when he comes out for the show."

"No friends?"

"None I want to call. If you want to leave—"

"I don't." Jack reached out for her hands. "I'm not going anywhere." He suspected she wouldn't appreciate him noticing the tears glistening in her eyes.

"Do you have any other family other than Ashley?"

Jack let her change the subject. "The typical. Mother, father, an older brother."

"Let me guess, he's a theoretical physicist."

"Try again."

"Rocket scientist?"

"Nope."

"An Indiana Jones wannabe?"

This time Jack snorted. "Hardly. He manages my parents' deli back in Chicago. Makes a killer pastrami."

"Wow." She frowned. "So a doctor, a small-business owner and a police officer. Quite the combination."

"You mean why is one of these things not like the other?"

"I guess. Why did you want to be a cop?"

She was trying to distract herself, he thought. Finally, she'd inadvertently given him something to do. "I think that—" he stood up as Ashley returned from Greta's bathroom "—is a discussion meant for a dinner date. Everything okay?" he asked his sister.

"Other than the fact I'm having an unrequited love affair with that bathroom, everything's peachy."

Jack didn't get the joke. What was it with women and bathrooms?

"I probably should have warned you." Greta sighed and started to roll onto her side but sucked in a breath so harsh Jack felt it in his own teeth. "Well, that hurts."

"Let's get that shirt off. Jack, do you want to go brew tea or something?" Ashley fluttered her lashes at him.

"No." He couldn't explain it, but he didn't want to let Greta out of his sight, either, especially since she'd told him more about her past in the prior few minutes than she ever had previously.

"Well, then, you get to play assistant," Ashley said. "Come on, Greta. Let's sit you up."

"If it's broken, I'm screwed," Greta groaned as she cradled her left arm in her hand. Jack pushed her up, and Ashley guided her feet to the floor. "I've got work to do before my showing."

"Let's not borrow trouble just yet. This is such a shame." Ashley fingered the ripped edges of the fabric. "It was a beautiful blouse."

"I'm not meant to wear pretty," Greta joked with a weak laugh. "The tie is just under here." She started to pull her left arm up.

"I've got it." Jack bent down and unknotted the fabric.

"So not how I imagined this evening ending," Greta

mumbled. "Ah, ow." She swore and dropped her head back. "Sorry. I sound like a baby."

"You sound like you're in pain," Ashley said as she drew the fabric apart and then gently slid it down her arms. She pressed her fingers gently into Greta's skin beginning at her wrist, moved up slowly, to her shoulder. Greta sucked in a breath. "The good news is it's not broken." She pressed harder. "Sorry. Need to…" Even as she prodded, Jack could see the bruises forming. "Nope, joint is fine. I thought maybe you'd dislocated it. Just a bad strain, but there you go."

"Awesome." Greta shifted her gaze to Jack's as Ashley helped her into a loose shirt she'd brought from the laundry, adjacent to the bathroom. "Doesn't compare to a bullet in the chest, though."

"You've got that right." Jack tried to smile through the concern. He didn't like seeing her hurt, so much so he had trouble focusing on anything other than her. "But Ash here helped fix me up. She's the best."

"He's sucking up because he keeps messing up my sushi order," Ashley teased. "I'm going to hold off on any pain meds until you sleep off the other pill you took. That okay?"

"More than." Greta scooted down on the sofa. "How about I start now?" Her eyes drifted closed.

"What the—" Jack's stomach lurched into his throat.

"She's okay." Ashley stood up and caught him before he pounced. "Let's let her sleep. We can get her into a sling later. If she's still in pain tonight, she can come in for X-rays tomorrow. Now." She planted her hands on her hips and pinned him with a look. "Where's my sushi?" Jack's phone jangled and at his helpless shrug, Ashley heaved a heavy sigh. "Fine. Answer it."

Seeing Vince's name blink onto the screen, he moved into the kitchen, sparing a last glance at a now sleeping Greta. "McTavish."

"Hey. I thought you'd want to know, I've got some information."

"On Fremont?" Vince's slight hesitation spoke volumes. "On Greta?"

"Yeah. Look, I don't know if this means anything, Jack, but it's something you're probably going to want to have a conversation with her about."

"Spit it out already," Jack kept his voice low as he pulled open the fridge and grabbed a soda. Then, remembering his sister was still here, exchanged it for a water. "What did you find?"

"It's more what I didn't find. For whatever reason, her past only goes back ten years. Before that? There's nothing on record."

Jack shouldered the phone and twisted open the bottle. "So, you're saying…?"

"I'm saying that before ten years ago, Greta Renault did not exist."

Chapter 7

Because he'd done little more than pace Greta's loft while she'd slept off the pain pill Ashley insisted Greta take, Jack found himself at the station at sunrise, determined to grab a few hours' sleep before resuming the investigation. If only his mind would stop spinning. The information Vince had given him about Greta was intriguing, although less than fruitful.

It wasn't so unusual, he kept telling himself. People reinvented themselves all the time; changed their names. Moved around. Kept to themselves. But that wasn't often done with teenagers. Not without a court-compelling reason. She'd mentioned her parents had died when she was a little girl, and she'd referred to her guardian as just that, her guardian. Reinventions like this were extraordinary and only fed Jack's stifled curiosity.

A curiosity he'd satisfy himself. He asked Vince to shift his focus completely on to Doyle Fremont. Whatever Greta was hiding, she'd been keeping it to herself for a long time. Or maybe that was it, Jack reasoned. Maybe she was *in* hiding. Witness protection, maybe? Who knew?

But he needed to know. Not only to satisfy his curiosity, but to make sure nothing in her past was going to interfere with any case they might bring against Doyle Fremont. Not asking her the questions would put his career and future at risk, not to mention the people he worked with. He was banking everything not only on the word of a witness who was being less than forthcoming about her past but on his own shaky judgment. It would take learning about one to solidify the other.

At least he could stop worrying about Greta for a little while. Ashley, who was tired of being cooped up in his condo, was more than happy to stay with her patient if it meant easing some of Jack's concern.

Greta. That wasn't her name. Not her real name. But so far, Vince hadn't been able to unearth who she might have been prior to ten years ago. Or, maybe and more importantly, what would have caused her to change her identity. Given the roadblocks Vince had encountered, Jack would bet the only thing that would give him the answers he needed was an honest tough-love conversation with Greta Renault.

Exhaustion crept over him, which was no doubt what had him falling into a deep sleep the second his head hit the anemic so-called pillow.

It felt like only minutes later when a sharp rap on the door to the coffee room dragged him awake. He bit back a groan, pressed hard fingers into his eyes and pushed himself up. "Yeah?" If whatever Bowie had to tell him wasn't case-altering, he was going to find out firsthand how long it took to strangle a man to death. "I'm up," he called. "What is it?" He shoved his head into his hands and scrubbed at his hair. When he looked up into the open doorway, he wasn't entirely sure he wasn't still dreaming. "Cole. You're back? But I thought—man, what time is it?" His head felt as if it had been wrapped in cotton. He rubbed a hand against his aching chest.

"Almost ten." Detective Cole Delaney lounged against the doorframe and looked at Jack with a critical, albeit friendly, eye. Why did the guy always look like he'd stepped out of a designer-menswear ad? The super-high-end kind. Not the *Here's the sales rack* kind. "I got an SOS from the LT yesterday."

"Why would he do that?" Jack asked.

"Other than Bowie's ditched you for a family emergency in San Francisco?" Cole aimed a doubtful look at Jack that told him his partner didn't buy that explanation for one second. "He didn't really say, just thought you could use some help with a new case. Man, you do look raw. Eden and I took a late flight back. Got in around midnight."

"Santos must think I'm going off the rails if he called you. You didn't have to do that. You were on vacation." Even as he said it, he was glad to have his partner back. After hearing Vince's report last night, the need for a steady rudder in this case was even more important.

"I was into my sick days," Cole shrugged. "So it's just as well. So are you?"

"Am I what? Coming off the rails? No." The response was automatic, but because he knew he could trust Cole, he slipped back into uncertainty. "Yes." This time yesterday he was brimming with optimism and excitement, ready to take on not only Doyle Fremont but also the world. Now? It was as if that car that missed hitting Greta had somehow slammed into him and thrown him completely out of whack. He sighed, dropped his hands and looked up at his friend. "I don't know."

"Let's get out of here. Find some coffee and talk."

Cole wasn't just back, Jack noticed of his partner and best friend, but he was also ready to work. Cole had his badge clipped to his belt and his sidearm in place. But it was the gold wedding band on his finger that Jack knew brought Cole the greatest sense of pride. Not to mention accomplishment, Jack thought as he dragged his jacket off the hook by the door and followed Cole into the bullpen, where he unearthed a clean shirt from the bottom drawer in his desk. Eden St. Claire had not made things easy on anyone over the years, especially Cole. In the end, though, it hadn't mattered. "Where's Eden?"

"Back on the boat." Cole's prized possession was the 1960s gentleman's cruiser he'd somehow convinced Eden to live on. "She's got new notes to organize on the cold case she's checking. She probably won't surface until tomorrow.

"Eden is a bit of a Rottweiler when it comes to her cases," Cole said. "Five kids, all from the same town, all vanished within a year. And no movement on the evidence at all. She won't let that stand. Solving cold cases, bringing closure to families, it's her calling."

Yes, Jack thought. Yes, it was.

"So." Cole pushed open the station-house door and they headed outside into the blissful, cool morning air. "You want to fill me in?"

"That depends." Jack smirked. "How fond are you of your career?"

"Either you move like a ghost or I sleep like the dead." Greta might have leaped ten feet in the air if she hadn't caught sight of Ashley, her Jack-appointed babysitter, moving into the studio out of the corner of her eye. "As I know it's not the latter," Ashley said, "you must be feeling better. How's the shoulder?"

Paintbrush in hand, Greta faced Jack's sister and tried to ignore the frown on the other woman's round face when she noticed Greta had ditched the makeshift sling. "Better." Truth be told, it still hurt, but she was pushing through. Focusing, however distractedly, on her painting was helping.

"Headache?"

"Barely noticeable," she lied, wondering what Ashley was thinking as the physician walked around her studio.

"You didn't take any more pain pills?"

"I told you, I don't like—"

"Pills." Ashley turned, all traces of sleep gone. She looked at Greta as if peering through a microscope to examine an unknown organism. "For someone who doesn't like taking them, you certainly have a stash of them."

"Everyone has a hobby." The joke didn't land, but Ashley didn't push back.

"How long have you been up?"

"Since—" Greta glanced at the clock on the counter by the door "—three, I think?"

Ashley nearly tripped on one of the tarps covering the floor. "Three this morning? That's almost seven hours."

"Okay." Greta paid special attention to swirling her paintbrush in the glass of paint thinner. Her stomach clenched as it always had when she was forced into a conversation she didn't want to have. "I'm most productive when the rest of the world is asleep." And she had been productive. For the first time in months. Just not in the way she'd expected.

"I was the same in med school," Ashley said. "Used to drive my roommate nuts. Greta, as your current medical provider, those pills—"

Greta closed her eyes. "I don't want to talk about it."

"Too bad. Those are powerful antipsychotics, Greta. Does Jack know?"

"No." That question got her attention. She blinked and glanced at Ashley. "Why would he?"

Ashley arched a brow. "Because you're involved. Or if you aren't yet, you soon will be. The two of you are like a flashing billboard when you're together."

"We are not." Greta's face went hot.

"Please." Ashley rolled her eyes.

Unfamiliar nerves fired under her skin. "Jack and I haven't known each other very long. We haven't reached the *are you sure you have a grip on reality?* phase of our relationship yet." Except they had. Yesterday. And they'd blasted beyond it. If she'd seen who she thought she saw yesterday, the same man she'd seen the first night… Terror slithered up her throat, but she swallowed hard. Greta rearranged the tools on her small worktable beside the nearly finished painting she'd done only hours before. It had been mountains that called to her this time. Fire-tipped mountains with a swirling blue smog and scaled, purple dragons in the distance. It all felt so much safer than the real world. *Afterburn*, she was calling it.

"You're the main witness in a case that, in his words, is a political powder keg. This case could destroy Jack's career if he's wrong about anything, Greta. If he's wrong about you." Ashley caught sight of the large canvas Greta had thought she'd hidden better. Most of the image was obscured by a bold, green fabric, but given Ashley was more than familiar with the subject, of course it would have captured her attention. "Well." She stooped down, pushed the fabric aside and stared into the eerily accurate image of her brother. "That's impressive. And quite personal. Not very long, you said?" She looked over her shoulder at Greta.

"Jack makes an impression." She wished he hadn't. She wished anyone other than Jack had been the one to turn up at her loft the other night. Whether they'd have believed her or not, she wouldn't be dealing with the added complication of developing, well, she guessed they were feelings for Jack McTavish. Feelings that went far beyond the desire of any kiss. Feelings neither of them could afford for her to have.

"He's certainly made an impression on you. This is stunning, Greta. Truly. I won't even try to comprehend how you captured everything about him in just his face. The strong jaw, that silent nobility in his eyes. He'd die of embarrassment if he ever knew about this, but he's always reminded me of one of those medieval soldiers, fighting against all the wrongs in the world, be it with a sword or spear or—" Ashley indicated the barely there yellow stars in his eyes "—a badge. Please don't tell him I said that. I'm kind of saving that bit of information for when I know it'll completely humiliate him." She grinned.

"There's nothing humiliating about nobility." Greta couldn't help it. The sight of him, even in a painting, drew her in. That Ashley saw him in roughly the same vein eased her mind.

"And there's nothing wrong with taking medication when you need it. But if you are taking—" Ashley turned, rested a gentle hand on Greta's arm.

"I'm not," Greta insisted. She was so tired of being doubted. Why didn't anyone ever believe her?

"Greta—"

"I'm not taking those pills. They're a…" How did she explain when she didn't understand it herself?

"They're a what?"

Greta drew a deep breath. She'd never told anyone. Not Uncle Lyndon. Not even Yvette. But maybe she needed to tell someone, if only to maybe have them help her make sense of it all. "They're a precaution."

"A precaution for what?"

Greta squeezed her eyes shut long enough to pray for strength. "For when I lose my mind."

"Well, okay then." Cole refolded the statement Greta had typed up and tapped the paper against his hand before returning it to him. Their coffee was long gone, but they remained seated at the small café table a few blocks from the station. "I can see why you're worried about career suicide. Doyle Fremont. Wow."

"Do you believe her?" Jack wasn't entirely sure what he wanted Cole's answer to be. Either way... Jack was in deep trouble.

"Oh, I believe her." Cole shrugged and even behind his sunglasses, Jack could see him flinch as he looked up at the sun. "There's no reason not to, given that picture you took and the conversation you had with Fremont. But that's also the problem, Jack. It's Doyle Fremont. That new complex alone is employing a good chunk of the population. It's done wonders for the city and only promises to do more. And let's not forget who he calls his friends and that his lawyers are already on alert. Now that you know Greta isn't exactly who she says she is? This could turn into a serious cluster— well, mess."

"This is why I'm glad you're back," Jack muttered. "To help clear things up for me."

"I do what I can." Cole's smile was quick. "What about this thing that happened at the Camellia, yesterday? Who did she see? Fremont?"

"I'm assuming. Not that I could get her to tell me. She shut down, like whatever she saw flipped an off switch inside of her." And try as he might, he hadn't been able to turn it back on.

"Did you see anyone?"

"I saw plenty of someones, but not Fremont. Besides, according to the LT, he's out of town. I can't believe he'd be so careless as to commit murder in front of a witness."

"He didn't expect a witness," Cole said. "The time and location pretty much solidify that."

"But what is all this about? If we could just figure out who the victim was, that has to be what unlocks this whole thing."

"If there was a victim."

Jack's blood went icy. "You don't believe her?"

"I don't not believe her. I'm also not so naive as to think you might have a bit of a hero complex and still blame yourself for what almost happened to Allie. Not to mention—"

"Don't go there, Cole." This was not a road he planned on going down. With anyone.

"Why not? You have. You're afraid of missing something again. Of someone getting hurt or, worse, killed. What happened in Chicago with your witness was not your fault, Jack. The DA underestimated how dangerous the defendant was. You couldn't protect her for the rest of your life."

It wasn't something he hadn't told himself a million times before. But nothing would convince him he hadn't failed Clara Pilsken. The fact the young woman had a grave marker rather than a college diploma was all the evidence he needed.

"You're worried if you don't cover all your bases, if you look away even for a second, something's going to happen and maybe this time you won't escape with your life intact."

He wouldn't call two months in the ICU followed by four months of physical therapy a life intact. "That's not it." For the first time since they'd met, Jack lied to his partner. A lie he tried to pull back almost immediately. "That's not entirely it. Greta needs someone to believe her, Cole. It's important to her."

"And that's important enough to you that you're willing to put your entire career on the line to make it happen."

"Is that a question or a statement?"

"You tell me. Look, I'm not saying don't believe her, but maybe let's look at this from a different angle. You've said yourself, she's eccentric, and I can see it on your face. You don't know what the heck happened at the gallery, and you were there. Maybe this is some kind of stalker situation? Are you sure she and Fremont have never met? She is an artist, after all. Didn't you say he has a pretty extensive art collection?"

Jack nodded. "He has a bunch of framed pieces boxed up in his office. I wouldn't be surprised if one of hers is in there. With her star on the rise, it's not out of the realm of possibility he'd see it as an investment in the future."

"Agreed. She's been building up a name, had some pretty prestigious placements, and one thing we know about Fremont is he enjoys the benefits of wealth. It's also possible it's some kind of obsession thing. Does he have any previous record or charges?"

"I have someone looking into that," Jack said. "Off the record."

"Huh. That's interesting."

"What is?"

"You going to Vince."

"Jeez, what am I? An open book?"

"No. You're a man willing to do whatever it takes to

protect someone who needs it, and we both know, outside the department, Vince is someone we can count on. Nothing's going to stand in your way of doing what you think is right. Even if it might not be."

"I don't want her hurt, Cole."

"Can that even be a factor? We're talking about a career make-it or end-it case. You bring in Doyle Fremont, and you'll either be a bright, shiny star in the department or out on your tail. We do what we have to do to close the case, fallout notwithstanding. Although, there's always collateral damage."

"Was there collateral damage with you and Eden?" Jack asked and tried to control his temper. "Or did you do whatever it took to protect her?"

"It's not the same thing." Cole waved dismissively. "I was in love with Eden, which meant my judgment wasn't exactly..." He trailed off, inclined his head and, after a long pause, let out a sigh they probably heard back at the station. "Well, dang, Jack. That was fast."

"Yeah," Jack agreed. "About sums it up."

"So, that's the issue." Cole looked a bit disbelieving. "You're in love with her."

"No." Jack altered his response at Cole's snort of disbelief. "Yes." He groaned. "Maybe. First time I saw her, bam! It was like she'd been branded into my brain. And no, before you say what you're thinking, there's nothing I can do about it. Even if I wanted to change things, and I don't, I couldn't. This stupid thing hasn't worked right since I was shot." He pounded his fist against his heart. "I would love to play bodyguard and let whatever this is happen without pushing anyone's buttons, but I can't shake the feeling there's something more going on, Cole. The pieces just don't fit. I need your help to make them fit."

"What if they don't fit the way you want them to?" Cole asked.

What if? Was there ever a more disturbing and challenging question? "If I'm wrong, then I'll take what comes. Me alone. You have my word."

"You just refuse to take the easy road, don't you, Jack? Even when it comes to the fall."

"I've always liked a challenge." And Jack had never met anyone as challenging, or as life-affirming, as Greta Renault. "Just promise me you'll do one thing for me."

"What's that?"

"Stop me from doing anything stupid."

"Sorry, partner." Cole shook his head. "Some things a man just has to do on his own."

Chapter 8

It wasn't until Greta opened the door later that night that she realized just how much she'd missed Jack. Even if he arrived with a bazillion questions about what—and who—she'd seen at the gallery yesterday, she was ready to answer them. It was the least she owed him.

"Hi." It felt as if it was the first time she'd smiled all day, and the simple action popped that balloon of unease that had been building inside of her.

He looked tired again, but that rumpled kind of tired rather than the utter exhaustion that had driven him to sleep on her sofa. She loved how the crisp white shirt was set off by the thin, black tie. How he slouched against her doorframe, how he held his hands in his pockets, and that it made her long to dive back into her studio and begin another painting. She reached out, nearly touched his cheek before he caught her hand.

"I hope you don't mind, but I've got my partner with me."

"Bowie?" She stepped back, motioned him in. The man who followed, however, was completely unfamiliar. If ever there was an epitome of a TV cop, she was looking at him. Tall, fit and looking back at her with a bit of reservation in his eyes. Funny. She couldn't remember the last time she'd had so many people in and out of her home. She tended to feel invaded by visitors, anxious for them to leave so she could be alone again, but not so much with Jack's friends. "Hello. I'm Greta Renault."

"Detective Cole Delaney." He offered his hand and when she took it, she had an immediate impression of controlled strength intermingling with casual acceptance. He dropped a small duffel by the door, held out a large paper bag. "Hope you don't mind. We brought dinner."

"Tell me it's sushi." Ashley launched off the sofa and dived for the bag in Cole's hand. "Ugh. Burgers from Vince's. Darn it! I cannot catch a break."

"I thought you liked his burgers," Jack accused. "You sure inhaled one the other night. Along with half my fries."

"A woman cannot live on burgers alone. You know what?" She held up a hand, then returned to the sofa and slipped into her shoes and jacket. "As much fun as this has been, I'm going to get my own dinner. And then I'm going to go back to your place, take a long shower and spend a few hours catching up with my favorite demon-hunting impala-riding brothers."

Greta rolled her eyes.

"She only watches old TV and movies. Can you believe it? Nothing from the last few decades." Ashley poked Greta on her uninjured arm. "I've been telling her all day she needs to branch out, and you can't go wrong with Sam and Dean…"

Whatever else Ashley said slipped right past Greta's ears. Greta reached down and lifted the bag out of Jack's hand, a sweet, secret exchange of smiles happening when their hands brushed. He'd been so good with her after the gallery scare, so kind and caring, as if whatever barrier he'd been trying to keep up between them had vanished. And so understanding that he hadn't pushed her to tell him who she'd seen. But she'd felt it: the doubt, the concern, the worry she didn't want to come between them. Despite Ashley's steadying presence, the residual fear that had been threatening all day finally subsided. Just seeing him, knowing he was here, made her feel…safe.

"Okay, yep." Ashley waved a hand in front of Greta's dazed face. "There she goes. I'm definitely out of here." She patted Cole's shoulder, murmured something on her way out. "I'll be by tomorrow to check on your shoulder, Greta." The meaningful look she shot Greta as she closed the door had Greta swallowing the lump in her throat.

"Come on in the kitchen," she managed after Ashley closed the door.

She was grateful for the reprieve. While Ashley had assured Greta she wouldn't be sharing any of Greta's earlier admissions, she made it clear she expected Greta to come clean with Jack. And the sooner, the better. Okay, fine. She'd tell Jack. When the time was right. When she had to.

But not tonight.

Greta focused on the two detectives opening cardboard containers in the kitchen. The room filled with the amazing aroma of well-cooked burgers and oil-slick sweet potato fries.

"Jack said you've been on vacation." Greta slipped onto one of the tall stools at the end of the kitchen island, while Jack and Cole sat across from her.

"I guess you could call it a vacation," Cole said easily. "My wife isn't exactly one to leave work behind. It kind of goes with us. Eden's a crime blogger," Cole clarified as he dumped a pile of fries onto his plate. "She investigates cold cases, then reports on them, tries to give departments new leads so they can finally give some closure to families. I'm sorry. I should have checked with you that you eat meat."

"Carnivore, through and through." She flashed him a smile. "This smells great. Thanks for bringing it. I didn't realize I was at the end of my food provisions until Ashley informed me the freezer was down to chicken soup and frostbitten hot dogs. Jessie's coming in tomorrow to cook, so I should be stocked up again. I bet she does something with shrimp and crab. Or maybe artichokes. Oh, I hope she makes those chicken dumplings with tarragon. Those are just delicious. What kinds of cold cases?"

Cole coughed, and he reached for a napkin. "That was a road map of information."

"Sorry. I'm a bit…distracted." She looked to Jack, but he didn't say a word. Simply kept his head bent and focused on his meal. Was something wrong? Had something happened?

"There's wine, beer and sodas in the fridge." Greta pointed Cole in that direction. "Help yourself."

"Thanks." Cole grabbed two bottles of beer and set one down in front of Jack. "Eden works all kinds of cases, but mostly anything having to do with kids. Kidnappings, murders. She can spend weeks, months, even years sometimes on the same case. She blogs about them as she goes."

"'Eden on Ice'? You're married to Eden St. Claire." She dug into the burger and felt every millimeter of her mouth rejoice. Aside from a few snacks, she hadn't eaten much today, despite Ashley's insistence.

"I am, indeed," Cole confirmed. "You're a fan?"

She wasn't big on social media, but as it was a necessary evil for her work, she spent some time on the internet. "I love her blog," she said after she swallowed. "Not really what she talks about, but she has this voice that just resonates, you know? It's like she gets you inside the head of the people—"

"The people left behind," Jack finished for her.

"Exactly." Greta nodded. "I'd love to meet her sometime."

"I'm sure you will." Cole cast a sly-eyed look at Jack. "How's your arm?" He pointed his bottle at her shoulder.

"Better. Hot and cold packs, and I painted, so it helped put it out of my head. Sitting around doing nothing just made it hurt more."

"You wor—" Jack began.

"What happened at the gallery?" Cole cut him off, pinning Greta with a steely-eyed stare that reminded her that he, just like Jack, was a cop.

His question hit her in the solar plexus. Greta took another bite of her burger and stalled. Fear wound its way back up her chest, into her throat.

"At least let her finish her dinner first," Jack complained.

"No, it's all right." Greta's heart pounded in her chest as she tried to push away those moments of terror when she'd been in the elevator, not knowing what would happen when it stopped. In one way, it was easier hearing the question from Cole, rather than Jack. "I know we didn't talk in detail yesterday once we were back here, so I've been expecting it." She wasn't entirely sure she could have had that conversation then, either.

"Painkillers knocked her out." Jack aimed the comment at Cole who continued to plow through his meal. "Whenever you're ready, Greta."

"Actually, now would be best," Cole corrected. "If it was Doyle, if he's following you or stalking—"

"It wasn't Doyle Fremont I saw at the gallery."

Jack's hands froze halfway to his mouth. He set his burger down. "It wasn't?"

"No. It wasn't." She'd been waiting for this moment, knew without a doubt it was going to arrive, and she'd prepared for it. She slipped from her stool and exited, ignoring the frustrated mutterings from the men left behind as she retrieved her sketchpad. Heart thudding, she flipped to the page she needed and returned to the kitchen. She handed the pad over. "This is who I saw."

Jack sputtered and nearly spit out the beer he was drinking as he accepted the notebook. "But—"

"I know." Greta steeled herself for the worst. For the doubt. The anger. And most of all, the disbelief. "I saw a dead man."

She replayed it, bit by bit in her mind, talked it out with the two men, what had happened from the moment she arrived at the gallery to when Jack brought her to his car. Neither detective interrupted, and by the time she was done she wasn't sure if she felt better or worse for the purge. She rubbed her shoulder as it seemed to throb in sympathy. She nibbled on a fry, waiting for a response.

"I'm only going to ask you this once," Cole said. "You're absolutely certain who you saw?"

The inquiry irritated her, mainly because she'd been asking herself the same thing in an unending loop in her head. But he, and Jack, had every reason to be skeptical. Except Jack had yet to utter a word.

"Yes." Did she sound as certain as she felt? "I saw him. He was there."

"Okay then." Cole nodded as if that closed the subject. "Your meeting with the curator—"

"Collette Sorenson," Greta clarified.

"Who knew about that?"

"Well, me. My friend Yvette, and Jessie, my assistant. Anyone Ms. Sorenson would have told. Jack, of course."

"Of course." Cole's smile was temper quick.

"And Lyndon. My family lawyer." Explaining who Lyndon really was always opened doors she wanted to keep locked. "But he's stuck in New York, which is why I took the meeting myself."

"He also became your guardian after your parents died, right?" Jack asked.

Greta's eyes went wide and her throat tightened. How did he—?

"Last night, before the pill kicked in. You told me you lost your parents when you were very young, that you were raised by an honorary uncle."

Because she had no words, she nodded. What else had she said last night? It must not have been much more since he was still sitting here.

"Did Ms. Sorenson walk you through the security layout?" Cole asked.

"No. Should she have? Should I have asked to do that? Was that a mistake?" Given all that was going on, should she have been paying attention to that?

"Not a mistake." Cole polished off his burger and wiped his mouth. "Not even an oversight. That's not where your mind goes. It's on your work, on the display. We need to find out what their setup is."

"Tammy's working on that." Jack shifted on his stool. "Our lab tech," he clarified to Greta. "She's also tracking social media in case anyone posted videos or pictures of the accident. If our victim was there—"

"If?" The word shot out of Greta's mouth like a bullet. "What do you mean if? I told you I saw him. You told me you…" She trailed off, her breath hitching in her chest as her mind raced. "Actually, you didn't. You didn't say you believed me." Even though she'd been expecting it, hearing it now felt like a slap. "I knew this would happen. You don't believe me."

"I didn't say that, either," Jack said.

"Well, pick one," she insisted. "It's not like this is important or anything."

"That's my cue to make a call to…anyone." Cole pulled out his phone and headed for the living room.

"Coward," Jack muttered as he picked up his container and carried it over to the sink, returned for Cole's and dumped the flatware in the sink. "I never said I didn't believe you, Greta. Stop putting words in my mouth."

"Do you really think I made it up?" Greta jumped off her stool and circled around the counter. "I know what I saw, Jack. What possible reason would I have to lie?"

"I don't know." He faced her, pinned her with a look she was certain he used when questioning criminals. "Why would you lie?"

"I—" The steel in his eyes, the way his jaw pulsed as he gnashed his teeth. Whatever was bothering him, it went deeper than what had happened at the gallery. "I haven't lied to you, Jack." Because she couldn't. She'd tried but found her only option was to remain silent, for fear all her secrets, secrets she'd struggled to keep for more than a decade, would come spilling out.

"You've lied to me from the moment we met." He dried his hands on the towel and set it aside with calm deliberation. "Who are you really? What's your real name, *Greta*?"

"My—real name?" The question hit her hard. "Why would you ask me that?"

"Because Greta Renault has only existed for the past ten years. Did you really think I wouldn't check into you? Did you think I'd just take your word on everything you've told me, risk my career, risk my future, my partner's future because of what you said you saw?"

"Yes." Her hands balled into skin-piercing fists. "You either believe me or you don't. My past doesn't have anything to do with what's going on now. It doesn't change what I saw."

"Given who you've accused of murder, the truth about who you are could very well have a lot to do with it. You asked me to believe you, to trust you, but you haven't really trusted me, have you?"

"It isn't about trust." Liar. This was about trust. It was about trust and so much more. She needed his help to find out the truth, to find out if what she'd seen had actually happened. But if he knew who she really was, would he continue to help her prove she wasn't making it all up? She couldn't take the risk. Not with her entire future on the line.

"Isn't it?" Jack's voice never rose but stayed at that frustratingly calm level that made her feel like a naughty but caught child. "Is it that you can't tell me? Are you in witness protection or something? I can't imagine you are, since you're ready to have a very public showing, but if it's—"

"That's not it. Exactly." She twisted her hand around her leather cuff until it hurt. Until this moment she never realized just how loud the past sounded as it roared in her ears. The screams. The sirens. The absolute dead silence of a happy home that echoed with the cries and tears of a six-year-old girl who was suddenly and completely alone. "I've never lied to you about anything important, Jack. Who I was before…" She struggled for breath. "It doesn't matter. Not to any of this."

"You've made it matter by not telling me about it. Do you know what a defense lawyer could do with the fact you've been living a lie for the past ten years?" His voice softer now, she felt her heart jump when he moved forward and placed his hands gently on her shoulders. "You can tell me, Greta. Let's get ahead of this. Let's prepare for it. Together. Or…" He gave her a quick squeeze, dropped his hands and stepped away. "Or we can wait and see what we find on the camera feeds at the gallery, and we'll go from there."

Greta gaped at his back as he turned on the water. Had he just *dismissed* her? Feeling whiplashed, she moved in behind him. "How about we don't do either. If you don't believe me, about what I saw, what are we even doing?"

"Right now, I'm going to do the dishes."

"More like playing your passive-aggressive card." She grabbed his arm and faced him. She needed to see him, to look into his eyes and find out if he felt anything remotely close to what she did. "You know what I'm doing? I'm trying to hold my life together. I'm trying not to call myself every kind of stupid for even contacting the police in the first place. If you're looking for an excuse to walk away from the case because it's politically inconvenient for you, feel free. Don't let me stop you."

Jack's smile set off a fire inside of her that all but exploded.

"What's that for?"

"I'm sorry." He tried to duck his head, but she stooped down so he couldn't look away. "It's just that you're really pretty when you're angry."

"You have got to be—" She shot back up to full

height. "Do you have any idea how condescending that sounds? Are you serious right now?"

"About you being pretty? Never been more."

"Oh, my God." She pushed her hands into her hair and resisted the urge to yank. "You have got to be the most confounding person I have ever met in my life. Of all the infuriating, mind-numbing… You do realize just a minute ago you were calling me a liar."

"Yes."

"And now you're just standing there smiling at me like you'd like nothing more than to…" She trailed off, realizing exactly what he wanted to do.

What she'd been wanting him to do ever since she'd first kissed him. The energy around them, between them, sizzled. She lifted her hand to his face.

"Aw, jeez." Cole stopped in the doorway. "I feel like I've time-traveled back to seventh grade. Maybe you two should just have a go already and get it over with."

"Get out."

"Shut up."

Jack and Greta ordered at the same time without looking at him.

Cole opened his mouth to respond when his phone rang. "Back in a moment. Carry on."

"Great idea," Jack said as he moved toward her.

"What is?" Greta demanded.

"Carrying on."

Whatever else she was going to say flew out of her head as his mouth landed on hers. Didn't just land, she thought, as her mind spun. Swooped down and invaded. His hands pressed into the base of her spine and pulled her solidly into him as he angled his head and deepened the kiss. The ache in her shoulder throbbed as she lifted her arms, dragged her hands up to hold his face gently and surrendered. Every bone in her body liquefied, and she clung to him, grateful for the support even as her mind rang with all the protestations he'd made about getting involved with her.

When he lifted his mouth, she cried out, unwilling to let him go just yet. She brought him back to her, down to her, under with her so she could take what she never realized she needed until she'd met him. The warm taste of him sank through her, drifting into her mind, singing through her blood even as she could feel him pulling away.

"Oh, for—"

Greta opened her eyes and spotted Cole standing with his back against the kitchen archway. She brushed her fingers lightly across Jack's lips and felt her own curve in a silent, wanton question. A question she saw answered in the depths of Jack's reluctant gaze.

"Do I need to remind you it's a violation of protocol to get personally involved with a witness?" Cole asked.

"No." Jack kept an arm around Greta.

"It is?" Greta asked.

Cole turned but rolled his eyes before he walked to his chair to retrieve his jacket. "As much as I'd love to play wet blanket and keep you two from being stupid—" he aimed a glare at Jack "—I need to head home. Eden's not feeling great."

Greta felt Jack's body tense beneath her hand. "Is she okay?"

"She's been fighting this weird bug. Comes and goes. I'm going to stop and pick up some soup on the way."

Cole patted his hands against his jacket looking a touch flustered. "Not sure where I put my keys."

"Left outside pocket," Jack told him.

"Wait. I can save you a trip." Greta dived for the bottom freezer drawer and pulled out two tall plastic containers. "It's chicken soup. All I've got left from Jessie's last batch." She put it into the paper bag Cole and Jack had brought dinner in. "Reheat it on the stove or in the microwave."

"Thank you." Cole accepted the bag. "Appreciate it. I know Eden will, too. I'll check in with Bowie and Tammy first thing in the morning. See if they've come up with something on those cameras and…the other thing."

"You don't sound very hopeful," Greta said, enjoying his transformation from inquisitive cop to devoted husband.

"I haven't been hopeful about anything since Jack here told me you saw Doyle Fremont murder someone. Speaking of which, where are we on finding out if he's bought one of Greta's paintings?" he asked at the door.

"I'm sorry, what?" Greta's voice vanished under a new wave of panic.

"We were just about to discuss that," Jack said.

"Yeah, it is difficult to talk with your mouths fused together. Talk away. And I suggest you keep all four feet on the floor. You two want to finish this once the case is over, fine, but don't make things more complicated than they already are." Cole pointed at their feet. "All of them. On the floor. At all times."

"You'd be surprised what I can do with my feet on the floor." Jack grinned as Greta blushed.

Cole's lips twitched. "Let's leave a bit of mystery, shall we? You." He pointed at Jack. "Call me every few hours, just so I know everything's okay. If I think for a second you can't keep the personal and professional separate, I'll get the chief to assign someone else to babysit her."

"Babysit me?" Greta pushed back and glared up at Jack. "Is that why Ashley stayed all day? You really asked her to do that? What the—"

"Perfect. I started a fight." Cole flipped up the collar on his jacket and headed out. "That should do the trick and keep things platonic. I'll see you in the morning. Night, Greta."

"Oh, good night." She closed the door and spun on Jack. "Explain."

"It can't come as a complete surprise." Jack's voice took on that strained-patience tone again. "We had a discussion—"

"*We* who? Because we did not include me, and me is very much involved in this situation."

"Me as in Cole, Bowie and our LT. Given what happened yesterday at the gallery, we decided—"

"You made a decision that affects me without me?" This was why she kept to herself. This was why she didn't get involved. So she wouldn't lose control of her life.

"Yes." He returned to the kitchen to clean up. "If what happened at the gallery—"

"There's that *if* again." She followed him around the island. "There was no if. I know what happened. I. Saw. Him. And don't even think about kissing me this time." She planted a hand firm on his chest when he leaned toward her. Big mistake. Big, big mistake. Her fingers flexed against the sudden warmth, and she cheered.

"Do you mean now or in the future?"

"Don't smirk at me like that. I mean it." And she did, despite the bubble of laughter caught in her chest. Darn it, she should be mad at him. She didn't need a babysitter! Whatever else might be going on, she was safe in her own home. She'd paid a small fortune to protect it.

"Okay then, let's finish our earlier conversation. About the regression therapy. Unless you can describe him more clearly now?"

He may as well have dumped the Arctic over her head. She stepped back and wrapped her arms around her waist. "I told you no."

"Discuss it or do it?"

She pressed her lips tight. "Both."

"Funny." He reached for the dish towel to dry his hands. "One thing I didn't take you for was a coward."

She'd never met anyone who triggered her temper faster. Or hotter. "Do you really think I'm dumb enough to fall for that?"

"Dumb enough, no. Angry enough? Determined? I thought maybe you might be feeling as anxious to get out from under this case as I am so we can see if there's anything between us on the other side."

"I—what?" Was this what she sounded like on one of her tangents? What did that even mean?

"Let me put this another way." He whipped a hand around her waist and dragged her against him, covering her mouth so completely, so deliberately, she almost melted into the floor. His fingers skimmed beneath the hem of her shirt, brushed against the bare skin of her spine, dipped slightly below the waistband of her pants. Her stomach tightened as anticipation built, heavy, hot and pulsing across every inch of her body. "That's as far as this goes," Jack murmured against her lips. "That's as far as it can go until I close this case."

"You're not playing fair and you know it." Desire battled against reason. She hooked a bare foot around the back of his calf, shifted her hips against his and made sure he knew exactly what he was walking away from.

"Now who's not playing fair?" But rather than getting angry or pushing her away, he brushed his mouth against hers. "Just think about talking to Allie, seeing what the session entails. Not only because it'll help us with the case but because I really, really want you in my bed." He cupped her face between his hands, his touch so tender, she almost surrendered then and there.

But she didn't. Not quite. There was no point in telling him he was right. There was no logical reason not to talk to his friend. But she wouldn't do so without doing some research first. Before knowing for certain that the secrets she'd struggled with all her life were going to stay locked safely away. "I'll think about it."

Jack dipped down, bored his steely, determined gaze into hers. "Think fast."

Chapter 9

In the gray haze of night, Greta opened her eyes. The woman's cries drifted into her ears and lodged hopelessly in her mind. A screech, a long wailing cut through the midnight hours that had blanketed her room, her loft, the city, in darkness. Her name. She heard her name before more sobs erupted.

"I'm coming." Head heavy, she pushed back the covers and slipped out of bed, the sad sound pulling at her, drawing her to it, achingly familiar. Greta stepped into the hall as the flash of gray light floated out of sight and around the corner.

"Wait. Don't go. Come back." Greta followed. The dim glow of the living room light didn't deter her. How could it when the only brightness she saw melted through her front door and disappeared? She could still hear it, calling to her, like a siren calling to a sailor in the moonlit fog of the sea. She flicked the padlock, pulled open the door and moved.

As she descended the stairs, somewhere in the distance she heard her name. But it was another voice. Louder. Determined. She walked, transfixed by the vision in white. The marble floor was chilly against her feet. Her hand brushed the banister. The lobby vanished; instead she saw them, her parents. Saw the blood-spattered walls, heard her mother's frantic wails. Greta looked down, saw the blood pooling around her feet.

"Greta!"

The image disappeared. Greta blinked, looked around. "Jack? What's going on?" Her voice left her as she looked at the dark lobby. "Oh, no. What did I do?" She struggled against his hold even as she wanted to cling to him. She shivered so hard her teeth hurt.

"Sleepwalked would be my guess." He bent down, reached for and held her hands. "You okay now?"

"I think so." She couldn't quite focus. "I'm sorry. I didn't mean to wake you."

"You didn't." He moved in, drew her to him and just held her. She squeezed her eyes shut, relaxing into him, resisting the urge to burrow into him. He was so safe. So perfect. So...

He picked her up and turned toward the steps.

"Your chest. Your breathing. You shouldn't—" She pressed her fingers against his heart.

"Don't ruin my Prince Charming moment." Joke aside, he seemed to be focusing intently on taking each step carefully.

The next thing she knew, she was back in the loft.

While he went to fix her some tea, she went into the bathroom to rinse her face, gripping the sink as she stared dazedly into eyes that didn't seem quite her own. She was back in bed when he appeared in her doorway, white tray in hand. She watched him while he poured her a cup of anemic tea, wondered what he was thinking, then told herself she didn't want to know. Instead, when he handed her a cup, she murmured, "Thank you."

"I'm glad I caught you before you called an Uber."

She couldn't help it. She laughed, then bit her lip as a wave of emotion crashed over her. The sight of this strong, determined, kind man pouring her a cup of tea had the tears burning her throat again. It would be so easy, she realized, so easy to fall in love with him.

She was already halfway there, she admitted, remembering how her heart had tumbled in her chest when she'd found him on the other side of the door hours before. But nothing could come of it, she told herself. She knew better than to let it, especially after what had just happened. Besides, love not only made people vulnerable, it was the sharpest and deadliest weapon anyone could ever use. And the bleeding never stopped.

Jack sat beside her, faced her, but didn't touch her. It was for the best, as all she wanted was for him to touch her, kiss her and make her forget…everything. She almost asked him to, the request rested on the tip of her tongue, but she held back. Being with him, making love with him would only make walking away worse. And she would walk away. She didn't have a choice.

"Has this happened before?"

"The sleepwalking?" She stared into the teacup. "Not for a while. It used to happen all the time, when I was little." She swiped at a tear that escaped. She sipped, had to force herself to swallow the barely brewed tea. He'd tried so hard and looked so expectant, she couldn't tell him the truth. About that, at least. "Then, when I was not so little. My doctors said it was my coping mechanism after my parents...died." How did she even begin? She didn't want to talk about it, but she had to tell him something. His sister, Ashley, had been right about that much. "Talking about...things earlier tonight...must have brought it all back." She took a deep breath.

"I'm sorry. That wasn't my intention."

"I know." And she did.

"Tell me something, anything, Greta." He did touch her now. Just a brush of fingers, but enough to soothe her. Part of her hated that it did. "Who did you think you were following?"

"My mother." The answer came so easily, she never thought twice. "It looked like her from the back." She shook her head. "Everything's all mixed up. Probably not the best thing for your case, huh?"

"I don't care about the case right now. I care about you." He curled his finger around a strand of her hair, the understanding smile on his face almost felt like a knife to the heart. She didn't want anyone—especially Jack—feeling sorry for her. Not for any reason. Nor did she want him to go.

"But I am still a detective," he reminded her. "I don't see any memories in your home, Greta. No photographs of family, no old books or mementos. You don't like to be reminded of anything that came before. Not even yesterday."

"No, I don't." He was the first person who had ever

picked up on that. Her first six years had been a festival of memories, a celebration of life and love. All of which had been shattered one balmy summer night. "The past should stay where it belongs. Behind us. And buried."

"It's an easy thing to say. Not always an easy thing to do." There it was again, that ghost that flitted across his face. "And given what happened tonight, I think we can agree you haven't buried anything. When was the last time you did something like this?"

"Sleepwalked?" She had to stop and think, confused by his statement. "About a year ago. Right before I moved here. I woke up in the backyard next door. Good thing I don't have neighbors anymore." She forced a laugh even as she swallowed the jarring terror at having been woken by a frantically barking dog. She twisted the leather band on her wrist until she felt it burn. To remind herself that she could always move beyond the past. She might not be able to outrun it completely, but she could stay a few steps ahead. "After that, I decided no more houses with pools. I guess I should be lucky I went downstairs to the lobby and didn't walk up to the roof."

He gave her a weak smile and slipped his hand around hers. She clung to him because she could. Because she needed to.

A headache crept up behind her eyes. "It started when I was in boarding school. My roommate Yvette saw me leaving the main house when she was sneaking in after curfew. I was already waist deep in lake water before she could dive in after me." She took a shuddering breath. She could still feel that frigid water coating her skin. "The school therapist said stress was a trigger, that I should learn to meditate. And lock my door when I went to bed. Helpful, huh?"

"Did it work?"

"Clearly not. Which is why I spent a few weeks the following summer at a…" She pulled herself back before she said too much. But even without looking at him she knew he'd filled in the blanks. The word *institution* wasn't often used these days, but at times it's what it seemed like to her. No matter how posh it might have been. She cleared her throat, determined to give him at least some of the answers he needed. He deserved that much. "When I eventually left, my guardian decided a clean slate was needed all around. He had my name legally changed. I transferred to another school and tried to start over. And it's worked. Mostly." Only now with Doyle Fremont, with the stress of needing to be right about what she'd seen, everything was all flooding back to her.

"And the sleepwalking stopped?"

"Not for a while." Finally, a bright memory cut through the darkness. "Yvette convinced her parents to transfer her, too, and they made sure we were roommates again. Yvette made sleeping a kind of game with her own winning strategy. Before we went to bed at night, she'd tie yarn or string around my ankle or wrist, attach me to various items in the room that, if I got up to walk, I'd knock over and wake both of us up. Now, that worked." She actually managed a laugh.

"She sounds like a good friend."

"She's the best." Greta pressed her hands against her face to stem the tears. "I hate the idea of disappointing her. That's why I don't want her to know about all this. She did a lot to help me get this place, help me settle down. She doesn't deserve to have to worry all the time." The lack of sleep the past few days, the pressure of the show, of watching a man die in front of her eyes only to rise from the dead and haunt her at the gallery, pressed down on her. She set her tea aside and, just as she had in the lobby, clung to him, her fingers gripping the soft fabric of his T-shirt. "You're sure I didn't wake you up?"

"I was reading. I called your name when you walked by the sofa, but you didn't hear me. So I followed you."

"*She* called my name. I heard *her* call my name." The dream was coming back now, in fragments, but it was there, hovering. "My real name. I didn't recognize it at first. It was as if I'd forgotten."

"What is your real name?" He asked so gently, she only wanted to ease the lines of concern on his face. Whatever he chose to do with the information, she'd deal with that later.

"Genevra," she whispered. "My real name is Genevra."

"We got a hit on the victim's face." Even over Jack's cell, Bowie couldn't have sounded more excited if he'd just been promoted to captain. "Eamon found him."

Jack stood up from the sofa he'd spent most of the morning and afternoon on, hunched over his laptop while Greta had locked herself in her studio. Workers were busy installing the carpeting in Doyle Fremont's office, unwrapping furniture and boxes and consulting what Jack assumed were detailed specs on the room. He'd checked frequently for signs of Fremont himself, but near as Jack could tell, the businessman hadn't made an appearance since the day Jack had met with him.

"What's our victim's name?" Because he needed to move, he headed into the kitchen.

"Paul Calhoun. He's been on the FBI watch list for a while. Lawyer, age fifty-two from New Jersey. Divorced, no kids. He was reported missing nine months ago by his nephew."

"What else do we know? Any connection to Fremont?"

"That's where things get interesting. According to Eamon," Bowie said, referring to the longtime FBI agent who had helped them last year, "Calhoun's been a member of the New Jersey Bar Association for twenty years. Bounced around a number of firms but landed his own big-fish client about six years ago and became the lead lawyer for the Mishenka crime family. And here's the part you're going to like. Or not like."

Jack's interest was piqued. Bowie had definitely investigated to impress.

"A little over three years ago, the Mishenkas were looking to invest in legitimate businesses, probably to get a new laundering scheme going, and they chose a bunch of up-and-coming companies including, but not limited to, a solar research and development company owned by…"

"Doyle Fremont." Jack did a fist pump and mouthed a *Yes!* "Finally. A thread to follow. Any details?"

"The deal fell apart about eighteen months ago when word leaked the Mishenkas were being investigated by the feds. Which is true, by the way. And guess who the star witness was going to be?"

"Paul Calhoun. Our missing dead man. Why? What made him turn?"

"Calhoun got a little greedy with the Mishenka finances. He stole about fifteen million from them. The family found out and put a price on his head. A pretty big one. He agreed to testify in exchange for witness protection. But before they could get him relocated—"

"Calhoun disappeared." Not that uncommon. And with fifteen mil at his disposal, he could have gone anywhere. Instead, he'd shown up here, in Sacramento. With Doyle Fremont. "If the deal fell through, why was Calhoun still in contact with Fremont?"

"That's what we have yet to figure out, but the simple answer is probably money. Doyle Fremont's broke, Jack. Property-rich but cash-poor. That failure wasn't his first, but it was one of the biggest. It got swept under the media rug. Can't get much more out of the FBI without telling someone other than Eamon why we're looking."

"This is enough." Enough for Jack to pass on to Vince as soon as he got off the phone. "This is great work, Bowie."

"No idea where any of this will lead, though."

"We'll figure it out. Let me know if you come up with anything else."

"Will do."

Jack clicked off, tapped his phone against his chin as he shifted the pieces of information around in his head. Fremont's lifestyle hadn't changed one iota despite the hit to his profit margin. Not entirely surprising, but maintaining a lifestyle like that didn't come cheap. And he'd continued expanding his empire, including the new home office right across the street from where Jack stood now. Had he killed Calhoun for the stolen money? Possible, Jack supposed. Either way, with a major organized-crime family potentially involved, that put a whole new twist on things.

A twist his boss needed to know about. But Lt. Santos's reaction wasn't exactly the one he'd been hoping for.

"This is getting too big for a handful of us to manage, Jack." Santos's clipped tone told Jack he wasn't happy about any of this. "I need to consider calling in another department to help run it."

"With all due respect, sir, we both know the more people involved, the more likely it is the investigation is going to leak. If what Bowie just told me gets out, we're going to be overrun not only by the media but by people connected to the Mishenkas. And while Greta's happy to help now, I don't think she'll be nearly as cooperative with a different group of detectives."

"Is that your personal or professional opinion, Detective?" Santos asked.

It was a reasonable question, but one he surprisingly had no trouble answering. "Both, sir. Although I'd be happy to find a way to keep her out of it, period. If we can make a case strong enough to not need eyewitness testimony to Paul Calhoun's murder, I think that would be the best solution for all involved."

"I'm sure you do. I'm sure I don't have to tell you that becoming personally involved with a witness puts a case like this in serious jeopardy."

Jack winced. Hadn't stopped him, though, had it? Nor had he told anyone beyond Cole and Bowie that

Calhoun might not be quite as dead as they thought. He was twisting himself up in professional knots to protect someone he cared for personally. It was Chicago all over again. But what was he supposed to do? Just walk away and leave Greta on her own? "No, sir, you don't have to tell me."

"I should pull you off this case altogether."

"Sir—"

"I said *should*, Jack. I spoke with Cole last night and we decided that while you're needed on this matter, Cole will be taking over as lead detective."

"What?" Jack's stomach dropped. "No, sir. This is my case. I don't want—"

"You don't want anyone else taking the fall if this goes belly-up. We're past that now, Jack. We're all stuck in the quicksand with you. So, before I make this official, I'm going to ask you one more time. Is Doyle Fremont a killer? Is Greta Renault a reliable witness? Are you willing to stake all of our futures on it?"

Jack looked down the hall, to the locked door where Greta had hidden herself in her studio at some unholy hour of the morning. She'd been so vulnerable last night, so scared, but she hadn't been fragile. She'd fought through the sleepwalking, pushed past her own reservations and told him something of her past. He'd also seen the desperation on her face when she'd begged him to believe her. She needed someone to, and Jack wanted—no, he *needed* to be that someone.

Beyond that, he'd looked Fremont in the eye and seen a killer.

"Jack?"

"Yeah." Jack glanced through the window at Doyle's office. "I'm still here."

"Answer my question. Is this case an official go?"

"Yes, sir." This time Jack didn't hesitate. "It is."

Chapter 10

She'd told him her name.

She hadn't meant to. She wasn't even sure she'd wanted to, but she'd needed to. Just enough to push him off the questions. Just enough to satisfy. It shouldn't matter, she told herself as she splashed paint against the canvas. She shouldn't care. How could she care what one man thought about something she couldn't change, something that had shaped her into the person she was today?

Normally the solitude worked to calm the rioting questions and doubts spinning in her mind. Normally she could go days, sometimes weeks, without having to admit anything had changed. That was the wonder of her work: she could hide in it, with it, for as long as she needed. As long as it took to keep the threat of darkness out of her mind.

Except it wasn't working. She picked up another brush, saturated it with the blue of a midnight sea and stabbed it against the canvas. It didn't matter how many layers of paint she added, how many slashes and gouges and streaks she made, she couldn't stop wishing she'd never looked out her window that night.

That damned window!

Another swipe, this one pure white, tinged with the blurred colors of the brush's previous puddles, cut across the expanse of the canvas, slicing the chaos into fragmented shards of fear.

She stepped back, set the brushes down and stared into the colors swirling and arcing as she wished for, prayed for, clarity. For an answer. What was the truth? What was a lie? She didn't know what was real anymore.

And that, she realized, was the fear lodged like a stone in the center of her chest, and the only thing that made her feel stable was… Jack.

Her music cut off, plunging the studio into an eerie silence she'd been trying to avoid all morning. She then spotted Jack standing in the open doorway, the emotion on his face unreadable.

"Too loud?" she asked.

One of the reasons she'd had soundproofing installed was that she liked her music indecently loud.

"I'd answer you, but my ears are still ringing." The slight tease in his voice didn't do anything to ease the worry coursing through her. She glanced at the door and frowned as Cerberus padded through and hopped onto the ledge by the window she'd kept her back to.

"I thought I locked that."

"You did." Jack shrugged. "I'm a man of many talents. You work it out?"

"Work what out?"

He leaned back, crossed his feet at the ankles and his arms over his chest. The arch of his brow had her squirming where she stood. No one, especially someone who had known her for such a short time, should understand her this well.

She didn't need him to tell her that her method of coping with complicated situations was to burrow into her studio and disappear. "I've been trying to work stuff like this out most of my life." She plucked up her brushes and set them in the thinner-filled jars. "It's not going to happen in a few hours."

"Maybe it could if you talked about it."

"What's to talk about? Obviously what I saw the other night wasn't real. Or what I saw at the gallery wasn't. He can't both be dead and alive." Something in the man's expression, just a tic, had chills running down her arms.

"Depends what the angle is," Jack said. "Speaking of angles, this canvas is full of them." He shifted his attention to her painting. "Is this what you've been working on all day?"

"All…day?" Greta looked to the clock on the far counter. "It's after four. In the afternoon?" She'd lost the entire day? That was part of it, wasn't it? Hallucinations? Losing time? Her future seemed to drop off into the same dark hole as her past. Was this it? Was she finally falling into the madness that had taken her…

"You need to get out of here."

"No!" She jumped back a step when he moved toward her. He stopped. "I just mean, I'm not done yet. I need to focus. I need to finish…" She motioned toward her paintings in the hopes he'd understand. But how could he when she didn't? She didn't want to be out there, where she had no control. And for the first time since she'd moved here, she didn't want to be in this loft, either. It felt tainted somehow. Dark. Like an extension of the nightmares she'd dealt with most of her life. No matter where she went, she felt trapped.

"Greta." Jack held out his hand, palm up, arm relaxed, giving her the choice she wanted to make. She looked at his hand, imagined how it would feel holding hers. Was this gratitude she was feeling over how caring and understanding he'd been last night? Or was this more? She wanted it to be more. So much more…

Her hand found his palm.

"Do you trust me?"

She did. It shocked her to realize it was true. It scared her. Once he learned the truth, he was going to turn his back on her. Leave her with a broken heart.

"Unless you want another pair of officers—"

"What officers?"

"Unless you want another pair of officers in your apartment while I'm gone—"

"Where are you going?"

He tugged her into his arms and locked his hands at the base of her spine. "Unless you want another pair of officers in your apartment while I'm gone, you're going to go in, take a shower, get dressed and come with me. Casual. Layers. There's always a breeze over the water."

"Water?" The word alone was enough to lull her into a trance. "I like the water."

"Then you're going to love where we're going for dinner."

Even after her sleepwalking event, even after telling him her real name, Jack didn't expect Greta to be a font of information. Not about her past. Not about much of anything. The fact she'd agreed to come with him, that she'd clutched at his hand as if he were the only stabilizing force in her universe weighed on both his shoulders and his heart. Doubt clung to that weight, which he could only hope to avoid dropping.

He didn't know what magic soap she used that erased every droplet of paint from her skin, but it left her smelling of spring flowers after a rainstorm and had Jack wishing he'd declined their hosts' dinner invitation. Greta had twisted her long, thick hair into some kind of intricate knotted braid and wore snug jeans and a loose apricot-colored shirt. As she sat beside him, the dimming light blanketing them as they drove down Garden Highway toward the Crest View Marina, she absently rubbed at her shoulder, wincing as she watched the passing trees and road.

"What did you mean when you said he could be alive and dead?"

"Took you long enough to ask." He glanced in his rearview mirror and saw their patrol car escort continue on once he turned onto the side road. "We ID'd your victim from Fremont's office."

"You did what?" The leather of her seat squeaked when she turned to face him. "You're just getting around to telling me this now? What's his name? Where did you find him?"

"Hang on." Jack maneuvered around the parked vehicles and switched on his headlamps so he could see to the end of the road. "I said we ID'd him, not that we found him. His name is Paul Calhoun. That sketch you gave us last night paid off. The FBI identified him almost immediately."

"FBI?" Greta squeaked. "What's the FBI got to do with this?"

Jack couldn't very well tell her the truth that they were trying to keep the investigation off the radar for another day or so. Not without her thinking it was because they didn't believe her. "We needed to use outside resources." Skirting the edge of the truth was okay, wasn't it? "We have a friend in the FBI's San Francisco office. They've actually been looking for Calhoun for a while." He managed a quick smile. "And you found him."

Her eyes flickered in the growing darkness. "Did I?"

"You gave them a lead they've been looking for months. He's an ex-mob attorney on the run. And we did find a connection to Fremont. We're working on fleshing it out, now."

Greta rubbed at her shoulder again. "He's real." The relief in her eyes was so bright he felt like shielding his eyes. "You're telling me the man I saw was real. You're sure?"

"He's real." Jack glanced over at her before he pulled into the space next to Ashley's ancient Camry. Cole's 1960s gentleman's cruiser bobbed gently in the water against the dock. The vessel had been refurbished and upgraded to a high polish, and this evening had been decked out with tiny white twinkle lights strung from stem to stern. He spotted Vince Sutton and Max Kellan lounging on the deck, beer bottles dangling from their hands. "There are a lot of unanswered questions, Greta. Enough that until we get those answers, my boss and I agreed you should be under police protection." He killed the engine and turned to look at her.

"Oh?" She inclined her head, and her braid fell over one shoulder. The curl at the bottom brushed against the top of her breast. "You just decided that on your own, did you?"

"Is that going to be a problem?"

"That depends. Are you my protection?" The smile that spread across her lips had the blood surging through his body and settling south of his belt.

"That's the plan." A really bad plan, but the more time he spent with her, the more time he wanted. She was like a drug to his system, a habit he had no inclination to kick. He reached out, intending to brush a solitary finger down the side of her face but instead his hand slipping into her hair, and cupped the back of her neck as he reached down and unhooked her seat belt. Oh, yeah, he thought as he hauled her closer. A really, really bad plan. He brushed his lips against hers, inhaled that intoxicating scent before sinking in to her.

He wasn't sure what spiked into his mind first. The feel of her mouth, the way she opened under him, or the way her hands slipped up his chest and gripped his shirt. He heard a moan and wasn't entirely sure who had made it; he didn't care. What he did care about was that he'd made a serious tactical error by leaving her apartment. There wasn't anything he wanted more at this moment than to be back in that bed of hers, with nothing between them other than need.

His hand slipped free, trailed down her arm to catch the hem of her shirt. The second his fingers brushed her warm flesh he nearly broke apart.

A sharp rap on his window had Jack jerking away. He cracked his head, hard enough to make him groan and Greta bite her lip against a smile before she looked around him, the humor sliding from her face even as the color drained from it. "Jack?" she whispered. "What's Cole doing here? Where are we?"

"Just…hang on a second." He shifted but winced as parts of him protested and strained. He clicked the key and lowered the window. "Sorry we're late."

"Uh-huh." Cole glared at him.

"All four feet are on the floor," Jack added.

"Grill's ready for the steaks." Cole left no doubt he didn't believe him. "Come on aboard. Greta, glad you could make it."

Jack glanced back in time to see her manage a smile.

"Two minutes." Cole backed away and held up two fingers. "Or I send in reinforcements."

Jack swore. Reinforcements probably meant his sister or Eden. Maybe both.

"Why would you bring me here?" Greta whispered when he came around to open her door. She sat facing forward, a hand locked around the base of her seat belt.

"Because we were invited."

She shook her head, and only then did he see the hint of fear in her eyes.

"Greta—"

"I thought it would just be the two of us. I'm not good around people."

"I hate to break it to you," he said, leaning his hands on the roof of the car, "but in a few days you're going to be surrounded by them at your show."

"That's different. That's…safe. I can talk about my art and the pieces, my inspiration or a million other things, but this is…me."

"Your paintings are you, too. Greta, do you really think I'd bring you someplace I didn't think you'd be safe? Either physically or emotionally?"

She pressed her lips together and leaned back for her seat belt. "Take me home."

Jack rested a hand on her trembling one. "No."

Greta finally looked at him. "What?"

"Not used to hearing that, are you? You're used to sitting alone in your protected space, painting and drinking tea and pretending there isn't a world outside your door."

"I…do not."

"Then, prove it." He pounced on the uncertainty he heard in her voice. "One hour. Give me one hour, and if you still want to go home, we'll leave."

She looked out toward the boat, her hands twisting in her lap. "How many people are there?"

"In the world? Billions. Should make tonight easier to deal with."

"Jack," she whispered.

"One hour." He turned her face to his and kissed her again.

"Fine." She grabbed her purse. "I don't like being tricked. There will be payback."

"Noted for future reference." He hadn't tricked her, exactly. He closed the door and, before she could think, slipped his hand around hers. "Relax. You already know Cole and Ashley. The rest are easy. Well, except Eden. She can be, well, unpredictable."

"Fabulous." The tension remained in her voice, but her hand relaxed a little in his. "One hour. Set your watch now."

There were few certainties in life, Greta supposed, but none as unifying as the male bonding ritual around the almighty grill. Not that Greta had much experience with the primal meeting among man, fire and meat. She didn't have much experience with a lot of things, but she had to admit, watching Jack debating the proper cooking techniques with three good-looking—not to mention intriguing—men was more entertaining and informative than expected.

She already knew Cole, of course, Jack's partner and fellow detective. Cole's wife, Eden, was what Greta had expected, given the woman's chosen profession, right down to Eden's cool edge of control and suspicion.

Manning the grill with a ferocious pair of tongs was former Marine turned private investigator Vince Sutton. He intrigued her, the surprising combination of intense physicality and good-natured ribbing making her fingers itch for a paintbrush or pencil, especially to capture the contrast between Vince and Simone, his elegant, put-together, district-attorney wife.

Max Kellan, a former firefighter who now worked with Vince at his investigation agency, was one of the most laid-back, jovial individuals she'd ever met. The man always seemed to be laughing or have a smile on his face, especially when his gaze landed on his wife, Dr. Allie Hollister-Kellan.

Greta wrapped her arms around her drawn-up knees, having shrunk as far into the corner of the padded bench at the back of the boat as possible. She glanced at her watch. Twenty-seven minutes to go. She'd survived the initial introductions, withstanding the curious gazes of the people Jack clearly considered his family. He'd been right. Already knowing Cole and Jack's doctor sister, Ashley, had taken a bit of the unease away, but that didn't mean she was ready to spend an entire evening inside the stylish yet somewhat claustrophobic boat.

Retreating to the deck had eased the tension knotting inside her. The cool night air circulated, tinged with an appetite-inducing aroma that set Greta's stomach to growling. She could hear the gentle sizzle of meat on metal along with the teasing banter and joking among the men. Jack's laughter rang in her ears, drawing a reluctant smile out of her. The setting was, Greta had to admit, however unfamiliar, somewhat…cozy.

"Pretty as a picture, aren't they?"

Greta blinked as a glass of white wine appeared in front of her face. Before even looking into the friendly dark eyes of the woman holding it, she accepted. "Thank you. And yes." She cleared her throat, tucked a stray strand of hair behind her ear. "They are." Greta studied the woman with a cap of dark hair, the gentle, passive expression on her face. The way she sat on the bench beside, but not too near, Greta. Those knots that had begun to slip loose tightened again. "You're Jack's psychiatrist friend." It couldn't be a coincidence she'd been the first to approach Greta. "Dr. Kellan. I don't want to do regression therapy."

"All right." Allie's expression didn't change, but Greta thought she saw a glint of surprise in the doctor's eyes. "As I don't usually solicit new clients at family events, that's good to know. And it's Allie, please." The way she moved, a light lifting of a dismissive hand, a gentle tug on the hem of the sunflower yellow cardigan she wore, called to mind a garden nymph or fairy looking for the perfect flower to perch upon. Greta's fingers twitched again, now that inspiration had struck. "Jack mentioned you were feeling a bit overwhelmed, and Ashley suggested giving you some space. I imagine we can be an intimidating bunch, but I promise we're friendly."

"It's not personal." Greta managed a quick smile and sipped the wine. "I don't, um, have many friends." She tugged her feet farther under her. "Crowds, groups just make me nervous. I never know what to do or say."

"You tuck in any tighter into that corner and you're going to turn into a turtle." Eden St. Claire—she hadn't changed her name after marrying Cole—popped into view. She tilted her head back, spilling strawberry blond hair down her back as she breathed in the cooling air. "Ah, that feels better." She fanned her flushed face. "I thought I was going to flambé down there." She sagged against the boat railing, a can of lemon-lime soda in her hand.

"Forgive Eden, Greta." The tall, slim blonde, introduced as Simone, emerged behind her friend and, after giving Eden a strong squeeze on her shoulder, walked past her to stand beside Greta. She moved like water, fluid and in smooth lines, encased in tailored white slacks and a bloodred blouse that set off the thin gold chain around her neck. "She has the personality of a sledgehammer. I'm afraid it doesn't get much better, so you'll have to get used to it. I only hope it doesn't take you almost thirty years like it did the rest of us."

Get used to it? Why would she have to... "Thirty years? You all have been friends that long?"

"They have," Ashley said as she checked her cell phone. "I'm a recent addition. Thanks to Jack."

"Simone, Eden and I met in kindergarten, if you can believe that," Allie told her.

Kindergarten. Greta's mind flashed. They'd been what? Five, six years old? An odd pang of envy sliced through her. She couldn't remember anyone from when she'd been that age other than...

"Hey." Allie reached over and touched her arm. "Are you all right, Greta?"

"Yeah." Greta took a shaky sip of wine. "Sorry. Memories. Ghosts. I've been seeing a lot of those recently." Too many. And all of them seemed to be walking over her grave.

"Anything to do with this case Jack and Cole are working?" Eden prodded.

"Wow, really?" Simone pinned her with an irritated glare that almost made Greta laugh. "You can't turn it off even for five minutes?"

"It's okay." Greta didn't want them to get into a squabble over her. "I don't know how much I can say, but yes, I've been working with them on an investigation. But that's all this is. Him, bringing me here. He thinks I need protection."

"Does he?" Eden grinned. "Funny. I've known him what? Three years? And he's never offered protection to anyone before. Let alone brought them to one of our dinners."

"What Eden's indelicately trying to say," Allie said, "is that we're glad Jack brought you and that we hope it isn't the last time we see you."

"Why?" Greta blinked. "You don't know me. I could be a raving lunatic, for all you know." She shifted her gaze to Ashley, half expecting Jack's sister to chime in in agreement, but Ashley simply sat back as if she were enjoying the conversation.

"Believe me, we've dealt with worse," Eden muttered. "I hear you have an art show coming up? You're a painter, right?"

"She's an exquisite *artist*." Simone settled herself between Allie and Greta. "We have a print of one of your paintings at the DA's office. The woman standing in the ocean. Those streaks of moonlight feel real every time I look at it. Gives me the shivers. In a good way."

"Moon Tide." Greta's chest relaxed. "I actually painted that one outside. I was living in South Carolina at the time. That stifling humidity, I couldn't sleep at night, so I'd paint."

"I've seen that picture," Eden said. "I like it."

"That's high praise." Allie leaned over Simone to tell Greta. "Eden isn't the biggest fan of art."

"Sure, I am," Eden said. "When it makes sense. You do good work, Greta." She toasted her with her can and earned another look from Simone, this one sparked with confusion. "What?"

"I just realized you aren't drinking," Simone said.

"And given the size of the wine fridge you had installed on this boat when you moved in—"

"And you hate lemon-lime," Allie added. "You say it's soda with an identity crisis. What gives?"

Eden's mouth twisted, but not enough to hide the smile. "Guess I gave myself away. Cole? I've been outed."

"What?"

Greta looked over with the other women as Cole looked up from the grill, oversize tongs in hand. He looked at his wife. "I thought you had this planned. I told you you'd blow it." But his smile mirrored Eden's.

Joy, Greta thought and felt almost as if she was intruding on a special moment. How Eden and Cole looked at each other, how they spoke without words, grabbed hold of Greta's heart. "Oh, that's just lovely," she whispered and earned a surprised glance from Allie and Simone.

"Eden?" Simone's hands gripped the edge of the bench. "What are you saying?"

"No sense in hedging now. I'm pregnant." Eden's laughter was muffled by Allie and Simone launching themselves at her, engulfing her in a hug that erased Eden from sight.

Greta unfolded her legs as Ashley came over to sit beside her, but Greta barely noticed. She was watching Jack congratulate his friend and partner with the most enthusiastic hug and smack on the back she'd ever seen. He was so unreservedly happy, and the sight warmed her from head to toe.

"Champagne is in the cooler," Cole announced.

"On it!" Max went to pull out not one but two bottles. Corks popped, glasses were filled, and once the hoots and hollers and celebratory cheers finally eased, Cole held up his glass.

"The only thing better than seeing that stick turn blue is making this announcement to our friends. Our family." He motioned to his wife, who, after a moment, gave him a quick nod. "And to our baby's godmothers." He nodded to an almost squealing Allie and Simone. "And her godfather." He turned back to Jack. "If you'll accept, of course."

Jack blinked and a slow smile spread across his face. "Of course, I accept. I'd be honored."

Greta's eyes misted. He looked so content and at ease, surrounded by his people. This was exactly where he belonged.

"That's just great." Ashley sniffed beside Greta. "First night in months I wear makeup, and now it's ruined."

"Nothing is ruined," Greta assured her and squeezed her hand. "Happy tears are never bad."

"He's always wanted to be a dad," Ashley told her as she dabbed at her eyes. "Even with everything he's seen, all the cases he's worked, just the idea of a houseful of kids brings a smile to his face. That smile."

Greta's own smile faltered as reality settled over her. Jack would make a wonderful father. But she could never be a mother. Not because she couldn't have children but because she knew, deep in her heart, she shouldn't.

"My brother's a good man, Greta."

"I know." Greta did know. As sure as she understood the sun would rise in the morning. That was the problem.

"Whatever anyone throws at him, he deals. He stands. You could not have a better person in your corner. Or at your side."

"Ashley—" Greta knew exactly what Ashley was trying to say and that there was no arguing with her. But even good men had their tipping points. Greta couldn't let herself believe, even for a moment, that there could be anything close to a future for the two of them. Not when the best thing for everyone was for her to be alone.

"Tell him, Greta," Ashley urged. "Whatever it is, whatever you're afraid of, just tell him. Let him help you."

She didn't want Jack's help, Greta almost said. She didn't want anyone's help. Even if she did, there wasn't anything they could do. No matter how she might wish otherwise, there wasn't anything anyone could do about the future that was hurtling toward her like a bullet in the dark.

One hour turned into three, which slipped into four. She hoped Jack wasn't an I-told-you-so type of person. Greta really hated that. But he had been right. Tonight had been…special. A night she didn't want to see end. But for now, she was content to leave the conversations, the huddling around phones in the search of the perfect baby items, the argument between Vince and Max over who the new arrival, boy or girl, would cheer for in the upcoming football season.

Greta headed down the steps into the confines of the boat, absorbing every perfect detail of the craft she learned Cole had refurbished himself. She didn't snoop, much. She didn't venture into the main bedroom but did admire the use of space in the very modern bathroom. The kitchen, galley-style for the most part, looked well used and cared for. The well-worn sofa and chairs, a small coffee table and big-screen TV completed all the amenities needed. One room, however, did catch her attention as she headed back toward the stairs. She ducked her head, pushed open the door that was slightly ajar and stepped inside.

Larger than expected, the room was filled to capacity with shelves, a desk and three large portable white boards currently covered in newspaper articles, scribbled notes, arrows and threads connecting them to various photographs of five children.

She couldn't help but admire Eden St. Claire, and what she did every day of her life in trying to bring closure to families of missing, exploited or murdered children. File folders sat stacked on top of one another, balanced on a straight-backed chair against the far wall. The filing-cabinet drawers remained slightly askew, with papers sticking out, but still relatively organized.

There were special touches, Greta realized, sitting on the shelves of the bookcases, on the desk. Photographs, some framed, including one of Eden and Cole on their wedding day, another of Eden, Simone and Allie years before, laughing into the camera. And another, off to the side, in a frame of abalone and silver. Four girls this time, Eden, Simone and Allie at about eight years old, with another girl with bright red hair and mismatched sneakers.

"Her name was Chloe."

Greta gasped and spun around, pressing the picture against her chest. Eden strode in. "I'm sorry. I didn't mean to intrude—" Greta said.

Eden waved off her concern. "Don't worry about it. Allie calls this my torture room." Eden smirked at Greta's frown. "She thinks I keep all this stuff up to torture myself because I haven't helped them."

"This is the case you're working on. The one in Arizona."

"Yep." Eden sat on the edge of her desk. "Local police chalked up the disappearances to a rash of runaways. Because seven-year-olds run away so often. Small town, limited resources. They didn't have the manpower to really investigate. Something I suspect the person responsible was counting on. Sorry." She held up a hand. "Soapbox. You don't need to hear all that. I know Allie's just teasing, mostly. She gets why I do it. I think."

"You do it because no one else will." Greta set the frame back down. "I didn't remember at first, but I do now. Chloe's case was recently solved, wasn't it?"

"Last year." Eden had an unnerving way of watching her, Greta thought. It was as if she could see right through her. "It took us twenty years, but we finally got her justice. Came at a pretty steep cost, though."

"Jack. That's when he was shot." Greta was both disappointed and relieved she hadn't known him then. She wasn't sure how she'd react to the man she loved being shot. Her breath caught in her throat. The man she loved? She loved Jack?

"He makes light of it," Eden continued as she began rummaging around in her desk. "But in all honesty, he shouldn't be alive. Makes me wonder what life has in store for him now."

Greta's eyes had long lost focus as she trailed her gaze across the rows of true crime books, criminology texts and an eclectic collection of movies. "Not me," Greta whispered.

"No?" If Eden was surprised by her answer, she didn't sound it. "Might want to clue Jack in on that."

"I'm just a witness in a case." Even as she said it, she knew it wasn't true. She swallowed the tears that threatened to fall. "Yes, there's something there. A spark."

"One that goes off every time he looks at you. And every time you look at him."

Greta couldn't tell if Eden thought that was a good or bad thing. She trailed her finger along the line of DVDs. History documentaries, science specials, big blow-'em-up action movies she suspected were more Eden's style than Cole's. They had quite a collection of classics from Bogart and Bacall, Marilyn Monroe, Errol Flynn. The *Thin Man* series, Sherlock Holmes and...

Her finger froze, as did the air in her lungs.

"Feel free to borrow whatever you want," Eden said as Greta slipped the movie free. "Those are more Cole's bailiwick than mine. He likes that film noir–type stuff. Chinatown meets Hitchcock. *Midnight Witness* is one of his favorites. He drags it out every few months. I've watched it a few times."

"Have you?" Greta stared down at the embracing couple, the throwback-Hollywood blonde bombshell entwined with the tooth-achingly handsome actor turned director. Her hand shook so hard she could hear the disk rattling in the case. "What did you think?"

"Honestly? I thought the lead actress…what was her name?"

"Serena Lamont." Greta's heart ached.

"Yeah, her. I thought she looked sad. Like she couldn't quite break through to the character, you know? Almost as if she was playing herself."

"The critics agreed." The film, made in the late eighties, was supposed to be the first in a series of new noir, an updated genre aimed at the fans of the Mike Hammer mysteries and *The Maltese Falcon*. It hadn't caught at the time but now was considered a cult classic. Especially, Greta thought, given what had happened to its stars.

"Seems to me, I remember something about a scandal with the actress and director. I'd forgotten about that. One of Hollywood's tragic stories. A suicide pact, I think?"

"Murder-suicide," Greta whispered, unable to let go of the movie. "It was a murder-suicide."

Eden snapped her fingers. "That's right. Serena and Anthony Lamont. She had a pretty good career going, then one night she just snapped. Killed her husband in some kind of rage, then herself. There were other details I don't remember. Riveting story. Tragic, but riveting." Eden swore, bent over and then crouched almost into a ball. "Uh-oh. Here we go again."

Greta set the case down, bent down to touch Eden's shoulder. "What's wrong?"

"Nothing. Just feel like I'm going to puke." She took in a long breath, let it out, keeping her eyes closed. To Greta, however, Eden looked a bit green. "Can you believe it? Motion sickness, even when we're docked. This kid hates our home."

"Sit down." Greta pushed her into the desk chair. "Can I get you another soda? Do you want me to get Cole?"

"No." She grabbed Greta's arm when she stood. "No, it'll pass. Eventually. Cole's stressed enough about this. He thinks we should find someplace else to live, which breaks my heart because he loves this boat. It's his one true home."

"If it makes you sick, maybe he's right."

"I never like Cole to know he's right. About anything." Eden managed a short laugh. "On dry land, I'm fine. I knew I should have held on to my town house, but I honestly didn't think we'd be doing this for another couple of years." She pointed at her stomach. "House prices are ridiculous these days, and I don't want Jack selling this boat to buy someplace he hates."

"So don't buy. Rent."

"Not exactly a lot of options out there. At least not in any area we want to live."

The idea formed in the blink of an eye. "How about midtown?"

Eden rolled her head to the side. "You're funny. Do you have any idea how much rent goes for in midtown?"

"No, actually. I own. In fact, the building I bought has a vacant second floor loft. Three bedrooms, lots of space. Tons of potential. If you want it, if it'll help, it's yours."

Eden looked genuinely baffled. "You can't be serious."

"Can't be serious about what?" Cole stopped in

the doorway, looked down at his wife, who was now crouching. "What's going on? Are you playing Twister again without me?"

Greta wasn't sure she'd ever seen something so sweet. There had been panic, a quick flash across Cole's face, but he'd covered, no doubt because Eden would have taken exception to his concern. He leaned down, covered her hand with his. "Junior giving you trouble again?"

"*Junior.* He thinks that's cute," Eden joked. "Greta just offered us an apartment."

"Did she?" Cole glanced up at Greta.

"If you want. It's another loft, actually. It's just sitting there empty. It's pretty much a duplicate of mine. You can come by and look at it whenever you want. Check it out. Whatever. The parking isn't great, but—"

"I don't think we can afford—"

Greta threw out a number. "And you pay utilities."

"That's ridiculous," Eden countered. "You have to make some money."

Greta shrugged. "I own the building outright and, well, I inherited a lot of money at a very young age. Investments have been good. You'd be doing me a favor. I'd prefer someone to move in, and I'd really prefer it be someone I know. Talk it over. If it makes sense, we can do a short-term or even month-to-month lease. Whatever works best for you. I can have my lawyer draw up the paperwork in no time." Because she rather enjoyed the dazed and confused look on both their faces, she left and closed the door behind her. When she turned, she collided with Jack. She squeaked, "What are you doing skulking...oh!"

The kiss happened so fast, took her under so deeply, she didn't think she'd ever surface.

"What was that for?" she asked when he broke the embrace. At some point he'd pushed her up against the wall, pressed his body against hers in a way that had her wishing they were somewhere—anywhere—else.

"You're wrong. You do really well with people, Greta." He stroked her cheek, ran his other hand along the curve of her hip. "But I think it's time I got you home and into bed." He kissed her again. "What do you think?"

What did she think? She thought he needed to slow down so she could think more. She thought that going to bed with him, making love with him, was going to open a whole lot of doors to problems she didn't want.

"What about protocol?"

He looked into her eyes so deeply she almost saw stars. "What about it?"

It would be a mistake. It would create a connection she might never be able to sever and yet...she didn't want to go into another day without having been with him. Embrace the now, she told herself. She'd worry about tomorrow...tomorrow.

She kissed him, deeply, drawing him against her, into her, wrapping herself around him so she could barely feel where she left off and he began. "Take me home, Jack," she murmured against his lips. "Take me home now."

Chapter 11

"I worried all the way up here that the elevator was going to stall." Greta arched her neck as Jack's mouth trailed down the side of her throat. They'd made it to her front door—barely—and all but tumbled through when she unlocked it.

"We would have found a way to entertain ourselves." His breath was hot against her skin and made her shiver. She'd been surprised he hadn't hit his light and siren as the drive home seemed to have taken forever. Greta had reached out to take his hand at one point because she'd needed to touch him, to feel that anticipation of having that hand all over her body. She'd threaded her fingers through his, moved closer and felt an unfamiliar surge of power when he'd let out a moan in the back of his throat.

The sound had thrilled her. Excited her.

Now, in the confines of her loft, he kicked the door shut before toeing off his shoes. His jacket came next, with her helping push it off his strong, broad shoulders. She brought his mouth back to hers as his hands worked their way beneath her shirt, inched up to slip under her bra. She felt it release, then he pushed her bra free. His palms rubbed against her bare nipples, and she gasped, the sensation shooting straight to the apex of her thighs.

"Oh." She bit her lip, squeezed her eyes so hard this time she did see stars.

"Off," Jack panted and grabbed her shirt to drag it over her head. He discarded her bra as well, then stood there, looking down at her as the cool air of the room circled them. "Beautiful," he murmured. "Exactly as I've imagined."

"You've been imagining my breasts?" Greta laughed until he bent to draw his tongue through the valley between them.

"I've been imagining more than that. I feel like I've been waiting for this for years."

"So have I. In fact," she said and trembled as his fingers flicked open the button of her jeans. "Jack, I need to tell you—"

"Tell me what?" He dropped to his knees, pressed a kiss against her navel.

"Something." Her brain was a fog, but not the fog she often got lost in. A fog that shrouded them both from the outside world. "Right. Jack. I meant I've been waiting *years*. Not just for you. For this."

His hands circled her waist, his fingers flexing. And then he stopped and looked up at her, those amazing blue eyes of his sparking in the dim light of the solitary lamp. "This is your first time?"

"Mmm-hmm." She caught her lower lip between her teeth. "In case it makes a difference."

"Oh, it makes a difference." He stood, and for a moment, she thought he might leave, might turn away from her. Instead, he kissed her deeply and erased every doubt, every ounce of tension, all the nerves from her entire body. "It makes a big difference." He scooped her into his arms and carried her into her bedroom. From a distance, she heard Cerberus's soft mew, followed by a gentle plunk. "Smart cat you have." He released her, though she kept her arms locked around him as he lowered her to the floor. "Lights. We need lights. I need to see you."

"Do you really?" Those nerves she thought were gone returned. "Can't you just feel your way—"

"Not now." He cupped her cheek, stared into her eyes, and she felt herself tumble over that last edge of reality. "I need to see you, I need to watch you make love to me. I need to look into your eyes when I'm inside of you."

The very words were enough to start the anticipation building inside of her. "Okay, lights it is." She slipped away and clicked the lights on, had just removed her shoes when he reappeared at her side. "Should I—oh, okay." He sat her on the edge of the bed, eased her down on the mattress to leave her legs dangling over the edge. "Is there something I'm supposed to, um, do?" The zipper on her jeans eased, and he curled his fingers over the waistband, gently drew the pants and her underwear off her body. She lay there, naked and exposed, but warm under his gaze. "One of us is overdressed." She reached out, wanted to bury her hands in that thick hair of his, wanted to kiss him again. She wanted to keep kissing him until time stopped.

"One of us has a lot of catching up to do." The smile that stretched his lips made his eyes shine.

"What do you—oh!" His lips returned to her stomach, his tongue dipping into her navel before he dropped down to his knees, trailed his lips lower, lower until… the room spun as he lifted her thighs, drew her open and kissed her. She convulsed, cried out, her back arching as her hands fisted in the bedspread.

She was on fire as his mouth moved over her, pleasured her, nibbled at her. He pushed her knees farther apart, moved close enough that she could feel his hair brushing against her inner thighs. That pulsing pleasure built again. She didn't want it to end, didn't want to go over, she wanted this moment to go on and on.

Eyes closed, she nearly lifted off the bed as his tongue circled and flicked against the nub of pleasure he paid special attention to. She panted. She moaned. She reached for him.

"Look at me, Greta," Jack whispered as his fingers replaced his mouth. She tried to respond but couldn't do anything more than breathe as he slipped one finger, then another inside of her. He shifted, angling his hand so his thumb could continue to stroke her. "Let me see you go over."

"Jack," she managed, unable to hold on to him any longer. "Jack, please." His touch, his fingers, weren't enough, she wanted more. She wanted all of him.

"Go over, Greta." He increased his tempo, sending

her higher and higher to that peak she didn't think was possible. Just as she felt herself tip, he pressed harder and sent her flying.

Her body exploded. She cried out, half sobbing, half laughing, but she forced herself to keep watching him, to lock gazes with him as her body trembled through the sensations from his touch.

When her heart rate slowed, when her body quivered and began to relax, he removed his hand, leaned up and brushed his lips against hers. "Beautiful. My beautiful, Greta."

A feeling of complete satisfaction had overtaken her, yet she reached for him. "More. I want more. I want it all."

"Oh, there will be more." He began to unbutton his shirt. She sat up, pushed his hands away, determined to do this part herself. He drew her to her feet, a small if not arrogant smile curving his lips when her knees almost buckled. He swooped her bedspread away, threw back the blankets.

She released button after button. When his shirt was open, she slipped her hands inside, flattened her palms against his chest and pushed the fabric down his arms. "This is what I've been dreaming of." His shirt drifted to the floor. His hands moved, circled up her back, making her shiver as she pressed her lips against the smooth expanse of skin. He was beautiful, too. Solid. Male. Everything she could have wanted in a lover.

He jolted when she laved at his nipple, her fingers dancing along the lines of his chest. She could taste his sweat, feel the tension coiled in his body, feel the hard promise of him pressing against her stomach. "Stop."

He reached up, caught her hand as it found the puckered, still-red skin of his wound. "It's ugly."

"No." She pressed her lips against the scar. "It's you." She slipped her arm around his neck, drew him down for a kiss that mimicked what he'd done to another part of her body moments before. "You're perfect, Jack." The admission nearly broke her in two. Because she knew he didn't believe it. And she knew it wouldn't matter. Tonight was just that. Tonight. And she was going to enjoy every moment of it. "About your pants." She wiggled her hips and loved watching that fevered haze cloud his vision. "Would you like to remove them or should I?"

"I think for both our sakes—" he caught her hands to draw them away from his belt "—I'd better." But before he did, he reached into his back pocket. He held up some condom packages. "I raided Cole's bathroom before we left. As he won't be needing them for a while." He tossed them onto the nightstand and finished undressing.

"I bet you've always been somebody's hero, haven't you?" She needed to talk about something while she watched him. She might have been a virgin, but she wasn't innocent. She'd seen plenty of the male form, one of the hormonal perks of being an art student. But seeing him now, in her bedroom, knowing he was there for her, and only for her, sent the remaining doubt and fear from her mind.

"What are you thinking?" Jack stroked a finger down her cheek.

"A lot of things. As usual," she added with a smile. She turned her head and kissed his finger. "But mostly I'm glad it's going to be you."

"So am I." He lifted her in his arms again and kissed her, then placed a knee on the bed and lowered her to the mattress. He tore open the package and covered himself. The instant he slid over her, the moment she felt his body pressed so completely against hers, her system began the low, deep humming once more. "We'll go slow."

"Please don't. I don't think I can take it." She brought one leg up, skimmed her foot up and down the back of his calf, then, seeing his eyes sharpen and fire, repeated with the other foot. She felt him settle, felt the hot, hard length of him. She watched him as she slipped a hand between them to wrap her fingers around him. There, she thought, as he gasped and moved. That was what she'd wanted to see. "Please, Jack." She kissed his nose, each cheek, came to rest at his lips and noticed he was straining to control himself. For perhaps the first time, she didn't want anyone controlling anything. "Love me." She placed her mouth against his lips as she welcomed him, waiting, wanting and finally breathing when she felt him press into her.

"Slow," he murmured, taking her mouth in a kiss so primal, so deep, so loving, she almost forgot what else was happening. Until she couldn't. His hips rocked against hers. He moved a hand down to catch her thigh, to pull her wider, open her farther so the length of him, the strength of him wouldn't be so overwhelming.

Greta groaned as he filled her, stretched her.

"Greta?"

"More," she panted, bringing her legs up to wrap around him. Her hands moved down his back, to cup his buttocks and pull him in deeper. There was pain, she thought, but he eased it smoothly, vanishing under his continuous movement. The peak felt further away this time, just out of reach, but she matched her breathing to his, opened her eyes and looked into his and shot to the top. "More," she answered the unspoken question in his eyes. "Give me more, Jack. Give me everything. Let go," she whispered and locked her mouth on his.

She lifted her hips, met him thrust for thrust as he sank into her. Her cry was caught in his mouth. Sweat coated their skin as she rocked with him, tangled with him, every thought, every fear that had become a part of her now faded beneath his touch until finally, after a life-altering moment, after one perfect kiss, he drove them over the edge.

It was, Jack thought, quite possibly the best night of his life. There had been something primal about their lovemaking; not in intensity, but knowing, feeling, that this amazing, smart woman had chosen him.

"I can hear you thinking." Greta's breath was warm against his chest, tucked against him so completely he didn't ever want to move. "Care to share?"

"In a bit." He lifted her hand, pressed his mouth to her fingers. Then turned her hand to admire the narrow leather cuff she always wore. "What is this? No, Greta." He held on when she tried to move away. "You don't have to tell me everything. Not yet. But tell me about this."

She leaned over him, her hair falling loose of her braid. In the depths of her eyes he saw the battle, saw her struggle, either with the truth or the reality. He drew her down, kissed her, waited until the tension melted away again. He flicked the snap free. The cuff fell onto the mattress, and beneath it, he found the scars.

"I was fourteen." Tears splashed onto his skin when she blinked.

"Greta."

"It was just all too much. Everything closed in. I wanted to be with them."

"Your parents?"

She nodded and, to his surprise and relief, she lay back down, her head nestled into his shoulder. "There wasn't any buildup. I don't even remember thinking about it, really. One day I just…" She took a deep breath. "Therapy helped. Uncle Lyndon helped, and Yvette. Now I wear the cuff to remember. When things get difficult or suffocating, I use it to remind myself there's always something on the other side. And there is." She tilted her head back to look up into his face. "There's something wonderful."

He slipped his fingers through hers, turned her hand and pressed his lips against the scars. He didn't think he'd ever met anyone braver than the woman he held in his arms.

"Now, about what you were thinking before." She inhaled deeply and shifted over him. He could feel her, all of her, pressed completely against him. "Care to share?"

"I do, indeed."

"What are you doing?" Greta mumbled a good while later when Jack rolled her over. He stood beside the bed, hands on his hips, looking down at the most beautiful, goddess-like perfection he'd ever seen.

"What do you think I'm doing?" He wrapped gentle

hands around her ankles and pulled her toward him. She laughed, the sound zinging through him.

"We need to pace ourselves, or we'll be out of condoms before the drugstore opens." She gasped when he bent down and slung her over his shoulder. "Jack! What on earth—put me down! I weigh a ton."

"Hardly." He probably shouldn't be lifting her again, but he was feeling rather invincible at the moment. He carried her into the bathroom and bent to set her on her feet beside the claw-foot tub. "Your bath, my lady."

"Oh." She blinked up at him, her mouth curving in that secretive way she had whenever she was especially happy. He loved that expression. He loved creating it. "That's just lovely."

"I thought so. Come on." He got in first, held out his hand to help her in and together they sank into the warm, soapy water.

"I could so get used to this," she murmured as he pulled her against him, settling her as comfortably as possible between his legs and against his chest.

"One thing I've been wanting to do."

"You still have a list?" she teased over her shoulder.

"You'd better believe I do." He reached for her braid, pulled off the elastic and using his fingers, untangled her hair until it spilled around her shoulders and into the water. "Now, that's a vision."

"You can't even see," she giggled and sat up to turn around. The second she did, the moment he looked into her shining, passion-filled eyes, he knew. It was over. He was done. All the way, head-deep in love. "Jack?"

"Yeah?" He cupped her cheek in his hand. He'd never get tired of looking at her.

"You're not worried, are you? About us getting involved. About what it might do to the case or your career."

"No." He stroked a thumb across her lips. "We'll figure it out. We'll figure a way to make this work." He drew her in for a kiss and caught the flash of doubt—or was that fear?—in her eyes. "No one's going to hurt you, Greta. I promise."

She smiled and nodded.

"You asked me to believe you, Greta. Now I'm asking you the same thing."

"I'll try."

"There is no try. There is only do."

She blinked, pulled back. "Huh?"

"It's Yoda."

"That's not yoga."

"Yo-*da*. You know, little green Muppet guy, lives in a swamp. Lifts spaceships with a single… You're kidding, right?" Jack dropped his hands so fast he splashed them both. "Are you telling me I've fallen in love with a woman who doesn't know Star Wars?"

It wasn't exactly how he'd expected to make the pronouncement. Given the way the color drained from her face, it wasn't what she expected, either. She moved to the other end of the tub, leaving him feeling rather abandoned. "Jack, you can't mean—"

His cell phone rang, cutting off whatever else she'd been about to say. Whatever he didn't want to hear her say. He reached behind him for where he'd left his phone and answered it. "It's two in the morning, and I am occupied," he told Cole. "This had better be—"

"Jack, stop." Cole's voice snapped through the line.

"What is it?" He sat up straight and splashed water over the edge of the tub. "What's wrong? Is it Eden? The baby?"

"Nothing like that. They found a body, Jack. We think it's Calhoun."

Chapter 12

For all the cop shows she'd watched over the years, Greta found nothing glamorous or entertaining about a crime scene. As there had been no way for Jack to keep what he'd heard a secret, he'd reluctantly agreed to let Greta come along, but only on the provision she remain in the car.

Spinning red and blue lights threatened to blind her as she stared out the windshield, heat blowing, but not warm enough to take the chill from her icy hands. As quickly as their clothes had come off hours before, clean ones went on. Her hair was still damp from where it had touched the water. Definitely not how she'd expected her night with Jack to end.

She'd lost track of the number of people on-site. Deputies and firefighters working to recover the up-side-down vehicle lying half-submerged in the river, paramedics on standby or maybe, Greta thought, to transport the body to the morgue. The entire thing could very well put her off dramas all together.

The yellow crime-scene tape had been stretched around the Green Bridge area of Discovery Park before they'd arrived, before Jack had dropped out of the car, a closed, almost stern expression on his face. "Stay here, you understand?"

"I'm not a poodle," she'd spat and earned a flash of regret. "But yes, I understand." She knew why he was on edge, and it didn't have anything to do with a late-night phone call or the body they'd found. She hadn't responded well to his declaration of love. A declaration that had brought her pure joy and more pain than expected. It didn't matter how much she cared for him, there could be no future for them. Not when she was so unpredictable.

The driver's door popped open. Greta yelped as Eden jumped in behind the wheel and slammed the door behind her. "Whew! Cold one tonight. Weird time of year to say that." She handed Greta a metal thermos. "Tea, right? Leaf-brewed? Jack might have mentioned. It's decaf. Same as mine. Yuck." She sipped and shook her head. "Don't know how you drink this stuff. No real jolt."

"There can be," Greta offered. "What are you doing here?"

"Two a.m. phone call about a body? Kind of its own special alarm clock. I tried to go back to sleep, but the mind already started spinning. You okay?"

"Yes." Greta unscrewed the cap on the thermos, lifted it to her nose and sniffed. "Mint. Nice choice."

"I read it calms the stomach." Eden turned and leaned back against the door. "You look different."

"Must be the moonlight," Greta suggested.

"Nope, that's not it." Eden inclined her head, narrowed her eyes. A few seconds later, during which Greta looked anywhere but at the crime blogger, she nodded and laughed. "Okay, got it."

Greta snapped her head around. "Got what?"

"You and Jack had sex. Explains why you two blew off dessert."

Greta's face went blue-flame hot. "You don't know that."

Eden snorted and looked out the window where her husband and Jack were speaking with a group of deputies. "Sure, I do. Good for you. And good for Jack. He hasn't had the best of luck with women."

Something about the way Eden said it reignited all those doubts Greta had managed to shove down. "Have there been a lot of women?"

Eden flinched, as if realizing she might have said the wrong thing. "Not a lot. A few. Mostly friendly, you know? Not well, sizzling like the two of you."

Sizzling might be an understatement, Greta thought. She'd never imagined how...creative Jack was. Or how addictive she'd find him.

"Actually, I've never seen him like how he is with you, Greta. He's different. Calm. Protective. That's good for him. And you, too. You seem to be a good fit."

"Fit for what?"

"I'm beginning to think I stuck my foot in my

mouth." Eden looked at her again. "Did things not go well?"

"They went fine." Greta shifted in her seat. "This is a strange conversation to have." She didn't do girl talk particularly well, not even with Yvette, who had always had far more experience at everything than Greta.

"Doesn't help that I'm nosy." She grinned into her tea. "*Fine*, huh? Never known *fine* to put a glow like yours on a person."

"Jack said you were many things." Greta refused to be baited into checking the mirror. "He didn't mention you were rude."

"I'm a learning curve." If she was offended by Greta's observation, she didn't show it. "Coroner's here. Time to join the gang."

"What?" Greta sputtered as Eden pushed open the door. "No, Jack said to wait here for him."

Eden planted a hand on her hip and glared at her. "Do not disappoint me by being someone who does as she's told. You've got spunk deep in there somewhere, Greta. And I'm making it my personal mission to excavate it. Beginning right now. Out. You can bring your tea."

"But—" Greta didn't see any way to argue. She climbed out of the SUV and walked around to join Eden. "Why do you care if I'm spunky?"

"I don't. I care that you're happy, seeing as you've made me and Cole that way." Eden cupped gloved hands around her cup. "Look, I know I can be an abrasive bi—er, person. But I'm also a good judge of people, which is usually determined by people's impulsive actions. What you offered me and Cole, that goes beyond expectations of even my closest friends. So, I'm sorry to say that makes you one of them now. I know." She shrugged. "You don't have a lot of friends, and you don't like people or crowds or—"

"I like some people." Greta couldn't help but look over at Jack.

"See? That there. You don't even realize you're doing it. You're over the moon about Jack, and that makes my heart flutter."

Greta laughed. "You are not one to flutter."

"Not typically, no. But I did mean it that you have more friends than you think. Any woman who can put that look of life back in that man's eye after what he's been through goes to the top of my list. So, get used to it, kid." She hip-bumped her and had Greta stumbling. "You're stuck with me. Us." She glanced behind her as two pairs of headlamps joined the growing throng of cars. "We're a package deal."

Greta almost balked at the sight of Simone and Vince along with Max and Allie heading toward them. "What are they all doing here?"

"Consider them a support system. You can figure out the rest along the way." She leaned forward, narrowed her gaze. "Looks like they're getting ready to pull the car out of the river. That bridge is looking worse for wear."

Now it was Greta's turn to lean over where she noticed a good section of the bridge's guardrail had broken away.

"Let's see what's going on with the body."

"No." Greta stayed back when Eden moved forward. The deafening beep of a truck backing up made her wince. "I'd rather just wait for what Jack wants to tell me."

"Suit yourself. You can hang out with them, then."

"Hey, Greta." Vince Sutton, Simone's husband, gave her a quick smile and nod as he trailed after Eden.

"Hi." The man made her nervous. Quiet people always did. They were always thinking, watching, observing. And heaven only knew what he thought about her.

"Did Eden ambush you already?" Simone asked when she, Allie and Max joined her. "Never mind. I recognize that expression. This is a shame." She sighed. "This part of the park is so lovely."

"You all didn't have to come out here for me," Greta said.

"Don't worry." Simone flashed her a grin. "We didn't. She told us what you did, by the way. Eden. About the apartment."

"That was really generous of you," Allie added.

"What an understatement," Simone said.

Greta shifted on her feet. If she'd known offering Eden an apartment was going to earn her a place in the pantheon of friendship she might have thought better of it.

"Don't overwhelm her, Simone," Allie said. "Greta, you doing okay?"

Was she? Overwhelmed seemed at apt description. "Jack didn't want to leave me alone at my place" was all she could manage. She did have to admit, getting some fresh air, no matter how cold, seemed to be clearing her head.

"If you'd rather go home, Max and I can take you."

"No." Being alone would give her too much time to think, and right now, she didn't want to do that. Because once she started thinking, she was going to have to decide what to do about Jack. She'd much rather find out whose body they found. "No, thank you. I should be fine here."

"If you change your mind, just say the word. I'm going to go." Max gave Allie's shoulder a quick squeeze and jerked a thumb in Jack and Cole's direction before he moved off.

"Morbid curiosity," Allie grumbled. "He's really got a taste for this investigator thing since Vince asked him to run those background checks on Fremont. It's like the training wheels are off."

"Doyle Fremont?" Greta turned on her. "Why is Vince, or rather Max, doing background checks on him? I thought the police were doing that."

"Ah." Allie cringed. "Shoot. Now I wish Max hadn't told me. Jack asked Vince to handle it to keep this off the official radar for now. Just in case…"

"Just in case what?" Greta asked. An odd sensation dropped into the pit of her stomach. "Simone? Do you know anything about this?"

"No," Simone said slowly. "I don't, but it sounds as if I should. Allie married Max the chatterbox. I married the strong, silent type."

Greta's mind raced. Why would Jack want to keep the Fremont case off the official radar unless… "He doesn't believe me."

"What?" Allie gasped. "Oh, Greta, no. I'm sure that's not what this is about."

"I'm sure it is." She shoved the thermos into Allie's hands. "Excuse me. I need to speak with Jack."

"Oh, but, Greta—"

"Nuh-uh." Simone held Allie back when she started to follow Allie. "Let her go."

"Jack!" Greta stomped through the muddied brush and soil surrounding the shore where the Sacramento and American Rivers met.

Jack spun on his heel. "Greta, I told you to wait in the car."

Eden snorted.

"Stifle it." Jack moved toward Greta, who had no intention of stopping. She was tired of everyone telling her what to do, of always waiting for answers.

"Is it him?" She tried to duck around Jack, but he caught her arms, held her in place.

"Greta, you don't want to see this."

Why? Because she had enough monsters in her head? "It's my case as much as yours. I saw him get killed. I'm the one who started this whole thing, remember?" She poked a finger into his chest. "Or does that not matter since it isn't an official case?"

He started, frowned. "Who told you that?" He shot a look at Eden who held up her hands and shook her head.

"You asked a private investigator to do background work on Fremont. Meaning you haven't done it. Meaning it isn't a real case, is it?"

"Oh, man," Vince muttered under his breath.

"Okay." Jack seemed to sag for a moment. "That's not entirely true."

Not entirely true. The words echoed in Greta's ears. "But some of it is. You didn't file it as a case, did you? You've been humoring me this whole time. Placating the unreliable witness. Is this what it took to convince you?"

Anger sparked in Jack's eyes. "Do not put words in

my mouth. We kept it off official records because we needed evidence before we could proceed. Do you know what would happen to me, to the department, to anyone involved, if this case went sideways? We needed proof."

"And my word wasn't enough."

"Without a body?" he sighed. "No, it wasn't."

She could see it on his face that he wasn't happy with his explanation. She stepped close enough so only he could hear. "Do you believe me now? There's a body. Does it match the description? Is it him?"

"Jack!" Cole called. "We're rolling him over."

"Wait here," Jack ordered.

"No." To stop from slipping and sliding in the mud, Greta grabbed hold of his jacket and tried to keep up. "I want to see this for myself. I need to know."

"Suit yourself."

The whirring of machinery as a car was dragged onto the bank nearly burst her eardrums. The glare of work lights cast the entire area in an odd array of shadows, and it was then that she realized what Simone meant. Not how you want to think of an area known, she supposed, for family picnics and summer outings. She felt every second tick by as the recovery crew removed the body from the passenger seat. Silence hung heavy in the air, pushing down on her.

"Didn't expect such a large crowd." A middle-aged woman with dark spectacles peered up from where she crouched over the waterlogged body. "You're new," she said to Greta.

"Greta, this is Dr. Mona Hendrix, city coroner," Jack said. "We need her to identify the body, Mona. For a case," he added.

"I need to see his face." Greta's stomach lurched. The body seemed distorted and had an odd gurgling sound to it as Mona turned him over. The clothes he wore seemed too big, but what did she know about what happened to bodies after death?

Eden murmured, coming to stand next to Greta. Without meaning to, Greta grabbed hold of Eden's hand and squeezed. "You think it's Calhoun?"

"It looks like him," Greta whispered, recognizing the odd-shaped birthmark. But his face and skin were so distorted.

"I'll check for an ID in a second." Mona used her gloved hands to move the curtain of dark hair away from the face. An odd bubble formed under the skin of his forehead. "That's odd." She pressed her gloved finger to the raised skin. The bubble moved. She pulled out a scalpel, pierced the skin. Water gushed out and down his sagging face.

Greta gagged, covered her mouth. "That's not normal, is it?" Even as she watched, more bubbles appeared on his face.

"Detectives!" One of the firefighters called over. The group turned as one. The fireman was standing over the open trunk as water spilled free. "We've got another body."

"Look at you." Eden squeezed Greta's hand. "First no bodies, now two. You're getting better at this." Greta glared at Eden. "Gallows humor. Annoying, but a pressure release for me." Rather than responding, Greta found herself squeezing Eden's hand again.

"You coming?" Jack asked with a touch of challenge in his voice.

"We'll wait here," Eden answered for her. "I want to know what those bubbles are." She crouched down as Jack, Cole, Vince and Max headed over to the car.

"This is fascinating," Mona muttered, reminding Greta of a certain Vulcan first officer. "Usually I'd wait until I had him on my table, but these pockets just keep... Hang on." Mud squelched as she sank onto her knees. She slid the point of the scalpel under his ear, angled it down. Greta heard a soft pop and release of air. "It isn't even Halloween."

"Greta?" Jack called. Greta had bent down beside Eden, who had put on a plastic medical glove and was slowly pulling apart the lapels of the tailored black suit jacket. The glimmer of a gold pen caught Greta's attention. It looked just like the one she'd... "Greta!"

"What?" Greta tucked her hair behind her ear and looked over. She saw enough emotion on Jack's face to leave Eden and Mona behind. "There's something strange..." She broke off, barely noticing Jack slip an arm around her waist. A body had been wedged into the trunk of a BMW so tightly, the legs had clearly been broken. The face and body was bloated but fit her memory of the man she'd seen better than the one on the shore.

Cole shined his light on the side of the man's face. "Looks like the birthmark you described. Is it him, Greta?"

"Yes." Even without seeing him upright, she knew without a doubt, this was the man she'd seen in Doyle Fremont's office and the gallery. She didn't have time to embrace the relief. "But if this is Paul Calhoun, who's that?"

"Let's see if Mona's found out." Jack steered her

away. Vince and Max stayed behind with the car while Cole, Jack and Greta returned just as Mona began using her sharp scalpel to trace around the man's face. "What in the—"

"I can't decide if it's grotesque or cool," Eden commented.

"I know which side I land on." Greta swallowed hard.

"Cole, hand me an evidence bag, please." Mona leaned over to finish tracing. The bubbles under the skin disappeared as more water dribbled free. She slipped the edge of the scalpel beneath a small cut she'd made and pried the skin up. Seconds later, she deposited a latex mask in the clear bag Cole held open.

"And now for bachelor number two." Eden glanced over her shoulder. "Greta?"

Eden's voice echoed as if from a distance. A distance Greta wasn't sure she'd ever return from. It wasn't possible. It didn't make any sense. She knew that face. That kind, understanding patient face that had helped guide her through most of her life. The face of a man she'd relied on every day for the past twenty years. Her body went cold. She only knew she was trembling because Jack's arm tightened and drew her in. She watched, dazed, as Mona reached over and gently removed the wallet from his inside pocket. But Greta didn't need to hear. She already knew.

Greta told them, "His name is Lyndon Thornwald." She pressed her fingers to her lips to stem the tears as Mona nodded and flipped the wallet open to confirm. "He's my uncle."

Chapter 13

"Let's ask Allie and Max to drive you home."

Was it possible to both loathe and desire the patient sympathy she heard in Jack's voice? Greta drew up her knees and wrapped her arms so tight they went numb. "I'm not leaving until I have some answers." As if answers were going to bring her any peace.

So much had happened in only a few hours. The announcement of Eden and Cole's baby, making love with Jack, being catapulted into literally one of her worst nightmares. She was almost afraid to touch a toe to the ground for fear of falling through the earth. "Unless I have to go?"

"You don't have to do anything you don't want to do." He reached across the table and held out his hand. She stared at it for a long moment, blanking the noise from the station. Everything inside her screamed at her to take it, to hold on and never let go. She turned her head, rested her cheek on her knees and willed time to speed up.

She'd lost track of the hours she'd spent in the Major Crimes break room, but given the morning shadows had moved past the dusty blinds, she figured it had been a while.

"Do you want to talk to Allie? Maybe she can—"

"I don't need a psychologist. Have you talked to Lyndon's office back in New York?" Jack's lack of immediate response started her stomach lurching again. She forced herself to look into the eyes of the man she'd been in bed with hours before. "He's dead, Jack. I don't think there's much else that can surprise me at this point."

But apparently there was. She could see that much on his face. "We need to ask you some questions. It can be just you and me, but I'll need to record it. Or I can bring in Cole and my LT so they can corroborate."

"Probably best to do both." Her eyes hurt from not letting the tears fall. What good would they do? "Do you want to talk in here?"

"It's more comfortable than the LT's office, believe me." He looked over her head, gestured for them to come in, then moved around to sit beside her. Her heartbeat matched the footsteps. When the door closed, she unfolded herself and straightened up.

"Ms. Renault, I'm Lt. Santos. No, please don't get up." He rested a hand on her shoulder and placed a paper cup of tea in front of her. "Jack mentioned you don't like our tea here, so I grabbed this from a cart. I hope it's okay."

Kindness. Greta blinked away a new rush of tears. There was always such kindness after death. She sipped and felt her lips curve. Orange. One of her favorites. "It's perfect, thank you." For some reason she expected Jack's boss to be huge in stature, but she thought him a rather ordinary-looking man, with dark eyes and hair and a purpose in his walk and gestures that spoke of authority. "Jack said you have some questions about Lyndon."

"About Mr. Thornwald, yes," the LT said and sat on the edge of a nearby table.

"Greta," Cole said across from her, "were you aware Lyndon Thornwald was fired from his firm more than three years ago?"

"What?" Her mind started to buzz in that way it did when there was too much information to process. "Fired? No, that's not possible. He's been there for almost thirty years. He was a partner."

"We spoke with the senior partner a while ago," Cole said. "They discovered he'd been stealing money from clients. Rewriting wills and trusts to make himself the beneficiary. People with no other living relatives or connections. It only came out when he made the mistake of trying to do the same to a woman who had a legitimate heir that came forward after the fact. He admitted to gambling debts, to owing people who had threatened to kill him. He said he got in over his head and that he'd pay every penny back. He did, and the law firm paid damages. It was all kept very quiet, not surprising given the status of the firm. He was disbarred soon after."

Disbarred? "I didn't know." Greta couldn't breathe. How could she not know? Was she that out of touch? That sheltered? That detached? "It sounds stupid, I suppose. He's never let on... He's handled everything for me for years."

"We suspect you've been his only client since he was disbarred, Greta," Lt. Santos said. "Somehow he was able to keep that from you."

Jack didn't offer to take her hand this time, he simply did. "Simone's filed an order with the courts in New York requesting access to his home. She and Vince are flying back today to be on scene to act as representatives of this jurisdiction."

"Okay." Greta didn't understand. "But if he hasn't worked at the firm for years, what is it you hope to find? What is it you aren't telling me?"

"The FBI is requesting to meet with me," Lt. Santos said. "Mr. Thornwald has been under surveillance as part of an ongoing investigation regarding Paul Calhoun and the Mishenka crime family. Calhoun worked for Lyndon at the same law firm on and off over the years. The evidence seems to suggest that Calhoun was in on Lyndon's thefts from the start. It may have all been his idea. There's no real way of knowing now."

"We think Lyndon was hiding Calhoun's stolen money in his clients' accounts. At least in the accounts he once had access to. But as your account is the only one that's been available to him for the past couple of years, it's possible it's been used as either a cleaning account for the family or as a hiding place. Which means the feds are going to put a freeze on your finances until we figure this out."

It served her right for turning a blind eye. For falling so deep into her own make-believe world she hadn't paid any attention. It had all seemed above her. Or was that what Lyndon had told her? He didn't want her to worry. He didn't want to distract her from her art. And she'd been so caught up in her own fear, she'd never questioned any of it. "Was he stealing from me?"

"It looks that way," Cole said. "Simone's in the process of gathering up all his banking and other financial records. We'll get access to his computer and whatever else he has, don't worry. We'll need you to sign off on some things—"

"Whatever you need." Her mind whirled. All her properties, all her investments. Was any of it real? Did she still own any of it? "Wait a minute. What does this have to do with Doyle Fremont and what I saw in his office?" And why would Lyndon have been wearing a mask to make him appear to be the man she'd seen killed? Why was Lyndon dead? Why was Calhoun?

Jack's hand moved up and squeezed her shoulder. "We have evidence that Calhoun was the middleman between Fremont and the Mishenkas. They planned to invest in one of his start-ups, only the deal went south. Fremont needed to give back money he didn't have. He knew Calhoun, Calhoun worked with Lyndon and Lyndon had access to one big account. Yours. And once Fremont got a taste of it, he wanted more. Needed more. Fremont is just about broke. He had to have the cash, and he wanted it from Lyndon. The only way for Lyndon to have complete control over that money was to get rid of you."

Greta closed her eyes. She didn't want to hear any

more. But she needed to know. "Who killed them? Calhoun and Lyn… Lyndon? Fremont or these Mishenka people?"

"They aren't going to hurt you, Greta." Jack shook his head. "I'm not—we aren't going to let them."

A knock sounded on the door. Greta jumped. Jack's hand tightened reassuringly. Lt. Santos answered the knock, had a quick, low-toned conversation, then returned, a file folder in his hand. "Mona just gave me her initial report. She's putting Calhoun's time of death five to eight days ago. The water makes it a bit dodgy, but she's pretty confident."

"That makes it well after Greta's call to 9-1-1," Jack said. "So it was Calhoun at the office but not at the gallery?"

"Looks like. Calhoun's cause of death?" Cole asked.

"Broken hyoid." Santos flipped through pages. "No other bruising other than this V-shaped mark. No handprint, so it wasn't strangulation. Must be some kind of weapon, something hinged or—"

"Fremont could have done it," Jack said. "He's an expert at Krav Maga. One strike like that wouldn't be a problem for him. And it would explain why Greta didn't see a gun or knife. Fremont is the weapon. But why the elaborate plot? Why not just kill her?"

Greta shivered. The man who had raised her, the man who had been there to pull her out of that darkness one horrible night, the man who had told her everything was going to be okay had been plotting to get rid of her. She would have helped him. She would have given him whatever money he'd needed. All he'd had to do was ask.

"Why go to all the trouble of Greta witnessing one murder, then seeing his ghost—"

"My trust." Greta felt the pieces slip together. And they all had dollar signs. "The trust says if I die or become incapable of signing documents, all the money goes to charity. All of it. But if I'm incapacitated or institutionalized—" her breath caught hard in her chest "—if I'm institutionalized, then all the money goes into a liquid account for my care. And Lyndon would have complete control and access." All this time. She squeezed her eyes shut and felt the tears escape. All this time he'd insisted he'd been protecting her, when all Lyndon wanted was for her to slip over that edge of sanity just like her mother.

"You mean they were trying to drive you mad?" Lt. Santos said. "That seems a lot more difficult than planning a murder to me."

"It would be." She swiped at the tears, her head dipped so she wouldn't have to look at Jack. "Unless there's a history of severe mental illness in your family."

The silence in the room hurt her ears.

"This has to do with why you changed your name." Jack released her arm, and for an instant, she felt cold and alone. Until his hand sank into her hair, cupped her face. "Greta, there's no reason for secrets anymore. They can't do any damage at this point. What happened, who you are, it won't change how I feel about you."

Wouldn't it? Would he ever look at her the same? Would he ever say her name and wonder if maybe this was the day she didn't know him, remember him? Love him?

"We can leave, if it would be easier."

"No." Greta managed a weak smile at Cole for offering. "No, I'd rather not go into it more than once. But if Allie's still here, she might be able to help me explain some things."

"I'll get her." Cole left the room and returned a few minutes later with both Allie and Eden. "Okay?"

"Yeah." She found Eden's calm, almost unreadable demeanor a comfort. When the door closed, she took a deep breath. "My real name is Genevra Lamont. My parents were Serena and Anthony Lamont. I think some of you might have heard of them."

"Hollywood power couple in the late eighties, early nineties," Cole explained at Lt. Santos's blank look. "They both met a pretty horrible end, if I remember."

"They did." Greta nodded. "I always knew my mother had problems. My father often tried to explain, but what do you tell a child about mental illness? I just remember him saying she had good days and bad, and that sometimes she needed to spend time away, where she couldn't hurt herself or anyone else. I remember that last year she was gone for a long time, but when she came back, she was different. Happy. Beautiful. She had this long, silver-blond hair and this silk dressing gown, shiny white. We used to play dress-up, and she'd pretend to be Veronica Lake or Gene Harlow. She loved classic movies, which is why my father wanted to direct her in *Midnight Witness* and, given his recent success, he was given the okay.

"It was a new writer, a new type of movie, and my mother was so excited. She was on top of the world. And then, the night of the premiere, I remember I was in bed when they got home. I heard a crash, screaming, yelling. And voices. So many voices."

"Greta, you don't have to do this." Allie bent down and took hold of her hand. "You don't have to—"

"But I do. Because I never have. I've never told anyone…" And maybe if she had, then none of this would be happening now. Maybe if she hadn't let herself believe no one would ever understand, life would have been different. "I remember standing on the steps and seeing my father lying on the floor of the living room, a jagged piece of glass from the table sticking out of his chest. And my mother, standing over him, her hands covered in blood. I knew enough to call 9-1-1, but after that, I only know what people told me.

"That the paramedics found me standing barefoot in my father's blood. That the police took my mother away, but when she realized what she'd done, she killed herself. Uncle Lyndon was my father's best friend. All of my grandparents were gone, and both my mother and father were only children. He took me in without a second thought. He took care of the funerals and the house, and he brought my nanny and made me feel safe again. Kept me away from the media circus, and then, when I was old enough, he sent me to boarding school so I could put it all behind me." Anger spiked through the grief. "And now I find out that all this time, all he cared about was my money. All he wanted…" Had he ever cared for her at all? Was there anyone she could trust?

Eden said, "None of this explains why Lyndon thought he could—"

"I found out later my mother wasn't the first in the family to suffer from mental illness. My great-grandmother had been committed to an asylum when she was in her late thirties. My grandmother at around the same age. It doesn't take much to see the pattern. Driving me mad, making me think I saw something that I didn't, making me think a dead man was still alive—Lyndon was counting on my fear of me turning into my mother. And what jury would believe me if the case went to court? I was discredited before this even started. Lyndon knew me too well. He knew I'd go willingly myself before I'd take the chance of ever hurting anyone. And once I did that, he'd have everything he wanted."

Suddenly Jack's hand felt hot on her skin. She couldn't look at him. Didn't want to see the disappointment, the shock on his face.

"That's why I was so adamant about what I had seen that night," she whispered. "I didn't just need the police to believe me, I needed to believe myself. But I didn't see this, did I? I didn't see the truth."

"You saw what they wanted you to see," Allie insisted. "You're a victim in all this, Greta. And there's nothing to blame yourself for. If anything, they underestimated you. They probably didn't count on you calling the police."

"None of this was about Calhoun or the Mishenkas," Cole said. "This was all about Greta and getting her money."

"Wouldn't my mother be proud?" Greta tried to joke. "I'm the star of the show." Was there anything she could believe in? Was there any part that wasn't a lie? "I need to get out of here." She shoved to her feet, stepped away from both Allie and Jack. "Unless there's something else you need from me?"

"No," Lt. Santos said. "No, if we have any other questions, we'll ask them later."

"Great. Thanks." She hugged her arms around her waist and tucked in. When she lifted her head, Eden was watching her, eyes narrowed. Eden walked over, grabbed Greta's wrists and pulled them apart, pushed her arms to her sides.

"No more turtle-tucking," Eden told her. "Contrary to what Allie said, you are not a victim. You are a survivor. You are a strong, capable, talented woman I admire more than I can say. Don't you dare let anyone, especially Uncle Lyndon, take that away from you." She looked hard into her eyes. "Don't you dare."

"I won't," Greta whispered. But she didn't know how.

Chapter 14

"Do you have to get back to the station right away?" Greta dropped her bag and purse on the table as Jack closed the door behind them. "I have some time if you want to talk or—"

Greta spun around, planted her hands on his shoulders, shoved him against the door. She kissed him. No, she didn't just kiss him, he thought, she devoured him. Her mouth, her tongue, her entire body sank into him. He went hard instantly, all of the blood draining from his brain as she hooked her foot around the back of his leg and pressed against him.

"I don't want to talk." She caught his lower lip between her teeth and bit. He gasped. "I don't want to think." Her hands dragged his shirt free of his pants, her fingers diving beneath to scrape against his bare skin. "I just want to feel. I want to feel you. On me." She kissed him again. "Inside of me." She shoved his jacket off his shoulders, then his shirt. Her hands, somewhat uncertain just last night, didn't tremble. Didn't hesitate. Not as she undid his pants. Not when her fingers slipped inside to grasp him.

"Greta—" Pleasure ripped through him, a chain reaction he couldn't and didn't want to stop. He hissed out a breath through clenched teeth and tilted his head back as he felt her mouth go around him. He could feel the frenzy building inside of her, the way she moved her lips, her tongue, the way her hands manipulated, tightened and squeezed. He vibrated under her touch, the sensation coursing through him, reaching new heights when he dragged his head forward to watch her. When he came, she let out a gasp of part triumph, part ecstasy and looked up at him, the smile on her face one of promise. And in that moment, he knew he'd never wanted anyone more. He'd never loved anyone more.

With a groan, he reached down, grabbed her arms and hauled her up. "You are one fast learner."

"I want more," she murmured against his lips as she hitched her legs around his hips and locked her hands around his neck. "Give me more, Jack. Make me forget. Make me forget everything."

His hands held her hips as she ground against him. When he moved, he could only hope he could make it to the bedroom. When they did, when he lowered her onto the mattress and stripped them both bare, he knew there would only ever be Greta.

It was an odd feeling, Greta thought days later as she stood back to examine the array of paintings she'd chosen for the gallery showing. An odd feeling indeed to not know where the ideas, the images came from.

She'd finished the final work, a completely new and different piece that stood both in stark contrast and in perfect harmony with the others. The pressure valve she'd been waiting to release hadn't burst but had sighed, letting the residual energy and adrenaline slowly disperse, like steam through a tea spout. The last painting, *Evergreen*, was perfect, maybe the best thing she'd ever done, and contained every bit of anger, every bit of resentment, every bit of love she'd felt surge through her system when Jack touched her. Held her. Made love to her.

He had opened unexpected and unexplored doors inside of her even as she'd closed them behind her. The morning he'd brought her home from the police station had given her what she'd needed to break through those final barriers of doubt, of fear and allowed her to accept the fact that she was, despite being hopelessly and utterly in love with him, destined to be alone.

She set her brush down, carried the tray table over to the sink and turned the music down. The throbbing beat of techno-classical had given way to the soft, pan-flute sounds that facilitated her drift into the new world her mind had created. But now, she wanted silence. She needed the void around her so she wouldn't make a mistake. This had to be done right. And it had to be done soon. Before walking away became impossible.

The knock on the door didn't surprise her. She'd been hearing it off and on over the past few days, when Jack—or Ashley or Yvette and one time even Bowie—had stepped inside to bring her food or tea or poked their heads in just to make sure she didn't need anything else. She hadn't locked her studio door. She'd never lock it again, and she was grateful these people in her life understood her need to be alone to work out everything that had gone wrong. It was Jack, however, she had the hardest time dealing with. Because he mattered the most.

"Music's off." Jack leaned against the doorjamb and crossed his arms. "You must be done sulking."

"I haven't been sulking." She didn't like the edge to her voice, but she attributed that to hunger and lack of sleep. She tried not to notice how just the sight of him, barefoot, wearing simple jeans and a white T-shirt, hair falling nearly over one eye, was the most beautiful sight she'd ever seen. She couldn't notice. She couldn't risk it. The other day, the day she'd begged him to make her forget, to push all the ugliness and fear and hurt out of her, had been a goodbye. The only way she could think to say it. "I had a job to finish. Now it's done."

"Great. Join me in the kitchen. I've got dinner waiting."

"Dinner?" Greta looked out the window only to find them blacked out with paper. She'd forgotten she'd done that to stop herself from obsessively looking into Doyle Fremont's office. She pried one corner of paper free and saw it was dark outside. "What time is it?" She looked at the clock and saw it was nearly eight. "Oh. Wow. Okay." No wonder she was hungry.

She picked up the plate someone—she thought it was Ashley—had left earlier and greeted an eager if not irritated Cerberus on her walk to the kitchen. "Sorry. Time got away from me. Smells good." She went over to the stove while Jack pulled down bowls from the cabinet. "Did you cook?"

"I can manage a mean pasta. Yvette had a spare set of keys to the building. I gave them to Cole so he and Eden could check out the apartment."

"Oh." Greta cringed. "I forgot about that. Yeah, good. That's good. Did they like it?"

Jack barely looked at her. "Yes. Can we talk now?"

"How about after dinner?" She had the lid half-off the pot of simmering meat sauce when he came up behind her.

"How about now?" He covered her hand, lowered the lid and pulled her away. "How about we talk about the fact that I told you I love you."

Everything inside of her slowed. Her blood, her heart. Her pulse. "I know you did."

"That's your only response?"

"Would you like me to say thank you? Did you get any bread?" She moved around him to the fridge. "I feel like bread. It's been a while since I—"

"Stop it." He leaned against the edge of the counter, stuffed his hands into his front pockets. "Just stop it, Greta. We both know what you're doing, and it won't work."

"What won't?"

"It's not going to make me stop loving you."

Wanna bet? "You don't know me well enough to love me."

His smile was brief and sad. "Figured you'd say that, too. I'm not going to argue the fact that this came on pretty quick. In fact, it happened in the first five minutes of meeting you. Of seeing you sitting right here, drawing me on that sketchpad of yours. Mumbling to yourself. I've never believed in love at first sight, but there you go. Proven wrong. Little did I know you'd end up being the most frustrating, confusing, challenging woman I've ever known."

"We all have our flaws."

"Yes, we do." He nodded. "And that's what's really scaring you, isn't it? Not my flaws, although there are plenty."

There were? Greta blinked. She certainly hadn't found any. Not that she'd tell him that.

"You're scared of your own," he told her. "Or rather, you're scared of what they might be."

Greta's face went hot. He was skirting just a bit too close to the truth for her liking.

"Take these, for instance." He leaned over and grabbed a paper bag off the counter, turned it over and dumped out the prescriptions she'd had in her medicine cabinet. "That's a lot of bottles of fear."

Greta couldn't move. She couldn't breathe. "Did Ashley—"

"Ashley?" Surprise flashed across his face, followed quickly by disappointment. "No. My sister did not tell me you had a cabinet full of antipsychotic drugs. I suppose she couldn't once you became her patient."

"No." But Ashley had pushed her to tell Jack the truth. And she had. About most of it. "Those pills aren't any of your business, Jack. They never were. What we were doing, it was just fun. It was easy. You were staying here, and I figured it was time I took that step. I mean, I am almost twenty-seven. And it isn't easy meeting a nice guy to, well, take care of that." Every word, every lie felt like a wound. It couldn't matter, she told herself. It only mattered that he believed her. She couldn't—she wouldn't—saddle him with a future of uncertainty. It was only a matter of time before what had happened to her grandmother, to her mother, happened to her. And she was not going to put him through that.

She loved him too much.

"So I was convenient. Is that what you're saying?"

"Yes." It took every ounce of energy she had to force the word free. Right now, at this moment, she knew he'd touched a part of her heart she never even thought she had. And she knew she'd never loved him more.

"Of all the things I've thought about you, I never took you for a coward."

"I am not—"

"What do you call these?" He sent every last bottle scattering to the floor. "Those pills are nothing but your fear in physical form. You think about them every day. You see them every time you open that cabinet. You worry if this is the day you're going to have to take one. If today is the day you finally slip over that edge."

"Yes," she bit out. "Yes, I do. And I would never let someone else also live that life." She hugged her arms around herself and squeezed. "They're my safety net, Jack. They're the only hope that I won't turn into my mother. That I won't hurt someone I lo—"

"Careful." Jack's eyes narrowed as he faced her. "You might start telling me the truth. You love me, Greta. I'm even arrogant enough to think you've loved me from the start. But you won't let me in. Not really. You didn't tell me the truth about anything important.

About yourself. Instead, you tried to stay locked up in that cocoon of yours, where nothing can touch you. You didn't trust me to love you so much so that I don't care."

It was useless to keep up the pretense. He was right, but mainly about him deserving the truth. "That's why this has to end. Jack, please. You need to understand, I won't let you live your life waiting for me to disappear. I'm not angry about it, but I am scared of it. Terrified, actually. Why do you think I was so desperate to prove what I'd seen was real? Because I wasn't ready to go. I'm not ready. But it will happen."

"You don't know that. You don't." His voice calmed as he approached her, held her. "You love me, Greta. Just tell me, admit it to yourself, out loud, and we can deal with the rest together."

She wanted to. She'd never wanted to do anything more in her entire life. The idea of a life with Jack, being with him, being near him, laughing and crying with him, embracing all that life had to offer, was everything she'd ever wanted. And yet... His face blurred against the tears. "It's not enough, Jack. You deserve so much more than a fraction of forever. I will not let you give up your life, your future, when I might not have one."

"You're wrong." He searched her face, his eyes pleading, his hands squeezing his arms as if stopping himself from drawing her closer. "Those pills aren't a precaution. They're your escape plan. You're using them as an excuse because you're too afraid to take the chance. I'd take whatever time we're given, Greta. I love you that much."

That he did filled every empty part of her with warm,

perfect light. Even as her heart broke. "And I love you too much to let you."

The sound of her front door opening and cheerful voices echoing had him dropping his hands. He stepped back, his face going stone-cold.

"Hey, look who's come out of her cave." Eden and Cole rounded the corner as Jack turned away. "What's going on? Are we interrupting something?"

"No," Jack said. "We're done. Cole, you can fill her in on the case. I'm going home."

"Yeah, sure, okay." Cole leaned back to watch Jack leave the kitchen. "You want to tell us?"

"No." Greta shook her head and swallowed the tears. She'd shed them later, in the dark. When she was alone in her bed. "How do you like the apartment?"

"How do we—?" Eden gaped at her. "Greta—"

"I haven't had a chance to find a new attorney to draw up the lease agreement." Greta's voice sounded strained. "I'll take care of all that after the show. If you like it, move in when you want. There's pasta on the stove. I'm going to go take a shower and get some sleep. Just show yourselves out when you're done."

"Greta." Cole moved to her side. "What happened?"

"What had to happen," she admitted. "Enjoy your evening." She hurried out of the room, scooped up a whining Cerberus and scurried down the hall to her bedroom. Only when she'd closed the door behind her did she let the tears fall.

"You look like crap on a cracker." Ashley stumbled into the kitchen just after nine the next morning, stretching and yawning and beelining for the coffee machine.

"And what are you doing here? I thought you were staying at Greta's."

"She's got patrols watching her place until we locate Fremont. I don't want her alone until we've got him in custody." Jack didn't move from his seat at the breakfast bar. He didn't move, period. He could very well be turning into a zombie with the lack of sleep and constant worry about Greta while she'd been holed up in her studio. Sitting here for who knew how long, staring at the print of Greta's painting hanging over his couch, seemed like his best option. "Better get used to having me around again."

"Oh?" Ashley hit the pod button and headed to the fridge. "You two wear each other out already?" Her snort of laughter broke off when she caught Jack's glare. "Oh. Sorry. First fight?"

"First, maybe last. Who knows?" He wasn't ready to walk away. Not completely. He had to find the right answer to convince her that an unknown future was better than no future. "I told her I loved her, but she's scared."

"Of course she is." His sister broke up a bunch of eggs and set the pan on the stove. "Who wouldn't be, given everything that's happened?"

He watched her over the rim of his coffee cup. "You knew about the pills."

"Ah, yeah." Ashley grimaced. "Sorry about that. I tried to get her to tell you—"

"I'm not mad." Not exactly.

"Oh. Good. What are you mad about, then?"

"I'm not mad," he repeated. "I'm disappointed. She won't even—"

"What? Take a chance? Given what's in her past,

can you blame her? And now the one person she truly trusted, her only parental figure, the one guy who helped her through all that, was using her? We're lucky she's talking to any of us."

"How do you know about all that?"

Ashley rolled her eyes. "Because you aren't the only person in my universe. And because Eden likes to talk."

"Yes, she does." He supposed he should be grateful not having to explain everything to his sister. "You're a female, Ash."

She looked down at her chest. "So that's what these are?"

Jack's lips twitched. "There has to be something I can do to convince her we're worth it."

"Worth what?"

"Worth everything. I want it all. With her. Only her."

"Nice." She toasted him with her own mug. "Did you tell her that?"

"I did." Didn't he?

"You might want to make sure before you go making new plans."

Since Greta seemed too scared to ask, he knew someone had to. "What are the chances she has the same illness as her mother?"

"Without having access to her mother's official diagnosis, there's no way of knowing really."

"Never stopped you from guessing before. She said her grandmother and great-grandmother were hit in their thirties when it happened. It must have struck her mother earlier, though, since Serena was only thirty when she died."

"And Greta's what? Midtwenties?"

"Nearly twenty-seven." As she'd informed him last night.

"She could be on the other side of it. The only way to know for sure would be to get some genetic testing done, a few therapy sessions. I'd want to look at her family history, as well. Allie would know better than me what's available. Jack, I'm sure she's already thought about all that."

"Meaning she doesn't want to know?"

"Meaning maybe she doesn't realize just what's at stake. It's a bit like Schrodinger's cat, isn't it? She's alive, but not really living. Give her some time to deal with this situation with her uncle, with Doyle Fremont. Maybe once all that's behind her, she'll be more open to it. Don't give up on her, Jack."

"Don't worry." He finished his cold coffee. "I won't."

Because she didn't want to take the chance of running into Jack, Greta headed directly to the DA's office just after the gallery picked up her paintings. Funny how not too long ago she'd been thinking about expanding where she traveled within the city, yet most of the new places she'd visited had something to do with law enforcement. She checked the directory, logged in with security to get a visitor's badge, caught sight of *Ice and Snow*, a painting she'd done when she'd been living in Vermont, then headed upstairs to the DA's office. Cubicles lined either side of the wide, multicolored carpet. Muted conversations filled the space as she wound around, searching for Simone.

She found the lawyer sitting on the edge of her receptionist's desk, dressed in sharp, crisp white slacks, killer heels and a silk blouse the color of raspberries. "Greta." Simone stood up and reached out to hug her, a greeting that took Greta completely off guard. "How lovely to see you. Greta, this is Kyla Bertrand, my soon-to-be former assistant."

"She loves introducing me that way," Kyla said with a smile and rose to shake Greta's hand. Greta couldn't help but stare. The young woman was stunning, with bright, lively dark eyes and rich black curls framing her face. The long scarf she wore floated against a dress of bright flowers and swirls. She looked like one of Greta's paintings come to life. "Is something wrong?" Kyla brushed nervous hands down the front of her dress.

"No, no, sorry. I just—" Greta laughed through the distraction. "You're stunning. I was just thinking about drawing you. And yes, I know how weird that sounds. Occupational hazard." One she really needed to get under control.

"You're Greta Renault. Oh, wow! I love your work. Can't afford it, but I'm a fan." Kyla reached out her hand. "It's great to meet you. I'm coming to your show tomorrow night. I'm so excited."

"It's nice to meet you." Greta laughed. Odd how that seemed to be happening more frequently.

"Was there something you needed to talk to me about?" Simone asked. "What brings you by?"

"I was wondering if you could tell me what you and Vince found out in New York? Jack didn't—hasn't gotten around to it yet."

"Been busy, have you?" Simone grinned and motioned her into her office. "No problem. Shut the door."

She took a seat behind her desk. "How much detail do you want?"

"As much as you can give me. Is there enough evidence to arrest Doyle Fremont?" She lowered herself into one of the chairs across from Simone, drew her gaze around the beautiful array of photographs, mementos and awards lining the walls and shelves.

"For murder? No. I know you heard the preliminary autopsy results. Calhoun's cause of death was confirmed. The broken hyoid. Lyndon Thornwald was killed by a blow to the back of the head. It would have been quick, if that's what's worrying you."

It wasn't, but Greta supposed it eased her mind a bit. "Was he stealing from me?"

"Yes. And no." Simone reached over and plucked a file folder loose. "The FBI is still investigating, and we're waiting on some information, but it looks as if the majority of the money left to you by your parents is still there. However, the properties you purchased in the past few years, all but the building here in Sacramento, those have all been sold off."

"Oh." Greta frowned. Odd. Despite having liked the idea of having properties around the country, she found she didn't care beyond the relief that her current home was secure. "What Lyndon was doing with your finances was more out of desperation than greed. He was trying to dig himself out of a hole and just couldn't get out."

"I can't believe he never told me. I would have helped him."

"Sometimes pride and embarrassment go hand in

hand. He probably didn't want you to look at him differently or to be disappointed in him."

"And because of that, he's dead."

"Yes." Simone nodded. "I've been working on a theory as to why Fremont targeted you as a witness to his so-called crime."

"To have me declared incompetent so he could get to my money through Lyndon."

"Partially. But also to discredit you in court if he was ever charged with Calhoun's murder. You'd have to admit, under oath, that you'd seen him at the gallery days after you saw him killed. No jury would ever convict hearing that. Honestly? No prosecutor would take it to trial. You were his—"

"Escape hatch," Greta whispered.

"Interesting phrase, but yes."

"And he killed Lyndon because?"

"Because according to Lyndon's will, Fremont inherits half his estate. Lyndon gets your money, he gets Lyndon's. You know you can talk to Jack about this, right?"

"I don't want to talk to Jack right now." She needed— no, she wanted him angry with her, separated from her. But the suggestion reminded her of why she'd come to see Simone in the first place. "None of this has been made public yet, right?"

"About Fremont?" Simone shook her head. "No. I hate to say it, but I'm not convinced we'll ever get him into custody. He has too many connections. He's probably already called in favors to help him disappear. We've asked for a warrant to search his office, properties and home, so if he didn't already know, he will soon. Why? What's all this about?"

Payback. Revenge. Justice. "I have the guest list for my show tomorrow night. Doyle Fremont hasn't canceled."

Simone blinked. "You think he might still show up? Even with—"

"He'll show up." That smile he'd sent her the first night, she could recall every minute detail, right down to the gleam of triumph in his eyes. "He's too arrogant not to. He'll want to see me in person. And I want to see him."

"Greta, I don't think—"

Greta held up her hand. "At some point, I will forgive Lyndon for what he did. I'll have to." If for no other reason than to move on with her life. "But I'll never be able to do that with Fremont. I want him locked up, where he'll never manipulate or hurt anyone ever again. And so do you."

Simone's eyebrow arched. "You have been talking to Jack."

"I've also been doing my homework. You've earned your nickname, Simone. Tenfold. I want the Avenging Angel on my side. I want you to help me take Fremont down. Will you do it?"

"I'd ask if you have any idea what you're getting yourself into but—"

"I do." She forced the fear and panic down to where she'd deal with it later. "But first I have to ask for a favor."

"Name it."

"I need a new lawyer. Preferably someone with an expertise with finances. Someone I can trust."

Simone's gaze sharpened. "How do you feel about

newbies? I have someone to suggest. She's reliable, determined and about ten times smarter than I am. She's also incorruptible."

"She sounds perfect. When can I meet her?"

"You already have. Kyla!"

Kyla knocked on the door before she entered. "You bellowed?"

"You were advised to bolster your résumé with varying legal work, were you not?"

"I was." Kyla's dark eyes narrowed. "Why?"

"Great." Simone stood and handed her off. "Here's your first client consultation. Use the conference room. I've got some other details to work out on our special project, Greta. I'll come get you when I'm done."

Chapter 15

"You didn't really think you'd do this without me, did you?"

Greta gasped and spun and spied Jack standing in the doorway of her bedroom. Love rushed over her and nearly pulled her under before she steeled herself and turned back to the mirror. She did a quick wiggle and brushed her fingers over the top of the small microphone attached to the center of her bra. Vince's suggestion for low-tech recordings. "I figured Simone or Cole would tell you about my plan."

"Good thing. Clearly you weren't going to tell me." He moved into the room, the tuxedo he wore making him look as if he'd stepped straight off the screen of a classic Hollywood movie. Thunder, deep and low, rumbled in the distance. "You look…" He stood behind her and stared at her in the full-length mirror. "There are no words."

Inside, she melted. He really always said the right thing.

She'd purposely chosen the turquoise dress because it reminded her of the one her mother had worn in *Midnight Witness*. It was fitted, perhaps too fitted, and ended just above her knees. Her feet were already killing her in the four-inch stilettos, but she'd persevere. After watching a few online tutorials, she'd twisted and knotted her hair like a 1940s pinup girl and added sparse but perfect makeup with Ashley's help.

"How did you get in? Never mind." She finished clipping on the gold and pearl earrings that had once belonged to her grandmother, a treasure she'd made herself unearth from one of the numerous boxes in the storage room just last night. She was done with running from the past. Hiding from it was what had gotten Lyndon killed. She owed it to him, despite what he'd done, to see this through. "I have to remind myself Ashley's your sister."

"Actually, it was Cole. He sent me in with these." He reached into his pocket and pulled out a small, beige device. "It's an earwig and a tracker. It's so Max and Allie can monitor you from the surveillance van. Wait to put it in, though. Otherwise everyone is going to hear this conversation."

"What conversation?" Nerves she'd banked since she'd left Simone's office yesterday surged to life.

"The conversation where I tell you, again, that I love you." He turned her to face him, looked at her with such affection she couldn't breathe. "I know that scares you. It scares me. But you know what else scares me? The

idea of losing you. So, I'm making you this promise."
He framed her face. "When this is all over, you and
I? We're going to sit down and figure out our future.
We're going to talk about all of it. Everything. Your
past. Mine. It's all going to come out, and we're going
to go from there."

"Jack—" She couldn't deal with this now, couldn't
even let herself begin to hope...

"No time to argue. We're due at the gallery. And despite wanting to kiss you right now more than I want to
breathe, I'm going to resist temptation and leave your
lipstick as it is." He brushed his thumb lightly across
her mouth. "We'll save that for later."

Tears pricked the back of her eyes. "Jack," she whispered, then jolted when Cole leaned in and rapped his
knuckles on the doorframe.

"Time to go, kids. Greta, last chance to back out."

"I'm not backing out." She frowned and glared at
him, earning a nod of approval.

"Just checking. Got an SUV downstairs waiting.
Once you're in the gallery, you stick close to Jack. When
we have Fremont in sight, we'll lock down the exits and
arrest him."

"How is Fremont supposed to approach me if I'm
hanging out with him?" She stuck her thumb at Jack.
"He won't confess to anything with cops around."

"As soon as we have you and Fremont in the same
room, Jack'll give him space. You won't be out of our
sight, though," Cole said. "Promise."

"I'm not worried." Not about that, at least. As arrogant as Fremont was, she had doubts he'd confess to all
his crimes simply because she asked him to. Who was

that stupid in real life? "Let's go already. The sooner this is over, the better."

The sooner this was over, the sooner she'd say good-bye to Jack and set him free. She followed Cole out of her loft, Jack right on her heels as they exited the building and headed to the car. She offered both men a tentative smile as she climbed inside before them.

And bid them a silent farewell.

"You're doing great," Jack murmured to Greta a few hours into the event. They made their way through the opening-night crowd. A crowd that didn't appear to have any qualms about venturing out on a dark and stormy night, a night that not so long ago would have acted as inspiration for one of Greta's paintings.

Lightning crackled in the air, flashing across the windows seconds before thunder rumbled its way over and through the valley. The last thing they needed tonight was more atmosphere to add to the tension. Tension that Jack wished he could make disappear with a mere thought.

Greta deserved the perfect show, the perfect evening. Instead, they had to worry about a killer stalking her and mother nature wreaking havoc.

Greta had done wonderfully with the attendees and the press. She shook hands and schmoozed like she'd been doing it all her life. From the mayor to the chief of police to countless faces of the wealthy and famous, Jack had yet to catch a glimpse of Doyle Fremont. From where he kept a hand at the small of her back, he could feel the tension riding off Greta in waves. When the receiving line was finally concluded, he steered her deeper into the exhibit, an open room lined with her beautiful, atmospheric paintings. "Just keep going about your normal routine."

"It's my first show, remember?" Greta plucked a flute of champagne off a passing server's tray and tipped it to her lips. "There is no routine yet."

"Well, stop looking as if everyone's here to attack you."

"Wait, was that—" Greta stepped around Jack and watched their server move away. "Was that Bowie?"

"Yes, ma'am." The officer's voice was clear in her ear.

"Kid had the night off and offered to help." Jack looked down to where Greta had laid her hand on his chest. An innocent gesture, he knew, but an instinctive one. One she probably didn't even realize she'd made. His skin warmed under her touch.

"At what point do I lose the kid part of that sentence?" Bowie asked.

Jack enjoyed the smile that played along Greta's perfectly painted lips. "When you've earned it. Let's keep moving. Just so you know, Greta, Vince's brother Jason is one of the bartenders, and we have two more patrol officers in the crowd. Cole and Eden are around here somewhere. Probably near the food, knowing Eden."

"I heard that," Eden's feminine growl clattered in their ears. "You do remember we're all synced, right?"

"So that must be your stomach I hear rumbling?" Jack teased, trying to keep Greta calm even as every cell in his body stayed on high alert.

"Hey, for once Junior here isn't making me want to puke, so I'm taking advantage. Simone?" Eden asked. "Where'd you go?"

"We're at the far end of the exhibit. Apologies. I

might have gotten distracted by one of the paintings."
Simone's voice held an undertone of awe.

"Yeah, well, keep your head in the game," Jack said.
"And your eyes open for Fremont."

"Yes, sir."

Jack winced. He knew that irritated tone.

"I feel like I should say something so people remember we're here." Allie's voice came in with a touch of static. "Can someone deliver a doggie bag to the van?"

"Max, fix that feed, please," Vince said.

"On it," Max confirmed. "Greta, I started recording as soon as you arrived."

"Understood." Greta looked about to say something to Jack, but something caught her attention. For a moment, Jack thought she'd spotted Fremont, but the smile that spread across her face held nothing but joy. "Yvette. You made it!" Greta stepped away from Jack toward a stunning brunette who looked equally pleased to see Greta.

"I'm sorry we're late," Yvette apologized as they hugged. "But I swear it was for a good reason. Richard's been headhunted."

"Sounds painful," Jack inserted.

Yvette's gaze slid to him before returning to Greta. "I think that's your man's way of suggesting you introduce us, Greta."

Jack grinned. He liked her already. "Jack McTavish." He held out his hand.

"Yvette Konstinopolis. And this is my husband, Richard."

"Pleasure." Richard, a few inches taller and quite a few pounds heavier than Jack, returned the greeting. "Yvette's right, Greta. It's entirely my fault we're late."

"So, you've found a new venture?" Greta asked him. "Tell me about it."

"Ah." Richard turned dubious eyes on his wife. "Maybe now isn't the time."

"What? Why not?" Greta asked.

Yvette's smile dimmed. "He's been offered a VP position in a tech company. In Singapore. We leave next month."

Jack moved in as Greta's shoulders drooped. "Oh."

"I know it's messed up," Yvette confessed. "I mean, here I finally talk you into moving here, and then I go and abandon you. I'm so sorry, Greta. The timing couldn't be worse, what with Lyndon's death and everything."

"Don't be silly," Greta insisted, but Jack heard the tightness in her voice. "It's a wonderful opportunity. For both of you. You deserve every bit of happiness you can grab. Congratulations, Richard."

"Thank you, Greta."

"I just hate leaving you alone," Yvette admitted and leaned into her husband as he moved closer.

"You won't be alone." Allie's voice echoed in both their ears. Jack could have kissed his psychologist friend for knowing exactly what to say.

"Singapore's just a plane ride away, right?" Greta said and moved off with Yvette to continue their conversation.

"Greta has an open invitation to visit anytime," Richard told Jack as he was handed a glass of Scotch. "And you, too, of course."

"Appreciate that." Jack kept his eyes moving about the room. He estimated a good three hundred people had shown up for the exhibition. But he still hadn't seen even an inkling of Doyle Fremont. He did see the gallery's curator placing red-circle stickers next to a number of Greta's paintings.

"Someone in particular you're looking for?" Richard asked.

Jack didn't realize he'd been so conspicuous. He debated for a second, then realized another pair of eyes couldn't hurt. "I'd heard Doyle Fremont might attend."

Richard cringed behind his glass.

"I take it you aren't a fan?" Jack liked Richard Konstinopolis more by the minute.

"Arrogant creep. And about as fake as a six-dollar bill. Sorry." Richard shook his head. "Must have forgotten my filter at home. A good friend of mine dated him for a while. Suffice it to say she was not treated well. I also don't carry an affinity for people who gobble up companies just to sell them off and put people out of work. You know, word has it he's not in as great financial shape as he says. I really hope that's true."

"You don't say?" Interesting. Everything he'd heard outside of law enforcement said Doyle Fremont walked on water.

"Oh, I do. And so do a lot of others. It's entirely possible the shine is finally wearing off. Speaking of shine—" Richard shifted his focus to one of Greta's paintings across the room "—I think I've just found the first addition to our new home. If you don't mind?"

"Please." Jack watched as Richard moved off to speak with Collette Sorenson. She nodded and, after a moment, placed a sticker next to the painting Richard had his eye on. "Well, I'll be. You guys seeing this?"

"No, actually," Allie mumbled. "See what?"

Pride surged through him. "Greta's paintings are almost all sold."

"Well, I know one that is," Vince said. "And you have my wife to thank."

"When art speaks to you, you listen," Simone added. "Has anyone seen Fremont yet?"

"No," Eden said. "And I'm running out of food."

"Perhaps you could stop doing your impression of a Hoover and focus?" Simone suggested.

Jack chuckled and scanned the room for Greta. His smile faded when he didn't see her. He did a walk-around and still didn't find her. He spotted Yvette heading over to her husband, but Greta was nowhere in sight. Pulse pounding, he set his glass on the closest table. "Yvette? Where's Greta?"

"Ladies' room. Why?"

Jack didn't answer. He headed into the hallway toward the restrooms.

"Jack? We may have a problem." Max's voice was too calm in Jack's ear. "We've lost all surveillance camera feed. Dead screens." Fingers tapped on computer keys. "All of them. Entire gallery."

"Does anyone have eyes on her? Greta, can you hear me?" Jack pressed his earwig deeper into his ear as if that would help connect with her. "Greta…"

"Jack." Someone touched his arm. Jack spun around and found the assistant DA and her PI husband right behind him. "She's not answering," Simone said.

"Check the ladies'."

"All right." She hurried down the hall.

Vince checked his watch. "Max, what is going on?" When there wasn't any answer, Vince's eyes went sharp.

"Something's wrong. I'm not getting anything from Max now." He tapped his ear. "Eden? Cole? Bowie? Anyone read?"

Dead silence.

Simone rushed up to them. "She's not in there. Someone said there was an out-of-order sign up until a few minutes ago. She must have gone upstairs or down."

Jack swore. Eden and Cole emerged from the closest display room and joined them. "We can't hear each other," Eden said.

"I'm guessing there's a signal jammer in play," Vince said, and as he looked around, they saw people trying to get signals on the cell phones. "First the cameras, now our coms and cells. We need to split up and find Greta. Now."

"Cole, call in the reinforcements. Have them watch every exit for a sign of Fremont. He must have gotten in when the cameras went down."

"Pretty high-risk move to try that," Simone observed as Cole and Eden headed down a level.

"He's dead broke," Jack reminded her. "And desperate." And he knew just how far desperate men were willing to go to protect themselves. "I'll head up. Vince—"

"Go. I've got this." Vince slapped him on the shoulder, and he and Simone hurried off.

Jack flew up the stairs, dread and fear locking hard around his chest.

Greta needed to get back downstairs. Finding the bathroom on her exhibit level closed for cleaning meant she'd had to look elsewhere. She shouldn't have drunk that second glass of champagne. She straightened her dress, stepped out of the stall and washed her hands, took an extra minute to refresh her lipstick and smooth her hair.

The voices in her ear had gone silent, another warning that she needed to get back to Jack and the others. Clearly she'd gone out of range, and Jack was not going to be happy about that.

She pulled open the door.

The scream froze in her throat. Her hands went slack, and her clutch dropped to the floor.

"Hello, Greta." Doyle Fremont stood there, hands clasped behind his back, as if he'd been waiting for her. "How nice to finally meet you in person."

Greta pressed a finger against her ear. "Jack? Vince? Allie?" Each name burned in her throat.

"They can't hear you." He reached into his suit-jacket pocket and pulled out a small device with a blinking green light. "Signal jammer."

"They aren't far away," Greta told him and tried to ignore the recognizable look in his dead eyes. She'd seen that same one weeks before. When he'd killed Calhoun. "They'll be looking for me."

"Don't worry. They'll find you soon enough." He dropped the jammer back into his pocket and locked his other hand around her upper arm. "Come with me."

"What? No!" She struggled, kicked out with her pointed stilettos and caught him hard on the shin.

He swore but didn't loosen his hold. Instead, he pulled a gun out of the back of his waistband and jabbed it into her ribs. "You're going to come with me." He moved in, his breath hot against the side of her face. "Or

I'm going to go downstairs and see if your boyfriend, Detective McTavish is as bulletproof as they say."

"In front of all those people?" Greta actually snorted. "I don't think so."

"The FBI is searching my home and businesses as we speak. Do you really believe I don't have anything left to lose?" He pressed the barrel of the gun harder into her ribs. "Now, move. Not that way." He yanked her back hard when she headed for the main stairs. "This way." He dragged her with him to an emergency stair-case. She could feel the thunder reverberating against the building, heard the rain pelting against the windows. Scrambling for an idea, she purposely caught her foot on the doorframe and tripped. One of her shoes went flying off.

She cried out, made a show of wanting to grab it, then clung to a fast-moving Fremont as he plunged up the stairs to the roof.

Jack hit the third floor at top speed, racing into the various bathrooms in the darkened hallway. Nothing. When he slammed open the last door, he saw the small handbag that matched Greta's dress. He grabbed it and exited.

His mind racing, he kept yelling into the silence, hoping the connection would pick back up. He didn't have time to go back downstairs to find backup. Greta was here, somewhere. And Doyle had her.

He could feel it as surely as he could feel his heart pounding against his rib cage.

Think like a cop! Jack tried to distance himself, tried

to forget this was Greta he needed to find. Greta. He was not going to let this happen.

Fremont wouldn't take her where there was a crowd. The staircase Jack had come up would be out of the question. The other staircases were blocked off, other display rooms locked. All except...he recalled the diagrams of the building. The emergency stairs.

He ran down the hall, made a left. There! He found her ridiculous stilt of a shoe lying discarded in front of the staircase door. He left her purse with it, reached behind him for his weapon and pulled it out.

Carefully, quietly, Jack took a deep breath, centered himself.

And pushed open the door.

"Stop. You have to stop," Greta gasped, trying to slow Fremont down by pulling and dragging him backward. If he got her outside, if he got her onto the roof, there would be nowhere to run. Nowhere to hide. "I can't breathe. I can't walk."

"Fine." He stopped long enough to bend down and yank her second shoe off. He threw it over the side of the staircase and took the last step at record pace. Hope burst to life when Greta saw the emergency bar. But when he shoved through it, the alarm didn't blare. Rain shot in through the open door as Fremont yanked her forward and sent her flying into the storm.

Soaked, Greta caught herself before she fell and tried to run, but he was too fast. He had his hand locked around her arm like a vise as he dragged her to the edge of the roof. Lightning snapped across the dark sky. Thick gray clouds sat heavy above downtown as thunder echoed and exploded around them.

"No!" She dropped low, pushed back with her bare feet and fought even as asphalt and rocks dug into her suddenly frozen skin.

"Stay there!" He released her and aimed the gun at her. "Just stay there."

The wildness in his eyes made her own panic grow. He was out of his mind, fueled by determination and rage.

"I still have a chance to salvage this." He cocked the hammer. She could barely hear him over the rain. "I can still get away. They'll all be thinking of you. The sad, mentally frail artist who couldn't take the pressure of success." He moved forward. "Now step up."

"No." Greta felt the ledge pressing against the back of her legs. Her hair dripped water into her face, and she swiped her hand over her eyes to keep her vision clear. "I won't jump. I won't make this easy for you. You won't get a penny. Not from me. Not from Lyndon." She touched the device in her ear again. And prayed. "You're finished. However this plays out, you're done." She looked behind her. Her stomach dropped as she glanced down and noted a half-dozen patrol cars with spinning lights and blaring sirens screech to a stop on the wet streets below.

Time seemed to slow. Her life, all those moments, all the pain and sorrow but also the joy and the successes, it would all come to an end. Could come to an end. Either by her stepping off the building's ledge or from Doyle Fremont's weapon.

She wasn't ready. She sobbed, an almost hysterical

smile forming as she forced a laugh. She wanted to live. She wanted to live a life with Jack. With his friends and his family. She wanted to be a part of something bigger than she'd ever experienced before. For as long as she had.

Her spine stiffened. She lowered her arms, which she'd held out to stave off Fremont. With the rain pouring down, she slowly faced him. "I won't help you."

She stepped away from the ledge.

"You can't force me to jump. I have too much to live for. But you have nothing. There's nothing left, Doyle." Anger built, exploding out with her words. "You've manipulated and conned people long enough. You killed the only family I had left. And for what? For money?"

"I had to kill him. Lyndon was a fool. He was going to tell you everything! He didn't understand the power of secrets. He let sentimentality and his feelings for your mother get in the way."

"His feelings for…" Pieces of her life fell into place. "Of course." She closed her eyes. "He loved her." No wonder he'd never married, never had a family of his own. Lyndon had loved Greta's mother.

"If you won't jump, you'll leave me no choice." Doyle lifted the gun another inch.

"And *you'll* leave me none."

Greta cried out as Jack stepped from the shadows, weapon raised and locked on Doyle. His wet tuxedo jacket shimmered against the moonlight. Despite the water pelting him, his hand and gun were steady. "Jack."

Jack moved in, circled around until he stood beside her. With Doyle's attention on them both, Doyle didn't see the shadows moving in behind him. Vince and Cole, both with their weapons drawn, their footfalls silenced by the storm.

"He confessed," Greta said, and Jack drew her around, forcing Doyle to circle closer to the edge of the roof.

"We know." Jack nodded. "That backup mic we wired you with did the trick. Max got it all."

Relief surged through her. "Then, it's over."

"No," Doyle Fremont said and raised his gun. "It's not."

Suddenly, Jack grabbed Greta around the waist, bringing her down to the ground just as Fremont fired.

"Police, Fremont!" Cole yelled, as Fremont spun and fired off a second shot.

Greta watched in horror as Cole and Vince both fired.

And hit Fremont square in the chest. He staggered away and turned. Blood spread and bloomed across his chest. For a moment, Fremont looked confused, as if it wasn't possible that he could have been hit. He stumbled back...

Jack pushed to his feet and launched himself forward, but it was too late.

Doyle was at the ledge of the roof and still moving, before he dropped out of sight.

Screams and cries ripped through the air before a sickening thud echoed up.

"We okay?" Cole demanded, racing forward.

"I'm good." Jack said and bent down to pluck Greta up off the ground as if she didn't weigh a thing.

She was drenched, a sopping mess, tears of fear mingling with the rain. But she was alive.

"Greta?" He cupped her face in his hands, looked into her eyes. "You okay? Did he hurt you? Are you—"

"I'm fine." A weight she didn't realize she'd been carrying lifted. "He wanted me to jump. He really thought if I did, he'd get it all. There was no...reasoning with him." She shook her head. "How could he not see...?"

Jack pulled her into his arms, wrapped her tightly against him. She held on to him, breathed him in. And smiled even as she trembled a little.

"The next time you have to go to the bathroom, tell me."

She laughed as he led her out of the storm. Laughed because she was alive. Because she was with him. Because she loved Jack McTavish and he loved her.

"Jack, wait." She stopped before he could open the door to the stairs. "I love you."

"Yeah." He squeezed her shoulders. "I know."

She scrunched her nose. "We back to Star Wars again?"

"Always," he grinned and pressed his lips to her temple.

"Marry me."

"What?" Jack jerked back and blinked down at her. "What did you say?"

"You heard me. I don't want to be afraid anymore, Jack." With her hands on his chest, she locked her eyes on his, she embraced the storm and her greatest fear. "I don't want to be alone. For however long we have, I want it."

"Fat chance of you being afraid with all of us around," Cole said, as he and Vince joined them at the door.

She caught Jack's face in her hands, drew him down

until he pressed his forehead against hers. "I don't want to wake up one more morning without you by my side. I love you, Jack McTavish. Please say you'll marry me."

He grinned. "Okay."

"Well, that's romantic," Vince chimed in.

"Tomorrow?" Greta whispered. "City Hall? I have an in with the mayor."

"So do I. Tomorrow." He stroked her cheek. "In the loft. With our family and friends."

"Our home?"

"If you don't mind?"

"I don't mind." She kissed him, then laughed as he dipped her backward. "I don't mind at all."

Epilogue

The next day...

"So, something's been bothering me about this whole Fremont thing." Simone held out her champagne glass for a refill.

Silence fell at her statement, and Jack, ever mindful of his friends' capacity for good deeds, hugged his bride of two hours against his side. The loft, thanks to everyone's work, had been transformed into a fairy world reminiscent of *Evergreen*, the painting of Greta's that had cost him a couple months' salary. Lush greenery abounded, and twinkling lights glistened. Cerberus strutted, and laughter filled the loft that only weeks before had housed only one heart. Now it housed countless. His friends. Hers. A perfect day.

He looked over at Greta, barefoot, her hair tied and twisted into braids and curls around her beaming face. The white flowing dress she wore was simple, with a high waist and delicate straps, and perfectly suited to her natural beauty. She looked radiant. She looked happy. And at peace. What more could he ask for?

"Is this a toast?" Kyla asked and nudged Jason Sutton with her elbow. "Should I get this on video?"

"No, you shouldn't." Simone suggested with an odd grin. "Given the short notice, it was hard to find a good gift, but I think I managed."

"Of course she did," Eden grumbled.

"I debated about doing this in private, but, seeing as we'll all find out eventually anyway... Greta, when you had me contact Lyndon's lawyer about his estate, he overnighted me the contents of Lyndon's safety deposit box. The rest is back at my office, but this I thought you'd like to see now."

Greta handed off her glass to Yvette, who had brought along her husband. It would only be a couple more weeks before the couple jetted off to Singapore.

"What is it?" Greta accepted the envelope, slipped her finger under the seal.

"Doyle said that Lyndon was going to tell you the truth. That there was power in secrets. This is the truth, Greta. This is what Lyndon wanted you to finally know."

Jack read over Greta's shoulder, his mind spinning. "This can't be true," she whispered, but the sob that erupted from her had her covering her mouth. She turned to him then, tears glistening in her eyes. "But... he never told me. My parents never—"

"Oh, for heaven's sake, what is it?" Allie, in an uncharacteristic move, snatched the paper from Greta's hands and read. "Oh. Oh, Greta."

"I'm adopted?" Greta's voice sounded as dismayed as Jack felt.

"Lyndon only found out after your parents' death," Simone explained. "They had to go overseas. No adoption agency would ever have put a child in your mother's care, but they found you. Whatever else happened, Greta, they chose you." Simone offered a smile.

Greta took a long breath, pressed a hand against her chest. "Oh, Jack. You know what this means?" She touched his face as his heart swelled with joy.

"I think it means our baby's going to have company soon," Eden chimed in and earned a hearty laugh from the guests.

"No. I mean yes," Greta said through the tears. "But it means something else, right, Jack?"

"It does." He kissed her, and his world settled. "It means we get forever."

* * * * *

*For more great romances from Anna J. Stewart
and the Honor Bound series,
visit www.Harlequin.com today!*

SPECIAL EXCERPT FROM

⬥ HARLEQUIN
ROMANTIC SUSPENSE

When a lead points security agency Rocky Mountain Justice in the direction of a posh resort in the hunt for a serial killer, operative and single dad Liam Alexander and child psychologist Holly Jacobs work together to hunt the huntress, eventually posing as a family to trap their prey. But as their plan backfires, Liam will do anything to save his child—and the woman he loves.

*Read on for a sneak preview of
the next book in the Wyoming Nights miniseries,
Agent's Mountain Rescue,
by Jennifer D. Bokal.*

"Look at us, we're quite the mismatched pair. Still, we make a decent team." Reaching for her hand, Liam stared at their joined fingers. "Plus," he added, "you're pretty easy to talk to and to trust. I don't do either of those things easily, but then I think you've figured that out already. I like that about you, Holly."

She inched closer, her breath caressing his cheek. "You're not so bad yourself."

He smiled a little. "That's better than you turning me down."

She licked her lips. Looking away, Holly stared at something just beyond Liam's shoulder. "I don't want to complicate things."

"I understand," he said, even though he didn't. He wanted her. She wanted him. It all seemed pretty simple and straightforward. "I'm not going to pressure you into anything here."

"Do you really understand?" she asked. "Because I'm not sure that I know what's going on myself."

"You have your life plan. You need money to keep your school open. A relationship is a complication. Besides, you could be leaving town, which means us getting involved could be difficult for Sophie."

Holly touched her fingertips to his lips, silencing him. "If I can't get the money to keep Saplings, then I'll definitely have to leave Pleasant Pines," she said. "You said it yourself—I might not be around much longer."

"Now I'm really confused. What are you saying?"

"Kiss me," she whispered.

It was all the invitation he needed.

Don't miss
Agent's Mountain Rescue *by Jennifer D. Bokal,*
available November 2020 wherever
Harlequin Romantic Suspense
books and ebooks are sold.

Harlequin.com

HRSEXP1020